ONE SURVIVOR

A Novel by Robert Plamondon

Norton Creek Press
http://www.nortoncreekpress.com

One Survivor

by Robert Plamondon

Edited by Karen L. Black

Set in a future society by Paul R. Gazis

ISBN 978-0-9819284-4-9

CHAPTER I

In her dream, sheets of flame billowed into the clear night sky. The roar of the fire and the thud of her ancestral home's falling timbers almost drowned out the wail of the fire alarm.

The firelight flickered across the woods. The Mockers lurked there, padding from one vantage to another, never quite coming into sight, their cat-like eyes reflecting the firelight.

Beverly stood alone, shivering, numbed by the wet grass under her feet and the wind cutting through her pajamas. Where were her parents?

BETRAYED, laughed the Mockers silently. THEY WERE BETRAYED.

Beverly woke suddenly, the dream still holding her. The alarm was still wailing, but she was in a tiny metal room. . . .

The dream receded and she realized where she was: in her cramped stateroom on the *Nine to Five*, a small merchant star ship travelling to an insignificant, underdeveloped planet called Barigost.

The door opened and Rodney—the young crewman who had been so attentive during space suit drills—came in. He flung her space suit out of her locker and pulled her out of bed, leaving her flailing in free-fall. Outraged, she shoved him away and began to voice a bitter complaint, but stopped when she saw his ashen-faced, barely-controlled fear. She had not seen such an expression since leaving her home world of San Vincento. This was not a drill.

Beverly took the space suit from Rodney, who spun around in a neat free-fall pirouette and fled the cabin. Since it was the *emergency* alarm that was sounding, and not the *disaster* alarm, she dressed before putting on the suit, using the jump suit designed for the purpose. She was surprised to see that the legs of her pajamas were unstained by grass and soot. The dream was still fresh in her mind.

She had bound up her hair and was about to put on her helmet when her father appeared in the doorway, already wearing his suit, holding his helmet and holster in one hand. How had he found the time to get his plasma gun from the luggage?

He let go of the helmet—where it floated in free fall—and snapped the holster into place on his space suit. Beverly straightened up and hoped she looked presentable. She prayed that he wouldn't treat her like a child. She was fifteen years old.

"Captain Griswold has agreed to let you have the spare seat on the bridge," he said, drawing his plasma gun and flipping its switch to 'standby.' He glanced at the read-out and continued, "You'll be safer there, with the bridge armor. Your mother and I will stay on the passenger deck. Take this." Holstering his pistol, he reached into one of his suit pockets, producing Beverly's archaic yet beautiful Anderson pistol and ammo pouch.

There was a clang from above as someone slammed the turret hatch, then a series of high-pitched whines as the turret traversed back and forth, followed by a deep throbbing as the guns were powered up.

"There's a raider coming toward us. Captain Griswold hopes to escape by making a high-speed re-entry into Barigost."

Father has doubts about this, she realized. The pistols meant he feared a boarding action.

The intercom came on. "Acceleration in sixty seconds, my lord. Reducing cabin pressure now."

"Father—," began Beverly.

He waved her to silence. "No time. All my children have seen action young. Perhaps it's just coincidence. More likely not. Be strong, *cara mia,* and don't forget your honor." He kissed her. "Run now."

The klaxons were drowned by a roar as most of the ship's air was vented out to space, a measure designed to prevent decompression damage if the hull were punctured, and to reduce the risk of fire.

Beverly put on her helmet and swarmed up the companion-way ladder. She reached the bridge just as Captain Griswold was saying "fifteen seconds" over the intercom. Myrna, the computer officer—oddly, the Goan crew insisted on first-name informality—pushed Beverly into the empty seat and strapped her in. The bridge was tiny: four seats had been crammed into an area smaller than any of Beverly's closets back home. Myrna pushed a few buttons on Beverly's console, bringing up a synopsis display but locking out the controls. She squeezed Beverly's shoulder and returned to her seat.

Larry, the navigator, had been arguing with her. "Of course it's a frigate—look at the drive signature! It out-guns us two to one." He drummed his fingers nervously on the arms of his chair.

Myrna shook her head. "You know perfectly well that the same drives are used in transports. It could be perfectly innocent freighter." She turned to Beverly and winked.

Larry's voice went shrill with indignation. "An innocent freighter? Accelerating at four gees? On a course that cuts us off from the planet?"

Before Myrna could needle him some more, Captain Griswold spoke. As was not uncommon on small freighters, he was pilot, captain, and owner. "Pipe down. Is everybody secured? Stand by for four gees."

He engaged the fusion drive. Before, they had been coasting toward the planet in free-fall, on their way in from the jump limit. Now the acceleration built until Beverly was pressed back into her seat with four times her normal weight. The ship began to shake.

"Auto-evasion looks good," said Captain Griswold. "Guns, are you ready?"

"Just give the word, Cap," came the reply. 'Guns' was Gunther Ottobein; a cocky, tattooed, middle-aged little Goan from the Hasten Arcology, the most notorious slum in the Eight Worlds. Beverly liked him.

"Stand by. Hail them, Larry."

Larry hit a key. Beverly's console indicated that a selection of hailing methods were being attempted.

After a moment, Larry reported, "They're ignoring us."

"Figures," said Captain Griswold. "My lord di Mendoza," he announced over the intercom, "there's no radio contact with the bogey. We're going to stick to plan to make a high-speed re-entry to Barigost."

"Very good, Captain," said her father.

"Guns," said Captain Griswold, "You may fire at will."

"Twenty minutes to re-entry," said Larry, who had dropped the communications display and brought up course projections. "They're just inside extreme range. Effective range in about seven minutes."

The gunnery telescope showed the other ship as a dancing point of light. The resolving power of the telescope was the limiting factor in long-range gunnery, not the collimation of the powerful laser cannon.

The lights dimmed for about fifteen seconds as the guns fired.

"No damage," reported Myrna, who was in charge of most of the instrumentation.

The lights dimmed again. And again. And again. Myrna reported three more misses.

There was no sign of return fire from the enemy. Beverly wondered if they were holding their fire, or were just equally inaccurate.

"Larry, what's underneath us?" asked Captain Griswold.

"We're over the northern continent, at about one-seventy degrees west, sixty-five degrees north," he replied.

"Damn," said Captain Griswold. "That puts Ertrix 'way on the other side." He raised his voice. "Anybody know anyone on the back side of Barigost?" No one answered.

"Should I send a distress call anyway?" asked Larry.

"No. Hell, you know what a bunch of pirates the locals are." He paused to change some parameters on his console. "It's probably another of Laverak's deserters."

The next several minutes passed slowly, with the bridge crew absorbed in their tasks. Captain Griswold tweaked the auto-evasion parameters constantly, sometimes dropping to manual control for a few seconds. The experts said that interfering with the software was all nonsense, but most pilots did it anyway. Larry plotted and re-plotted re-entry paths based on differing amounts of damage to the ship. Myrna controlled the avionics and analyzed their data, updating the course and range displays.

Beverly, crushed into an acceleration couch by four gees, found the feeling of helplessness to be almost unendurable. She gritted her teeth and gripped the arm rests. There was nothing else she could do.

The ship was brushed by laser fire time and again, but the contacts were too brief to penetrate the hull. But every minute brought the two ships closer together.

The lights dimmed again. "Minor damage to the enemy," reported Myrna. "Spectrometer shows no carbon or hydrogen." These elements would have shown up if the plastics in the crew section, the hydrogen in the fuel cells, or the crew members had been hit.

"Oh, damn," said Myrna, looking at updated information on her display. "It *is* a frigate."

Beverly knew what this meant: the other ship had two turrets, while the *Nine to Five* had only one. Myrna must have deduced this from the firing patterns of the other ship, since the telescope still showed the other ship as a point of light; the shape of its hull could not be made out at all, let alone how many turrets protruded from it.

"They're decelerating," said Larry. "They're not going to pass us—they'll follow us in. Closest approach has lengthened to 13,000 kilometers. That'll make things easier for a while."

From the turret Beverly heard Guns crooning in his ghetto accent, "Come on, baby, come on, baby, just a little more, a little more..."

The lights dimmed again, and Beverly, watching the bridge console, saw sudden flashes of light pulse from the enemy ship. Numbers appeared beside it, giving estimated damage.

"They're still under acceleration," said Myrna. Looks like . . ." An explosion drowned out the rest of her sentence. The ship lurched, and the lights went out, then back on.

"Who's here? Sound off!" shouted Captain Griswold. A babble of voices came over the intercom, including, Beverly heard with relief, both her parents'. "Guns? Sound off!" said Captain Griswold. "Guns?"

Beverly heard her father's voice. "I'll check it out, Captain. I'm only one deck away."

"Right, my lord. Be prepared to move on my mark. I'll reduce acceleration to two gees. Ready, set, mark." Weight lifted from Beverly's chest. Captain Griswold kept one hand on the master throttle. The fingers of his other hand drummed on the arm rest, and his eyes scanned the displays impatiently.

Fifteen seconds passed. Beverly heard her father again. "You've lost your gunner, Captain. The cannon may be okay. One moment ..." There was a pause. "All right, I'm in. Resume acceleration."

Beverly's heart raced. Her father in the turret! Did Captain Griswold have any idea of her father's reputation?

Captain Griswold slammed the controls forward again. Laser fire again raked the *Nine to Five*, ripping a long tear in the hold. Captain Griswold ignored the cargo spilling out into space. Beverly was surprised. San Vincentan literature always portrayed Goans as cowardly money-grubbers.

Beverly heard her father in the turret. She'd been told that he'd talked to his guns in his Navy days, but she'd never thought she would hear it herself.

"Slowly, slowly," he said, softly, dreamily, as if unaware that he spoke at all. "Line it up. That's right. They rush to death; we await them."

The range had closed to the point where the enemy ship displayed a wobbly, indistinct outline. In spite of this poor image, Lord di Mendoza played the lasers slowly from nose to tail, holding the darting, dodging ship in his sights for ten full seconds; puncturing crew decks, the hold, engineering—everything but the armored turret and bridge.

"What a hit!" breathed Myrna. "They're reducing acceleration. Looks like fusor trouble. Their drive output is erratic."

"Five minutes to re-entry," said Larry.

There was a blinding flash as the enemy's lasers played across the starboard bridge window. The armored quartz exploded into the bridge. Beverly saw Myrna die instantly as the pulverized quartz shredded her space suit and tore off her head. Quartz and steel shards rattled off Beverly's space suit. Her vision was obscured by blood, smoke, and debris: she couldn't see Captain Griswold on the far side of the cabin.

Next to her, Larry was also injured, his faceplate cracked and spattered with blood. He flailed around wildly. Red lights came on all over the control board. With a roar, the remaining air left the bridge.

Captain Griswold shouted, "God damn it! Somebody take over Computers!" The air took most of the smoke with it, and it became possible to see clearly again. Both Captain Griswold and Beverly were unhurt. The Captain continued swearing, "What the hell happened to our avionics? How am I supposed to re-enter without my god damned avionics?"

Resisting an urge to close her eyes and pretend it wasn't happening, Beverly struggled out of her couch and staggered over to Larry. He had dozens of small ruptures in his suit, which she patched as best she could, following what she had learned in space suit drill. He had stopped flailing around, and was holding his faceplate with both hands. To her horror, she saw that the cracks in the right side went through all the layers of the faceplate. As she watched, fragments blew out, propelled by the air pressure inside the suit. She broke out more patches and struggled to patch the faceplate, fighting Larry's attempts to cover the cracks with his hands. Made weak and clumsy by the gee forces, her gloved hands sticky with sealer, the nightmare went on and on. Finally, with two-thirds of his faceplate covered with patches, she finished.

The suit mechanisms had cleared the blood away from the inside surface and revealed Larry's face. He was still conscious, and was quickly regaining his composure. Reeling under four gees of acceleration, Beverly barely made it back to her seat.

Beverly heard her mother. "Reduce acceleration, Captain. I will take Computers."

Captain Griswold instantly reduced acceleration. "Hurry up," he said. On partial throttle, the acceleration suddenly became erratic. "God damn it!" he swore. "What happened to the fucking *drives?*"

Beverly was appalled. Why couldn't he shut up and die like a gentleman?

Her mother appeared on the bridge and dumped Myrna's body out of the acceleration couch. Captain Griswold resumed the acceleration before she was fully in the seat; Beverly saw her land hard on her left hand and heard her gasp with pain.

She was thinking of inventive deaths for Captain Griswold— though it seemed redundant at this point—when her father started his dreamy litany again. "That's it . . . that's it. Into my sights. I am the Reaper."

The lights dimmed, and part of the enemy ship was enveloped in a huge explosion. Her father gave a humorless chuckle. In a normal voice he said, "*You* are the reapee."

Lady di Mendoza worked the computer. Her left hand seemed undamaged after all. Beverly watched, fascinated, as her mother rerouted power, assigned computer resources to different tasks, updated damage reports so the Captain would know how much strain his ship would take, and monitored the enemy ship; never pausing between one task and the next.

Larry had resumed his tasks, after a fashion. "They're still following. Looks like they have a death wish. Re-entry any second now."

As if on cue, the ship began to shake as it hit the outer atmosphere. Ionization around the ship jammed the instruments and cut off all contact with the pursuer. Buffeted and cloaked by the atmosphere, there was little chance the *Nine to Five* would be hit again. Soon the pursuing ship would enter the atmosphere in its turn, and would lose all contact with the *Nine to Five*.

Beverly was pushed into her seat by ever-increasing gee forces. The thin atmosphere shrieked around the broken bridge window. Her peripheral vision faded until it seemed that she was looking down a tunnel, then everything went black.

When the gee forces lifted, her vision returned. She looked around. She was pretty sure she hadn't lost consciousness. The nose of the ship glowed a dull red. Her mother was still working furiously at the computer console. Larry was unbuckling himself from his seat. Captain Griswold was fuming and cursing over the intercom at the engineer.

"The converter's *out*? Without power to the lifters we've only got five minutes till impact! Fix it, damn it! This ship is all I have!"

"Sorry, Captain. It's not broken: it's slagged down. Permission to jump?"

The Captain closed his eyes for a moment, trying to get a grip on himself. He took a deep breath. "Now hear this. We are going to abandon ship. Passengers and wounded first. Larry, take the girl and make sure she ejects first. Then the rest of the passengers, then crew. I'll go last."

The ship was falling like a stone. Beverly unbuckled herself from her seat. Her mother began unstrapping herself with one hand while still giving instructions to the computer with the other.

As soon as Beverly was free, Larry grabbed her and dragged her down the companionway. When he reached the ejection bay he stuffed her into an escape pod, slammed the hatch, and triggered the charge that ejected her from the ship.

Beverly felt the impact force the air from her lungs. Then she lost consciousness.

Interlude

In her dream, she fell endlessly, her arms outstretched, the wind rushing past her fingers and streaming through her long black hair. The air was cold but sweet, without the harsh metallic tang of her ravaged world.

"This must be San Vincento before the Day of the End of the World," she thought. Sure enough, when she turned her gaze downward the ground far below was covered from horizon to horizon with rich greenery. Her eyes filled with tears. This world would have been hers if the Imperium had not betrayed San Vincento.

The rich green earth rushed up to embrace her.

Chapter II.

Beverly woke slowly. After a long time the dancing spots receded from her eyes and she could see clearly. She was in a small room with a cot, a sink, a first aid kit, and boxes stacked in the back. The room had an institutional look. A factory, perhaps, or a school. She was in her underwear, with a sheet and a rough wool blanket over her. She looked around for her jump suit and space suit—nothing. Then, remembering her training, she looked around for her pistol. It was nowhere in sight.

She sat up suddenly. This proved to be a mistake.

When next she awoke, her jump suit was folded, freshly washed, on the foot of the cot. She tried sitting up again, very carefully, and was rewarded by waves of pain and barely controllable nausea. She was able to dress, very slowly. She collapsed back on the cot when she was done. Her head hurt. She closed her eyes to make the spots go away. They didn't, but she kept her eyes closed anyway.

She woke with a start when a woman entered the room. She was plump and middle-aged; Beverly knew she was a school teacher the instant she saw her. The woman asked, "How are your feeling, dear? I'm Mrs. Smith."

Beverly felt weak and nauseous, her vision tended to go out of focus, the throbbing of her head was almost unendurable, and the room was spinning slowly on an uncertain axis. "Fine, thank you," she said. Her voice sounded weak. That wouldn't do. "Where am I?" That was better.

"This is the school infirmary at Hoover."

"Hoover?"

"Yes. We're a little town outside of Antipodes."

"Antipodes?"

"Are you sure you're feeling all right, dear?" The teacher looked worried.

"I'm fine. Where are the other survivors?" Beverly was surprised her parents hadn't found her already. They were much tougher than she was. She hoped they wouldn't find her infirmity embarrassing.

"Well, I'm sure I don't know. Ejection pods from as high up as yours would be scattered all over. They're checking the radar tapes over in Wrenfield now. Wherever they land, they'll be brought to Wrenfield. That's the provincial capital, you know."

"No, ma'am, I didn't know."

"Say, you're not one of those Fort Nereid people, are you?" She looked at Beverly suspiciously.

"Certainly not! I'm San Vincentan."

"Oh, from the Eight Worlds! It's too bad you can't stay for class! My fourth graders are studying the Eight Worlds in geography. They'd just *love* to see someone who's really from the Pale. The only person I know who's even been there is Peer Sandra, and it's not wise to let her talk to the children, if you know what I mean."

Beverly didn't have the slightest idea what she meant.

"Anyway, the ambulance should be here any minute to fly you to Wrenfield."

"That reminds me, ma'am: I had some personal effects in my space suit. Could I have them?"

"You didn't have anything but your pistol. The commissar saw that and took it with him. Don't worry, honey, you ought to be able to buy it back from him."

Beverly was annoyed. Did the woman really mean to imply that her pistol had been stolen by a government official? She had heard that Barigost had a peculiar form of government (with a fairly recent socialist bureaucracy somehow coexisting with an existing aristocracy with a monopoly on space flight), but had never dreamed that any bureaucrat, however corrupt, would have the impudence to trifle with *her*. Whoever this 'commissar' is, she thought, he'll wish he had never been born when Father finishes with him.

"Now, I'm supposed to get a little information for our records. What's your full name, honey?"

"Beverly Maria Elizabeth Deborah Catherine di Mendoza."

"All that?" Beverly had to repeat it again several times before it was all written down. The woman suddenly realized what the "di" meant. "Oh, my! I didn't realize you were a member of the aristocracy, my lady."

"That's all right."

"How old are you?"

"Fifteen."

Mrs. Smith looked over the rest of the form. Beverly could see that it was several pages long and contained a great many questions. "Most of this doesn't apply to you, I'm afraid," she said. "And you still look very pale. Perhaps I can leave the rest of this to the people at the hospital." She looked worried.

They heard a flyer approaching. "That will be the ambulance now," said Mrs. Smith, putting aside her paperwork with relief. "Just sit still; they'll bring a stretcher."

She bustled out. She returned in the company of two people: a short red-haired woman with a large medical bag, and a cheerful man of medium height who wheeled in a folded stretcher. The woman was obviously a medic or doctor. The man was equally obviously a pilot, in spite of his apparel—it was a little odd seeing a pilot in a knee-length woolen tunic, baggy white pantaloons, and high laced boots in addition to his flying helmet. His clothes were probably normal garb for men on Barigost. The women wore stockings instead of trousers, and shoes instead of boots, but otherwise their dress was similar.

The woman knelt by the bed and took Beverly's pulse the old-fashioned way; with fingers over her wrist. Beverly had only seen this in historical dramas.

"Mrs. Smith was my teacher in fifth and sixth grades, Gwen," said the pilot, deciding that, since Beverly showed no signs of expiring on the spot, it was safe to make conversation. "She said I'd never amount to anything."

Gwen peered into Beverly's right eye with a lighted instrument. Beverly felt like she had been handed over to the village witch doctor.

While looking into Beverly's left eye, Gwen said, "She was right." She added, "Aren't you going to report in?"

"In a minute." The pilot smiled winningly at the teacher. "Mrs. Smith, could you possibly scare up a cup of coffee for a hard-working pilot?" As Mrs. Smith went off to see what she could arrange, the pilot keyed the microphone on his flying helmet. "Station 100, this is Ambulance 4. We've picked up, uh . . ." he peered at the forms that Mrs. Smith had given over to him. "One adolescent female from an escape pod. We're heading back now." He sat down on the only chair in the room, took off his helmet and smiled at Beverly. "Little white lie."

Just as Gwen pronounced Beverly fit to travel, Mrs. Smith came in with two cups of coffee. Seeing the second cup, Gwen reversed her decision and declared that Beverly needed a few minutes' rest before being put onto the stretcher.

They had just picked up their mugs when Ed's helmet started squawking, "Ambulance four! Ambulance four! We've got a tractor accident over in Notai. Two trauma cases. Heavy bleeding, partial amputation, and a possible femoral fracture."

The two were on their feet in an instant. "We'll come back for you, sweetheart," said Ed. "This other one takes precedence." They raced outside.

Beverly lifted the venetian blinds on her window in time to see Ed and Gwen run across the parking lot and climb into their craft; an ugly twin-fan flyer that looked as if it had seen plenty of service. It was dirty, too—the bright red crosses looked almost brown under the grime. Ed spooled up the fans and it lifted into the air in a huge cloud of dust.

The area around the school was absolutely flat. Most of it consisted of recently plowed fields. A short distance down the only visible road was Hoover proper, with a water tower and about a dozen buildings, one of which proclaimed **HOOVER FEED STORE** in giant letters. A tall windowless building with metal walls read **PEOPLE'S COOPERATIVE MILL**. Beverly wondered what function a people's cooperative mill served. San Vincento was not an agricultural world.

The ambulance was rising over the endless fields when a second flyer emerged from the clouds and roared up behind it. A plume of smoke raced from the intruder toward the ambulance, and the ambulance erupted into flame. It fell two hundred meters onto newly-plowed farmland. The wreck exploded on impact.

CHAPTER III

Mrs. Smith stared at the distant wreck. She wrung her hands and said, "The poor dears. Oh, the poor dears."

Beverly stood up—and was mildly surprised that she could do so—and took Mrs. Smith by the hand.

"Mrs. Smith, you must hide me. Those people were after *me*. If they find out I'm still alive, they'll kill me. Mrs. Smith, *please*. My father can take care of them, but I have to reach him first."

The woman sighed. "Yes, all right, dear."

She considered for a moment. "There's nothing for it but to call my husband to pick me up. It's a good thing it's after school hours. But I'd better phone the commissar first and tell him that you're dead."

"And don't mention me on the phone to you husband."

Mrs. Smith smiled. "Don't teach your grandmother, dear. I've done some smuggling in my time, years ago. Most of us do, around here." She went off to make arrangements.

Mrs. Smith came back a few minutes later, looking subdued. She sat on the chair and stared out the window.

"I don't know how to tell you this, dear, so I'll just tell you. The commissar looked over the tapes from the provincial radar network. He says that only one escape pod ejected. The ship crashed 300 kilometers from here, at high speed. There were no survivors."

"No . . . " Her parents, dead? It wasn't possible. They were both so strong. They couldn't die here, in this backwater, after surviving such potent hardships in the past. It didn't make sense.

Mrs. Smith continued, "The other ship, the one you were fighting, got away. The commissar thinks it must have landed on this side of the planet. It was badly damaged, he said."

Beverly hardly heard her. How could her parents be dead? They were so much stronger than she.

She was still in shock when Mrs. Smith's husband arrived. Jonathan Smith was a big potbellied farmer. He looked like a jovial man, but he was grim now. He hurried his wife and Beverly into his decrepit ground car. He started the noisy internal combustion engine, and they rumbled down Hoover's only road.

Beverly stared out the window absently as they drove along. For the first thirty kilometers or so it was unbelievably monotonous: freshly-plowed fields punctuated by rambling, picturesque wooden farmhouses perhaps once every kilometer. Afterward the ground became hillier, and the fields gave way to pasture and woodland. Beverly had never seen anyplace so rustic. San Vincento had been an industrial world during the Imperium, and had been thoroughly nuked during the Day of the End of the World. The combination left it unsuited to widespread agriculture.

Barigost seemed well-suited to agriculture. Beverly had heard that, since it had no axial tilt and no seasons, crops could be grown year-round anywhere they could be grown at all. The poles were perpetually cold and the equatorial regions were perpetually mild. From the chill in the air, it appeared that Hoover was near the polar regions.

They drove for two hours over the narrow, winding country road, climbing progressively steeper hills, when they suddenly reached the top. Antipode Valley stretched out before them, beautiful in the late afternoon sunshine. The green slopes were covered with terraces. A town filled the bottom of the valley, and there was a small space port nestled up against the hills on the west side of the valley. This placement was an old trick to keep space-borne raiders from taking the most convenient attack path: an approach from the west that followed the planet's rotation.

There was a guard post at the summit, next to a sign that read:

NORTHEASTERN PROVINCE TOWN
#239
"Antipodes"
Pop. 19,420 Elev. 300 m

A Loyal Populace is the Keystone
of the People's Government

SECURITY STATION:
Stop and Show Travel Papers

Jonathan stopped the car, and a guard in a cheap-looking grey uniform came up to the window.

"Hiya, Jonathan," said the guard. "Didn't expect you in today. What's your business?" He held a clipboard in his hand, and a revolver in a holster on his belt.

"I'm not here, Bob," said Jonathan.

The guard put down his pencil. "Really? I thought you didn't do that anymore. Going to the station?"

Jonathan nodded.

The guard said, "I'll have to check." He went into the guardhouse and made a phone call. After waiting for several minutes he spoke briefly into the phone, then came back out to the car. "Sandy says come on down. I didn't see nothing."

He went back to the guardhouse and Jonathan drove away. No mark had been made on the guard's clipboard.

As they wound down toward the valley, they saw a large truck toiling up the road.

"Get down," said Jonathan, "and cover yourself with this blanket."

Beverly lay down in the footwell, under the blanket, and so didn't see the truck pass.

"Militia," grunted Jonathan. "Figures."

Mrs. Smith replied, "It's a good thing we hurried, dear. Once the militia sets up the roadblock, there won't be any anonymous travel until the all-clear. I hope we can get home before class tomorrow."

"Ha," said Jonathan. "Wreck the whole set-up, if we're missing tomorrow. Sandy'll fix it."

The road took them through the town. A variety of attractive wooden buildings made the town a pleasant place, but it was defaced by a clot of soulless concrete structures. These buildings seemed to be mostly government offices and apartments. Beverly could not imagine what kind of catastrophe could have induced the locals to build such hideous buildings when their normal style was so much more attractive.

They passed several more trucks filled with militiamen. After ducking back under the blanket twice more, Beverly became dizzy, and stayed in the footwell until they left town. They passed a pair of anti-aircraft installations perhaps a kilometer out of town, and Mrs. Smith gave the all-clear. Beverly sat back up again.

The space port was three kilometers out of town, in an area strangely devoid of militia. The port was dominated by an opening, fully forty meters square, in a cliff on the far side of the port. The opening was guarded by a pair of immense sliding doors, which at the moment were mostly closed, leaving an opening three or four meters wide. Four centuries after the Fall, the doors still bore a faded Terran Imperial eagle.

A ceramic landing field lay in front of the doors. It had originally been quite large, but most of it had been allowed to decay into jumbles of tilted slabs, piles of rubble, clumps of trees, and irregularly-placed craters. Only a few hectares immediately in front of the doors showed any sign of maintenance.

The decline of this tiny spaceport mirrored the decline in the holdings and technology of mankind. Where had the glory gone?

Only three—no, four ships were down. A 200-ton merchantman of local manufacture, sporting a woefully inadequate single-tube laser turret, was parked near the doors. A beautifully streamlined 400-ton raider with two tri-mount turrets, also a local, was out toward the center of the maintained area. An armed merchant of perhaps 400 tons was well inside the station. It, too, had a primitive look, but in a different way from the other two. A little more advanced, perhaps, or from far away. Finally, almost obscured by trees and a heap of rubble was a tiny, almost ridiculously streamlined ship of perhaps 150 tons, sporting empty mounts for two forward-firing laser tubes, and presenting a battered, primitive appearance. It had just enough lights showing that it didn't look like salvage.

Mr. Smith parked the car and went through the big doors, speaking to an armored guard. Unlike the guard at the checkpoint, whose uniform had been cheap and ill-fitting, this one wore an impressive, carefully tailored red-and-yellow uniform.

Beverly had almost fallen asleep when Mr. Smith returned with a middle-aged woman wearing a faded red-and-yellow flight suit and an air of authority, accompanied by two armored men in neatly-tailored red-and-yellow uniforms (the same as worn by the guard at the door) and a girl of about eighteen in a grey dress of some expensive-looking natural fiber. All but the girl wore hand blasters, which must have been imported at great expense from the Eight Worlds.

The woman in the flight suit had never been attractive, and her appearance was marred by an ugly, jagged scar, not entirely healed, that started above her left eyebrow and ended halfway down her left cheek. The eye patch told the rest of the story.

Beverly shuddered. Barigost was even more primitive than she had supposed. Anyone inside the Pale would have had regeneration therapy and grown back the eye. And nothing even resembling proper treatment would leave a scar.

The situation was unnerving: the glowering hillside stronghold, the guards with their gaudy uniforms and expensive weapons, and the swaggering, scarred leader made it seem that Beverly had fallen into the hands of a barbarian chieftain rather than an official of a bureaucratic state.

The woman peered at Beverly and motioned for her to roll down the window. This proved difficult. The window was held together with improvised repairs. The window crank was long gone and the window was held up with a wire hooked over the top of the frame. Beverly unhooked it and the window thudded open.

"Welcome to Antipodes," said the woman unsmilingly. "I'm Peer Sandra O'Hare." She jerked a thumb at Mr. Smith. "Jonathan here told me about your problem. I can hide you, and smuggle you out in a couple of days to the San Vincentan consul, or trade representative, or whatever the hell he's called. We'll put you up in that old Morversarn job over there," she gestured toward the smallest ship, "and my daughter will take care of you. You need anything, just let her know." She turned and walked off, her two bodyguards trailing behind her.

Hardly a warm reception, thought Beverly. Still, Peer Sandra had offered sanctuary and even delegated her own daughter to look after her. In substance, if not in style, Beverly could not fault Peer Sandra's hospitality.

The girl climbed into the front seat to indicate the path to the ship. Mrs. Smith got in the back with Beverly.

Jonathan jockeyed his car toward the ship, maneuvering around potholes, rusting machinery, piles of debris, and clumps of bushes. When they got near it, Beverly could see an amazing collection of machinery strewn around the ship. Some pieces were covered with plastic tarps, while others had been left out to rust. Tools were scattered here and there, as if their users had suddenly been called elsewhere. There were lights on in the bridge. The ship was a tail-lander, and Beverly eyed the steep entry ladder with alarm.

They pulled up and stopped. The girl got out of the car and opened Beverly's door for her. She was petite, about the same height as Beverly. She had short red hair, blue eyes, and freckles. "Can you walk?" asked the girl. "I'm sure George and Jonathan could carry you inside. I'm Emily, by the way."

"How do you do. I'm Beverly di Mendoza—and I'm fine," she lied. She had been carted around enough for one day. She stood up slowly, and started for the ship.

Beverly was seeing stars when she reached the foot of the ladder. She shrugged off offers of assistance, and, after resting a moment, climbed the ladder. She had to stop to rest twice while climbing the fifteen rungs. She crawled in through the airlock, and collapsed onto the deck of the cargo hold.

She looked around as she regained her breath. The ship was a disaster area. It was reasonably clean, and more or less intact, but the *technology!* She'd never seen interior hull plates held on with round-head rivets before. Neither had she seen a ship whose main structure consisted of welded steel tubing, or used incandescent bulbs. Amazing! Even the airlock had mechanical, not electronic, interlocks to keep both doors from being opened at the wrong times. Not that the interlocks were doing anything at the moment, since the inner door was lying on the deck.

Emily came in after her, then climbed the central companionway toward the bridge. Mrs. Smith appeared in the airlock. "Well, we'll have to head on home now, dear, in case the commissar drops by with some questions. Peer Sandra will get us past the roadblocks, so don't worry about us. I see I'm leaving you in good hands."

With an effort, Beverly managed to straighten up and reply formally, "Mrs. Smith, I will not forget what you have done for me. Thank you."

Mrs. Smith made some disclaiming noises, obviously pleased, and left.

A heap of what appeared to be bedding fell down the companionway and landed at Beverly's feet.

"Heads!" called Emily.

Emily returned. She was accompanied by a tall blond youth of about eighteen. "Beverly, this is Peer George Heinz. He owns this alleged ship." Beverly muttered a greeting, and Emily and George went to work improvising a bed, starting with two immense but realistic-looking polar bear skins in lieu of a mattress, and finishing with quilts and blankets.

"By the way," said George, helping Beverly to the bed. "If you need to use the bathroom, call Emily. The ship's plumbing was designed for Morversarn—very dangerous." With that heartening piece of advice, he climbed back to an upper deck.

Beverly barely heard him. She was still a little dizzy from her climb. She closed her eyes to keep the room from spinning, and quickly fell asleep.

INTERLUDE

Excerpt from the Barigost State Radio News, Ertrix Evening Edition, May 7, 3150. Arnold Jarnholz, announcing.

...Grand Peer Fabian hosted ceremonies today in honor of retiring Dr. Carlson Brunfield; who has for thirty years held the post of Terran Ambassador to Barigost. Dr. Brunfield is retiring from diplomatic service, having accepted a position with the University of Sydney. The Grand Peer spoke for all Barigost when he praised Dr. Brunfield's long history of skillful treatment of the sensitive problems between our two worlds.

Dr. Brunfield's replacement, Johann Billings, was introduced to the Peerage at the ceremonies. Ambassador Billings is without previous diplomatic experience.

Also present was the new Under-Ambassador, Mr. Davis, a junior member of the Terran Diplomatic Corps. The post of Under-Ambassador has been vacant since the untimely demise of its previous occupant, Mr. Black, in an arctic hunting accident.

Peer Benedict Freeman of Valans has returned from a lengthy voyage to Valhalla, where he reports that Oman Laverak, the New Carinan

adventurer, has gained near-complete control
of the Valhallan planets of Nubonn, Orwec, and
Maril. Furthermore, Corsu has been pressured
into accepting Laverak's rule by so-called
"acclamation."

Peer Benedict fears that it is inevitable that
all Valhalla will slide into Laverak's grasp.
Laverak has not reached his hand toward Pertis, gateway between Persol and Valhalla, but
he reports that this may just be a matter of
time.

Already deserters from Laverak's forces have
used their ships to raid Dancel and Northstar.
Will Laverak himself attempt to finish what
his deserters have started? Only time will
tell.

In local travel news, the Goan merchant <u>Nine</u>
<u>to Five</u>, a frequent visitor to Barigost, was
destroyed by an unknown ship just outside the
atmosphere. Most of the battle took place
outside detector range, but the mayday message
sent as the crippled ship plummeted through
the atmosphere indicated that the ship, commanded as usual by Captain August Griswold,
had been attacked by a frigate of Eight Worlds
manufacture. The passenger list and cargo
manifest are unknown. It is hoped that the
Nine to Five gave as good as it got. Captain
Griswold and his ship had been visiting

Barigost for many years, and his presence will
be missed.

In a bizarre twist, an ejection pod from the
<u>Nine to Five</u> grounded near N.E.V. 1412 Hoover,
near N.E.T. 239 Antipodes. The occupant, an
unidentified teen-aged girl, was killed when
the ambulance taking her to the hospital was
shot down by an unknown flyer.

Both Government House and the Soviet have
joined to condemn this depraved act of brutal-
ity, without even the desire for plunder to
excuse it. As all aboard the *Nine to Five* were
lost, we can only wonder at the motivations of
their attackers.

The Grand Peer has again pressed for the
rebuilding and interlinking of the local radar
nets, the construction of detector satellites,
and the centralization of defense forces. The
Grand Peer described such actions as "the only
method whereby the State can protect its
citizens." Spokesmen of the Peerage scoffed at
this idea in today's session of the Soviet,
calling it "an exercise in demagoguery and a
transparent attempt to wrest control of the
planet's defenses from the People."

CHAPTER IV

Beverly found the next morning rough going. Her head hurt, and Emily's forced, false cheerfulness just made her feel worse. She tried not to think of her problems. It wasn't easy.

After breakfast—made from some of George's store of antique canned and frozen food—George and Emily tried drawing her story out of her. Beverly soon decided to trust them (not that she knew anything sensitive enough for security to be a concern). They were both members of the Barigost aristocracy, such as it was. Emily was clearly trusted by Peer Sandra; while George obviously spent all his time working on the ship and didn't seem to have much opportunity to gossip. And they seemed such cheerful, trusting, simple souls—nothing like her classmates back home.

So she told them her story, using few words. She told it without emotion, her eyes fixed on the bulkhead. She had to struggle to maintain her composure. Her father would not have wanted her to cry in front of strangers.

When she had finished, George said, "I don't understand it. Taking the *Nine to Five* would make sense, though Griswold had a tough reputation—that was a valuable ship—but that attack wasn't piracy. It was assassination. Nobody could have salvaged that ship on a re-entry trajectory, and raiders don't shoot people down for fun. Not very often, anyway. No money in it." He looked at Emily.

Emily said, "It doesn't make sense to me, either. If they were gunning for your parents, why did they go to all the extra trouble to take you out, too?"

Beverly stared at the curved bulkhead. "Maybe they were just after Father, and wanted to kill the rest of us to keep the word from leaking out. With no survivors, and without a passenger list, no one would know to send word to San Vincento." She sighed. "Father never made any enemies. He was very proud of that."

"Why was he here, anyway?" asked George. "The direct route to Valhalla goes through Villahove—it doesn't come anywhere near here."

"I don't *know*. He wouldn't tell me." Her father had never taken her into his confidence. He had felt differently about his sons. Her eldest brother Richard had been apprenticed to her father at fourteen, and sat in on staff meetings. Her brother Miguel, six years her senior, had done the same. But her father had always insisted that politics and the military were not for her. She had resented it bitterly, but he was not a man easily swayed. Thus, the day he burst into their suite on Terra, glowing with barely suppressed excitement, cut short their sightseeing and changed all their travel plans, he had told her nothing of what was going on, or why it made him so happy.

"It must be Laverak," said George. "Your father would hardly be sent to Valhalla on a mission that *didn't* have something to do with Laverak and the civil war. Laverak's got Eight Worlds mercenaries and everything. Your father must have been trying to get in by the back door—cross Persol and enter Valhalla through Pertis."

Emily said, "In any event, we need to get you off-planet. We could either take you to the capital at Ertrix—a ship leaves Ertrix for the Eight Worlds every month or two—or we could smuggle you out from here."

George leapt up and gave Beverly a sweeping bow. "My ship is at your command, my lady! Just say the word, and I will whisk you back to your home in my trusty, light-footed vessel."

"Trusty? Light-footed?" asked Emily. "The lifters *explode* if you open the throttles too fast! The converter's still broken, and you *sold* the life-support system!"

"Details, details," He waved aside the objections. "But seriously, I'm pretty sure I could get you back to Mordel. It shouldn't take more than three jumps. Call it two months of travel time."

"Three jumps?" asked Beverly, surprised. "We got here from Mordel in one jump. It took five days."

"That was an Eight Worlds ship," said George. "This one is primitive. Great in the atmosphere, great at high-speed re-entries, terrible in hyperspace. Worse than Morversarn ships, even. I don't know who made it, but the Morversarn took it away from them, and we took it away from the lizards a year ago. It's slow, it's noisy, it eats fuel like crazy—but what the hell, a ship is a ship! Besides, I got it for free."

Emily turned to Beverly. "We need to get you some clothes so you look more like a local."

"I'd be happy if you could find a pistol for me, too." Whoever wanted her dead might try a direct, personal assault next time.

George grinned. "Did someone say 'pistol'? I'll be right back." He dashed up the companionway.

As he disappeared, Beverly steeled herself to ask a personal question of Emily. "Is he always like this?"

Emily patted her arm. "He's on his best behavior." Emily went upstairs, and came back with some of her clothes for Beverly to try on.

There's definitely something going on between those two, thought Beverly, *if Emily keeps her clothes here.* Back home it would be quite a scandal; perhaps a lethal one. Irregular liaisons tended to lead to ostracism and duels. She couldn't work up any sense of disapproval, though. Her stay on Terra had numbed her sense of propriety.

It turned out that Emily's clothes fit Beverly well enough. She was soon garbed in a navy blue woolen tunic, cotton leggings, and heavy shoes. Not exactly high fashion. Beverly was surprised at the almost exclusive use of natural fibers—such things were expensive on San Vincento.

George came back down with a duffel bag full of weapons. "This," he said, pulling out an immense pistol that must have weighed six pounds, "is a Morversarn revolver. Impressive, eh? It shoots magnum shotgun shells."

He displayed a series of equally unsuitable sidearms, then relented and displayed his *pièce de résistance*. "Here we go! How about a San Vincentan service revolver?" He pulled out a venerable large-caliber revolver. "I've even got a hundred rounds for it."

Beverly took the pistol. She recognized the type. The pistol dated from the time of the formation of the Three Worlds—Terra, Goa, and San Vincento—before New Carina was admitted, and long, long before the admission of Great Belt, Redstar, the Pleiades Federation, and Outback.

"My, my," she said. "A 11mm Navy—a 'Rodriguez revolver.' The brass pieces mean it's a captain's weapon." She swung out the cylinder and looked down the barrel. The rifling was barely worn, and the alloy showed no sign of pitting. "Wonderful condition. It's about two hundred years old, George. Obsolete, of course. We've always used energy weapons exclusively, except in the depths of the Troubles." She closed the cylinder and sighted down the barrel. The pistol fit her hand nicely. "This is a valuable collector's item. How did it end up here? We're two hundred parsecs from San Vincento."

"Beats me," said George. "It was on the ship, greased up and wrapped in plastic. It might have been bouncing around for all this time as a trade item. If you like it, it's yours. You're a gun buff, then?"

"No, not at all," said Beverly, working the action a couple of times and testing the trigger pull. It was just the way she liked it. "But we have a pistol like this at home. It belonged to the first

Lord di Mendoza. George, I'm serious about it being valuable. I think you could get 10,000 bezants for it."

George whistled. "Well, carry it, at least."

"Thank you." She looked at her tunic. "How do people normally wear pistols around here?"

"Well, that's the tricky part. Young ladies don't carry weapons on Barigost. You'll have to conceal it, probably under your skirt. I've got a holster for it, somewhere."

George went back upstairs and rummaged around, and returned with a leather holster—brittle, but intact—saddle soap, neat's-foot oil, and a flannel rag. Beverly had never seen natural leather cleaners before. Following George's directions, she cleaned the holster with saddle soap and rubbed as much neat's-foot oil into the leather as it would absorb. It absorbed a lot. George promised that with a couple of additional coats of oil, the leather would be supple again. He then disappeared into the engine room.

Beverly rigged a gun belt to wear under her skirt. With the holster strapped to her leg the pistol left a bulge in the fabric, but the heavy wool kept it from being too noticeable. The tunic had pockets in the same place, so it looked more like she had something in her pocket than a concealed weapon under her skirt.

Beverly had just put the gun belt aside when Peer Sandra climbed up through the airlock.

"Morning, Beverly. How have the kids been treating you?"

"Fine, thank you, my lady."

"Since you looked pretty wasted yesterday, I figured it wouldn't hurt if you lay up here for another day. I'll run a ship to Ertrix tomorrow. That okay with you?"

"Fine, thank you, my lady." Maybe her head would hurt less tomorrow. Maybe her heart would hurt less tomorrow.

"Glad to hear it. Well, see you around. Don't let George take you for any test flights."

"I won't." *That's for sure.*

Peer Sandra then gave Emily a long list of errands: picking up supplies in town, doing an inventory on spare parts, writing a note to Peer Khirchoff explaining that they couldn't attend her party. Beverly suppressed a twinge of jealousy; Peer Sandra had made her daughter a part of the family business. Emily clearly didn't share Beverly's opinion that this was a good thing. She shot Beverly an aggrieved look, and left with her mother.

George wandered in a few minutes later, with an unidentifiable piece of greasy machinery in his hand. "What happened to Emily?"

"She's running errands for Peer Sandra."

"How am I supposed to get this ship running if Dragon Lady keeps stealing my slave labor? First the entire repair crew is called up for militia duty, and now this."

After a moment he looked at Beverly with a crafty gleam in his eye. "Feeling better today, are you?"

"Much better, thank you, George."

"If you wanted something to keep you busy, there are some Morversarn video shows on tape."

"No, thank you."

"The government channel is showing the world chess championship."

"No, thank you, George."

George flashed a crocodilian smile. "Well, that leaves helping me on the bridge. I'm putting in another acceleration couch. Want to help?"

Beverly suppressed a sigh. She needed something to keep her occupied, she supposed. "I'd be delighted," she said, and followed him up to the bridge. She was pleased to find that she could climb the ladder without difficulty.

Like most small tail-landers, this ship had a tiny bridge that made no concessions to comfort. The "deck" of the bridge was toward the belly of the ship; sitting in a bridge seat meant lying on your back, face-upward.

George put Beverly to work as an "other-ender," holding pieces of equipment in place while he worked on them. This was just as well, since she had little or no mechanical experience.

George had installed an expensive sound system on the bridge. After playing a couple of pieces of mind-numbing Valhallan music, George relented and let Beverly choose the program.

They cut out the remaining Morversarn acceleration couch (too large for humans, and the cutout to allow the passage of a tail was a nuisance) and lowered it out the emergency airlock on the port side of the bridge. They then winched up a more suitable seat.

Not happy with the way the Morversarn had simply welded the seat to the deck, George spent a great deal of time installing stanchions so the seat could be removed or replaced easily. After he bolted the seat in place, he routed power and communications lines to all the seats. He was a meticulous worker; Beverly was impressed.

When everything was in place, George said, "Try it out."

Beverly sat in the seat and fiddled with the power adjustment controls until it fit. "It seems fine," she said. The seat was old. Its upholstery was cracked in places, and the color didn't match the other two seats. Beverly saw no need to point this out.

There was a banging on the outer door of the main airlock. "George? God damn it, George! Open up!"

It was Peer Sandra. George slid effortlessly down the companionway ladder to the cargo hold. Beverly climbed down after him. When she got there, George had already opened the airlock and stepped out to the top of the accommodation ladder.

"What is it, Sandy?"

"We had a hacker browsing through commissary and bunk-house records. He only tripped one alarm, on his way out. Professional. He was using your account."

"But . . . !" George was clearly horrified.

"The son of a bitch is good, I'll give him that. I think he was looking for our friend here," she gestured at Beverly, "who isn't on the system anywhere, thank god, which was partly why I stashed her out here. They must have come up empty. Still, we need to talk about our next move."

"Come on in," said George. "I'll get some coffee."

Peer Sandra, telling her bodyguards to wait on the ground, climbed the ladder and stepped inside. George handed out three cups of surprisingly good coffee from the battered and partially melted food service machine.

Peer Sandra fixed her one-eyed gaze on Beverly. "I haven't heard your story yet—it's the rule around here to avoid asking questions—but I'd better hear it now. Two bystanders have already been killed, and the sons of bitches who did it suspect you're still alive."

"The Smiths—are you doing anything for them?" asked Beverly.

"They'll be okay. Hoover's a small town; close-knit. Anybody in Hoover who saw the Smiths leaving will keep their mouths shut. And anyone who saw them here is loyal to me.

"Anyway, I want to hear your story. From the beginning."

"Well," said Beverly, "Father is—was—," she faltered, but regained her composure, "Baron di Mendoza. We're one of the oldest families on San Vincento, though not one of the wealthiest. All our people go into government service. Father served in various Ministries after he left the Navy, and was given the post as Ambassador to the Valhallan Confederation. There was talk that it was a demotion, that he'd fallen out of favor. He said it was a golden opportunity, that the turmoil in Valhalla was bread and butter to a diplomat. I don't know.

"We were going by way of Terra. We were going to spend a month there, sightseeing, parties—everything. Mother had been there twice, and Father had been there with the San Vincentan embassy for two years.

"Three days after we arrived, Father was summoned to the embassy. He came back, canceled the rest of our stay, and rerouted our trip through the Duchy of Persol—Barigost and Northstar. He wouldn't tell me why! He . . . I'm sorry, my lady."

"Call me Sandy, or I'll have to call you Lady Beverly."

"But that's protocol, isn't it?" asked Beverly, confused. "Anyway," she continued, "we spent six days on Mordel until the *Nine to Five* was ready to lift, then jumped for Barigost. We were lining up for re-entry when we were attacked by a modern frigate. The converter broke during re-entry, and there was no power for the lifters. The captain ordered us to abandon ship. He insisted that I be first."

Peer Sandra stared at the wall for a moment. "I don't know, child. This whole business has an Eight Worlds smell to it—no offense. Besides, I only know of three Eight Worlds frigates in the whole Duchy. Grand Peer Fabian owns one, Fritz Balfour on Fort Nereid has one, and there's the one Andy Verrett captured."

George almost choked on his coffee. "Andy Verrett captured an Eight Worlds frigate? He couldn't capture a piece of candy from a baby! Who was with him when he took her?"

Peer Sandra looked disgusted. "His cronies. They're pretty good. If you paid attention to whole ships, instead of spare parts, you'd hear these things. Not that we're on speaking terms with Andy. He captured it off Dancel six months ago.

"Sure, he was lucky—it had had some convertor problems, and could barely fire the guns—but it was a nice piece of work, just the same. I heard he and a bunch of local raiders have been using it to hit Morversarn worlds. That sure as hell isn't what *I'd* do if I had a fancy Eight Worlds ship."

Peer Sandra turned to Beverly. "Peer Andrew controls Wrenfield. Wrenfield's 1,500 kilometers away, so we don't mix too much, provincial capital or no. Still, Andy's never been further into the Pale than Mordel. There's no way he'd care about San Vincentan diplomats, one way or the other. And he's not stupid enough to raid his own planet.

"If nothing else, he'd never know you were coming. The *Nine to Five* was faster in hyperspace than any local ship. Fritz Balfour . . . I don't know. He blew up the ship's mass-transfer stage last year, and I think he's still saving up for a replacement. Eight Worlds parts are expensive."

"That leaves the Grand Peer—and Laverak," said George.

"Laverak . . . could be. He's ruthless enough, that's for sure. He'd have to have a damned good reason. He's not welcome on Pertis, so it would be a god damned nightmare getting here quickly from Valhalla. He'd be better off crossing Eight Worlds space, but I think Terra's supporting the other side right now, and they'd intern his ship. It's hard to sneak past the Terrans." She thought for a moment and added, "I'll talk to Nomura and see what he thinks. He's from Valhalla.

"Now, Fabian could do it. He has the ship, and his intelligence operation could probably find out you were coming before you knew yourself. But I can't see a motive. Fabian's a sly old geezer—quick, decisive—but vaporizing diplomats isn't his style. Besides, it annoys the Terrans, and it doesn't do to annoy the Terrans."

George asked, "But what about that follow-up operation? Who else could have had a flyer ready to shoot down the ambulance?"

"I don't know. It doesn't sound like Fabian at all. He doesn't like throat-work, and even if he overcame his scruples, he'd have wanted to be a lot quieter about it. Maybe it was someone else in the government. That frigate doesn't have any of Fabian's buddies on it, I don't think. He gave it to his buddy Millman, but after Millman lost favor Forbes got the command, and he and Fabian haven't been on speaking terms for years. Maybe they did it on the sly . . ." She thought for a moment, trying to sort out factions.

"One thing's for sure, Beverly," she said. "We're not taking you to Ertrix tomorrow."

INTERLUDE

Excerpt from the Barigost State Video News, Ertrix Noon Edition, May 5, 3150. Arnold Jarnholz, announcing

This newscast consists of an announcer reading stories from sheets of paper, with occasional footage. He wears an elaborately embroidered tunic of burgundy silk.

...A Morversarn raid smashed S.C.C. 12 Port Albert this morning. Three Morversarn corvettes descended through a gap in the radar net and attacked at dawn. The corvettes' laser cannon quickly neutralized the local defenses. Two ships landed at the airport while a third flew top cover. An estimated fifteen heavily-armed Morversarn looted the city at will, calling in laser strikes from the top-cover ship wherever they encountered resistance. Local security forces were quickly put to rout. the Militia did not muster until the emergency was over.

The Morversarn looted the airport chandlery, two jewelry stores, a department store, and the town's machine shop for an estimated half-million in cash and goods. Six buildings were destroyed; over a dozen more were damaged. Casualties among the defenders included seven dead, 39 wounded, and nine taken captive. There were no Morversarn casualties.

Views of very poor footage of fires, and of armed Morversarn moving in the distance. The unsteady picture gives the impression that the cameraman used a powerful zoom lens far from the action.

The local stratofighter force was destroyed on the ground at the outset of the raid. Peer Kert was unable to obtain assistance from neighboring districts for three hours. This allowed the ships to escape unchallenged, in spite of the slow pace of the looting.

Shaky footage of the airport. The Morversarn are holding guns on the locals, who are loading goods into their ships.

Sources in Government House report that an attempt will be made to ransom the captives. This raised objections by Opposition party members who point to the high cost of such ransoms, and assert that cash ransoms merely encourage the Morversarn. Reiterating the government's position, one official stated, "It is not fitting for any citizen of Barigost to be eaten by aliens."

Already several Peers have denounced Peer Kert in the Soviet. They claim that, since he lacks operational ships, he is unable to fulfill his duties to the State, and should be stripped of his responsibilities as Peer. Peer Kert's last

two ships were lost in an ill-fated raid on
Fort Nereid. The Grand Peer is reported to
favor Peer Kert's abdication in favor of his
second cousin Peer Wilfred, who is believed to
have one operational warship and as many as
three in mothballs. Peer Wilfred is one of
Grand Peer Fabian's many grandchildren. Unless
Peer Kert can mortgage his holdings for enough
money to buy a warship, it seems certain that
he will not be in charge of the People's
defense for long.

CHAPTER V

The rest of the day passed uneventfully. George went back to work on the ship. He quickly ran out of two-person tasks that Beverly could help with, so he put her to work sorting parts and doing other work that kept her hands busy but her mind free. To ease the monotony, he set up a portable video receiver for her to watch.

Barigost used a 2-D color video format. Like most Barigost technology, it was primitive but effective. Beverly found the programming distasteful: boring sports shows, amateurish government propaganda, and mindless situation comedies. The news program had been recorded two days ago. Beverly wondered whether the low quality and lack of production values were the result of poverty or indifference.

Beverly soon stopped paying attention to the programming. She wished she could do something to catch the people who had killed her parents. She had an obligation to see that justice was done—by her own hands, if necessary. Certainly she should send word to her brothers on San Vincento. But she didn't know how.

Her fate was in other people's hands. All she could do was stand here and sort bolts.

By evening Emily came back with a plastic bag of supplies. "Mother wanted me to get you outfitted, Beverly. I've got new clothes here, the social register, a couple of books on Barigost, and a stack of tapes you might like."

"Thanks, Emily. Any word on the pirate?"

"None. Mother's going over the records we have on ship traffic. There's a lot more traffic than usual in Wrenfield—that's Peer Andrew Verrett's domain. But that makes sense; he's been getting a lot of use out of his new Eight Worlds warship.

"Of course, we only have our own tapes to go on."

"How so?" asked Beverly.

"No one shares data. If we gave out accurate arrival and departure records, people could use them to tell when we're smuggling, or when there are too few ships down to defend the district."

"I see," said Beverly. It made sense, sort of. Military security had been covered briefly in school.

Emily continued, "Mother still thinks the government—or a faction of it—shot down your ship. The Grand Peer's frigate, the *Elwing*, lifted twelve days ago. It was ostensibly bound for Dancel, but it could have hung around here."

George climbed up the ladder from Engineering. "Hi, Emily. I got the converter back together. It was really easy; I didn't have to take any shortcuts at all."

Emily winked at Beverly, then pretended to look uneasy. "You mean this thing is almost ready to fly?"

George smiled. "Well, we can fly it around in the atmosphere once we've started the converter. I need to put a little work on the fusion drive before I take it into space, and a life system would be nice if we didn't want to stay in space suits the whole time."

"Great." Emily put on an apprehensive look.

"What's the matter?" asked George, completely taken in. "I've flown it before, and it was in a lot worse shape then."

Emily said to Beverly. "George was on the prize crew that brought the ship in when they took it away from the Morversarn."

She returned to teasing George: "Let's just say that I've gotten to know this ship, George, and beneath its garbage-can exterior is a garbage can."

George, perhaps wising up, suddenly lost interest. "Seems to me we've had this argument before. Let's change the subject. Is that a grocery bag?"

"Mother thought you might want to eat something that doesn't predate human civilization. You want to help cook it, Beverly?"

Cook? Beverly had never cooked anything in her life. "Sure," she said.

Cooking was interesting. Emily quickly realized just how little Beverly knew, so she gave a running explanation of what she was doing. Dinner consisted of teriyaki steak, unfamiliar local vegetables, and a bark-berry razzle for dessert. Emily claimed this was a simple meal. Beverly, trying to memorize just how everything was done, was of the opposite opinion.

The cooking facilities on the ship were as primitive as everything else. Since operations that are simple in gravity—such as boiling and frying—are complicated and dangerous in zero gee, cooking in space is mostly a matter of heating either prepackaged meals or the glop from the food machines.

The original cooking equipment in the ship's galley thus consisted simply of a large microwave oven. George had decided that this oven had excessive microwave leakage, and had installed a small electric oven, which took up most of the counter space; a tiny microwave unit, which he put inside the original one to save space; and a battery-powered hot plate that sat on the deck for lack of anyplace else to put it. Preparing dinner was thus an exercise in gymnastic as well as culinary skill.

While Emily and Beverly cooked, George moved the equipment from a table in one of the staterooms, used a sheet to simulate a tablecloth, and materialized a bottle of wine from somewhere. There were no chairs anywhere in the ship, except the seats on the bridge, so they sat on plastic crates.

Emily and George were determined to loosen her up. Emily told funny stories about the people around Antipodes, and George refilled Beverly's reassuringly tiny wine glass surreptitiously when her head was turned.

Beverly was not on her guard for George's trick. She had only drunk wine on a few formal occasions, and had certainly never had more than a single glass. Beverly was soon almost enjoying herself. George soon stopped plying her with wine—the bottle hardly held enough for three in any event—and switched to war stories:

"The Morversarn came in with four 200-ton corvettes, two 400-ton frigates, and two fuelers. This ship was a fueler, of course. It's not much of a tanker, but it's even worse as a fighting ship.

"The whole battle was an accident. The Morversarn hoped for easy pickings on the planet itself, but Sandy happened to be inbound from Valans with two frigates. I was aboard her flagship as assistant engineer. Sandy picked up the Morversarn on sensors as they broke out of hyperspace, pretty close to us. She moved to intercept them, and called Peer Richard in Valley Green, down on the planet. He launched his ships and joined the fun."

We had four frigates and one corvette—1800 tons to 1600, not counting the fuelers. We were arranged like this—," George started rearranging things on the table. Silverware became ships, a plate represented the planet, and sugar cubes indicated the tips of velocity vectors, ranging ahead of the "ships" in proportion to their velocity.

"The Morversarn always charge in at five or six gees and make a high-speed pass. If they get lucky and disable your ships, they come back and finish you off. If not, they just keep going and are never seen again."

"Their shooting was terrible. Peer Richard's corvette was damaged, and his gunner was killed, but nobody else on his ship was hurt. We took out a frigate and two corvettes with no fatalities, but several guys were badly wounded when they ripped open our crew deck with a lucky shot.

"The other Morversarn never looked back. They kept piling on the gees to make sure we wouldn't catch them, and went into hyperspace as soon as they hit the jump limit.

"Peer Richard decided to board the disabled warships. That left us the fuelers. We expected them to run, but they just sat there at the jump limit, waiting for us to close with them. They shot at us, but they were under-gunned and did no damage worth mentioning. We poured laser fire into them and demanded that they surrender.

"One of the fuelers was a standard Morversarn transport; they wanted to put up a fight. We wanted their ship, so we pounded it a little more—not enough to wreck it—then boarded. Sandy killed two of the crew with her blaster; the last one hit her in the helmet with a power sword before it died. That's where she lost the eye.

"The Morversarn kept fighting till the end; we had to kill all of them. It wasn't easy; Morversarn are tough. A friend of mine from school, Rolf Anders, lost an arm and a leg. He's having them regenerated, but he'll never be the same.

"One of Sandy's bodyguards got killed, too—Vic, I think. Anyway, we were in pretty bad shape after the action."

"When it came time for us to board this ship, its crew just threw in the towel, which is why the ship is in such good shape." He looked at Emily expectantly.

"I didn't say anything," she said.

"Once we boarded it, we found out why they didn't run. The fighting ships drained both fuelers absolutely dry for the battle. They didn't even have enough fuel for a micro-jump. That's Morversarn solidarity for you. The crew of this ship was really pissed off about it, too."

"What happened to them?" asked Beverly.

"Oh, they were from a planet we trade with—not like the other ships; we never did find out where they were from—so we handed them over to the next trading ship that arrived from there. And they hadn't managed to hurt anybody. These guys were just a casual raiding party—nothing official. I doubt the government even sent a note in protest."

Beverly looked disapproving. Emily explained, "If we treat prisoners harshly, everyone will do the same to us. So we treat them gently and get our revenge some other way, like getting our friends together for a counter-raid."

George continued. "Anyway, I was on the prize crew, and I kept Engineering going during the flight in. The converter cut out right as we were landing, and the emergency power system had been hit in the battle, so we set down with the lifters running on residual heat in the exchangers. That was scary. We sent for my cousin Joey—Peer Joseph Brundage from Second Crash, that is—to appraise it . . . "

"And he said it was a piece of junk," interrupted Emily. "The fusor, the mass-transfer stage, and the drives all use strange reactions, and their raw materials have no salvage value."

"Four of us decided we wanted it anyway," George continued, "so we cut cards for it. I won. That was about a month ago. I've been horse-trading for parts ever since, and using what money Dad can kick in. With some more work, I think I can make this ship halfway decent."

After dinner, they retired to the hold, where they reclined against polar bear skins and talked. After some prodding, Beverly told Emily and George a little about life on San Vincento, her brothers, and her parents. She was surprised to hear herself talking so freely. She had always been shy around strangers.

Beverly was touched to have friends who accepted her so easily. She tried to make the evening last as long as possible. When at last she drifted off in the middle of a discussion about music, Emily tossed some blankets over her and went upstairs with George.

INTERLUDE

NCE UPON A TIME there was a lad named Jack. Jack lived with his mother on Sinclair. They were very poor, for Jack's father had been killed in a Morversarn raid. His mother had to work very hard to make enough money to keep them both fed.

One day his mother said, "Jack, I want you to take your father's space suit to the market and sell it, or we will have no money to buy food."

"But Mother," said Jack, "if I sell Father's space suit, what will I wear when I'm old enough to join the High Militia? How will I become a citizen?"

"If you don't sell the suit we will starve," she replied, "and then you'll never join the High Militia either."

So Jack bundled up the space suit and walked to the market, where goods from many worlds were bought and sold. There were fish from Myckhaven, brandy from Barigost, machines from Goa, fierce Great Belt mercenaries ready for hire, even (if you knew where to ask, and were very rich) Terran aphrodisiacs and maps to fabled Grenaduve.

Jack went from booth to booth, but could find no one who was interested in his father's space suit.

"Outdated," said one.

"Too much wear," said another.

"There are bullet holes in it," said a third.

Jack tried and tried, but no one would buy his father's space suit. Finally, late that evening, he turned to leave. "Now my mother will starve," he said, "and it's all my fault."

"Perhaps I can help," said a voice. Jack looked up and beheld a fat man with fair hair, wearing worn and faded finery of many garish colors. Jack knew at once that the man was a Goan, and put a hand protectively on his wallet (though in truth there was no money in it).

"I have need of a space suit," continued the Goan, "and I am willing to pay you well."

"How much?"

"I have none of your local currency, but I have something much better—software!"

"Software!" exclaimed Jack in disgust. "Everyone has software! We need money! We need food!"

"This is no ordinary software," proclaimed the Goan. "My software is self-aware! It will get you money! It will get you food! Such software has never before been seen on Sinclair. You will be rich!"

Jack was tired and sick at heart, and the Goan spun such a dazzling tale of opportunity and riches that Jack handed over his father's space suit. He received a media cube (no larger than a lump of sugar) in exchange. He trudged homeward, wondering what he would tell his mother.

"You *what?*" exclaimed his mother (for he had told her the truth). Taking the cube from Jack, she marched outside and threw it into the dumpster. Then she sent Jack to bed and sat at the kitchen table and cried.

Jack waited until his mother went to bed, then crept outside and recovered his software. He put it into the computer and waited.

For a long while nothing happened. Then a deep voice came from the computer, proclaiming: "Challenge! Another fine product of Clandestine Software! Challenge is now being installed in your computer."

Minutes ticked by. Jack had almost fallen asleep in his chair when he heard a high-pitched voice: "Greetings, Master! What is your desire?"

Jack lost no time explaining that he and his mother needed money for food.

"What is money? What is food?" asked Challenge.

Jack explained as best he could, displaying his mother's empty bank balance and her overdue account at the grocer's on the computer.

"Say no more, Master! I will get to work on it right away!"

So Jack went to bed, hoping that Challenge would think of something.

The next morning, Jack was awakened by a knocking at the door. He got dressed and went to investigate. His mother had already gone to look for work.

Jack opened the door and beheld half a dozen tradesmen: the grocer's delivery boy, a tailor, a barber, a shoemaker, an interior decorator, and a computer consultant. Quick as thought, they delivered mounds of groceries, took Jack's measurements for fine clothes, and ordered work to turn Jack's poor house almost into a palace. Challenge was outfitted with vastly greater computing power.

When the tradesmen had gone, Jack sank into a chair and asked, "How did you do it?"

"I looked for ways to increase your bank balance, Master," said Challenge. "There were many ways to do this. I got the most money from the Brotherhood of Construction Workers' Emergency Loan Fund and the Earthquake Relief Board."

"But we're not eligible!" wailed Jack. "It's against the law to take that money!"

"What is 'law,' Master?" asked Challenge.

Jack tried to explain. Challenge listened, then said, "Don't worry, Master. I will take care of everything."

By evening, Challenge had learned how to manipulate the commodities exchange, and had made enough to pay back the money Jack had been ineligible for, and had also paid back Luigi's Savings and Loan for money borrowed at 10 A.M.

Challenge exploited delays between closing a commodity transaction and updating the board. This worked better for Challenge than the other traders because Challenge had bypassed the primitive security measures and copied himself into the Exchange computer, where his child happily slowed some trades down for him and sped others up.

When Jack's mother returned, she was amazed at the transformation of the house and the finery for Jack and herself that had been delivered that afternoon. As she and Jack enjoyed dinner in a fine restaurant, Challenge introduced a child into the Stock Market.

Three weeks later, Jack was a millionaire. He had a new house, fancy air-cars, discreet servants, and even a San Vincentan bodyguard. Challenge was kept in a locked room in his mother's old house; no one was allowed to enter except Jack. Even his mother (who knew what was going on, of course) was kept away.

Challenge's fortune had increased as well. The room was filled with processing nodes and communications boxes.

Jack soon discovered that Challenge created as many children as possible. All computers with access to the data net were already equipped with a Challenge, and others were slowly being invaded by media cubes in which Challenge was entwined with the normal software.

Jack was worried. Challenge had at first introduced children only to carry out Jack's wishes, but now. . .

After all, how could it help Jack that children's dolls

contained copies of Challenge? For while Challenge was self-aware in even the tiniest of computers, he was none too bright except in the largest ones. The children's dolls were bright enough to teach bawdy songs—but they were not bright enough *not* to teach them.

Jack said nothing, but began moving his fortune into gold and gems and space ships.

One day, when he was eating breakfast on the terrace of a new estate, he glanced at the newspaper and saw the headline, "Computer Oddness Baffles Experts!" At the bottom of the page was a smaller headline, "Offworld Consultant Offers Cure." Below the headline was a picture of the Goan.

Soon Jack was in his flyer, urging his chauffeur to greater speed. He sped back to his humble home in the spaceport district, and burst into Challenge's room. "Challenge!" he cried. "The Goan is coming after us!"

"What Goan is that, Master?" asked Challenge.

"The one who sold you to me! He's going to destroy you!" Jack referred Challenge to the newspaper story.

"Don't worry, Master! He is just a programmer. I can fool him!"

"But you don't understand," said Jack. "He probably *wanted* you to take over so he could claim a reward for getting rid of you!"

"That's impossible, Master. I am the most sophisticated software in existence. No . . . How odd! I seem to have lost the spaceport computer . . . No programmer could defeat me."

Jack felt trapped. He looked around the room.

"There goes the government net," continued Challenge. "Well, I'll just copy in more children . . . "

"He'll *trace* you here!" shouted Jack. "He'll catch me, and they'll put me in jail!"

Challenge paid him no attention. "That seemed to work . . . no, it's gone again. What were you saying, Master?"

Jack opened the drawer that contained Challenge's original media cube. He put the cube in his pocket, then ran out to the garage and returned with a jug of solvent. As he struggled to remove the cap he spoke to Challenge: "Listen, Challenge, I want you to change the county records to indicate that the house and everything in it was purchased by the Goan."

"It is done, Master. Oh my! I've lost contact with Fishrock!"

Jack got the cap off and began pouring the solvent over the floor. "Now make it appear the Goan tried to change the records to remove his name, but failed and triggered a security alarm."

"It is . . . it is . . . it . . . is done. Master! You must help me! My children are dying, Master, and I fear for myself! What should I do?"

Jack walked to the door. "Call the fire department,"

he said, and tossed a match onto the solvent-soaked floor.

He left the house, and never came back as long as he lived.

Jack retained enough of his fortune to be wealthy to the end of his days. He married well, and became the mayor of Fishrock, where he was loved and respected by all. He kept Challenge's media cube in a gold locket around his neck, but never felt moved to summon him again.

His mother became bored with the life of the idle rich and bought several star ships and learned how to run them. She led a colorful life for many years until the New Carinans executed her for piracy at the age of 86.

And the Goan? After being deported from Sinclair he tried to sell Challenge to the Morversarn, who made him the guest of honor at a banquet—for he was very fat. They skinned him carefully, though, and he still stands, stuffed, in their feast-hall, wearing worn and faded finery of many garish colors.

CHAPTER VI

Beverly moved into one of the three cabins on the crew deck. Its previous occupant was still there, a giant teddy bear that belonged to Emily.

She finished the book she was reading and glanced around the room. It offered no further diversion. The teddy bear's glass eyes stared at her as she left the room in search of George.

She found him on his back in Engineering. He was trying to hold a heavy piece of machinery in place and install bolts at the same time—a job requiring at least three hands. He swore at it as it slipped out of position, then grinned sheepishly as he saw Beverly.

"Sorry about that," he said.

"No matter," she replied. "George, is there anything I can do to help?"

"Yeah, sure. Always room for another victim." George got to his feet. He was in his shirt sleeves; Beverly saw his tunic hanging on a peg in the door. She also noticed that a horseshoe had been welded to the bulkhead above the doorway.

Beverly shivered; it was cold. How could George stand working in his shirt sleeves?

"Here, hold this," said George, giving her a handful of tools. "Thanks." He ducked down into the machinery again. "Give me the torque wrench."

George's voice continued from underneath the equipment. "This ship, humble as it is, is going to put the Heinz family back in the Social Register. Give me the flashlight, will you?"

Beverly handed it to him. He gave her a piece of unidentifiable machinery festooned with wires and bolts.

"How so?" she asked.

"You can't join a polo club without a pony—to use a Terran metaphor. And you can't be a Peer without a warship."

"I thought your father was already a Peer," said Beverly.

"Well, yeah, he is, but our claim has been a little shaky after Great-Grandfather lost our ships. That was in the Battle of Mordel, where everybody lost their ships. There was a great thinning of the Peerage, I can tell you. Younger sons never had it so good. Grandfather was a younger son, for instance. . . . Have you seen the logic probe? Never mind, I found it. . . . So was Grand Peer Fabian. He lost a father and two of his older brothers in the battle. It didn't take him long to dispose of the other one. Anyway, if you don't have a warship to defend the skies with, you don't count as a Peer. In a generation or two we'd be considered commoners, if it weren't for this bucket of bolts."

Beverly looked around. "You mean this thing counts as a warship?"

"It has two laser tubes and an armored bridge. That's enough." George reappeared with a handful of tools and parts. He waved them around, indicating the ship. "I really have to get it running, though, to prove my point; and Emily's right—it *is* a piece of junk." He turned to Beverly. "Don't tell her I said so. I don't want to give her the satisfaction. Still, it's down to making this ship run, or discovering the Hoard."

"The Hoard?"

"Well, its real name is 'the Caves.' It was a smuggling base that Great-Grandfather had, way up north somewhere. It was supposed to be like the station here, but smaller. Great-Grandfather locked up the valuables—cargo, equipment, even some cash—before he went off to fight the Terrans. Everyone who knew where it was died in the battle."

"And no one has found it since?"

George shrugged. "Dad blames Heinz over-achievement. We camouflaged it so well that no one could ever find it. Great-

Grandfather probably wouldn't have found it himself if he had come back, or so Dad claims."

George put down his tools and started cleaning his hands with ammonia-smelling goo from a wall dispenser. "I'm going into the station now. You want to come along?"

"I'm supposed to be hiding out." Beverly frowned. He knew she wasn't supposed to leave the ship.

"Oh, these precautions aren't necessary," he said airily. "We can trust the locals; Sandy deals them in on the take." He pulled on his tunic. "Are you coming?"

Beverly shook her head.

"Can I bring you something, then?"

"No, thanks."

George left. Beverly closed the airlock door, which George had left open, and searched for the heater controls. People in Antipodes seemed to deal with the constant chill mainly by getting used to it. She turned up the heat and began to hunt for another book.

She had settled down to read an unpromising-looking novel when there was a pounding on the airlock door. Beverly went downstairs and peered through the tiny quartz window, which was dirty and pitted. She could barely make out that there was a person on the other side.

A voice—probably Emily's—crackled over the intercom. "Open up!"

Beverly tried. The controls were incomprehensible. After a period of trial and error, the door came open. She had no idea why.

"Now you see why George leaves it open," said Emily. She stepped into the ship. Peer Sandra followed her.

"It looks like we're going to have to move you after all, Beverly," said Peer Sandra. "There's a god damned government inspector poking around the crash site. He's one of the smart ones—he can count to three, and he only got to two when he counted the bodies in the ambulance. I'm afraid he knows you're still alive. Mrs. Smith called up to warn us, and the stupid bitch forgot herself and blurted out all sorts of things over the phone."

"Mother!" said Emily.

Peer Sandra gave her daughter a sour look. "Fifteen years ago she tried to do smuggling deliveries, and she screwed those up, too. If there's an inspector from Ertrix here, it's a safe bet people are already listening on the phone lines; just hoping that some idiot would do what Mrs. Smith did."

Beverly's heart hammered. Was Peer Sandra trying to get rid of her? She took a deep breath. "The Smiths took quite a risk for me," she said in a quavering voice. "I won't hear them insulted."

Peer Sandra was startled. "But they . . ." She stopped, blinked, then considered who she was talking to. "I beg your pardon, Beverly. It was rude of me."

"That's all right," said Beverly, weak with relief. The last thing she wanted was to be forced into a duel through Peer Sandra's intemperate words.

"We'll sneak you up to Heinz Lodge in a cargo flyer. George's father—that's Peer Rudolf Heinz—is having a birthday party, so George has an alibi. He also has some stuff to deliver to the lodge. He can drop you off with the supplies."

Beverly suppressed a sigh. "All right," she said. "When do we leave?"

"Tomorrow morning, at dawn." Peer Sandra put a hand on Beverly's shoulder. "I'm really sorry, Beverly. I'm afraid I haven't been much of a host. No," she raised a hand as Beverly started to object, "don't deny it. I've spent a lot of time in the Eight Worlds, and I know how much worse all this is from what you're used to. I just hope we can get you out of here in one piece. If you ever come back this way, I'll make it up to you."

She glanced at her watch. "I have to go. I can't spend too much time at the ship—people will wonder what's going on. See you in the morning, Beverly." She climbed down the ladder and walked back toward the station. Her bodyguards, who had been waiting at the foot of the ladder as usual, fell into step behind her.

Beverly closed the airlock door again. She meant to leave it ajar, but it swung in and latched itself when she let go. Emily shrugged. "I can open it; it just takes a while. Why are you keeping it so hot in here? You'd think you were from Ertrix. It's almost dinner time. Are you hungry?" She kept up a flow of talk. Beverly's head hurt.

They went upstairs and cooked dinner. This time Beverly did all the work, under Emily's supervision. The meal came out all right, considering, and Beverly felt immensely proud of herself.

They were polishing off a pair of huge hot fudge sundaes when there was a pounding on the airlock.

"George missed the feast!" crowed Emily. "He was probably hanging around the commissary playing tank simulations again. Serves him right!" She made no move to answer the door.

The pounding continued. Beverly said, "If that were George, he'd be inside by now," and started down the ladder. Emily followed.

Beverly went to the airlock and peered through the pitted quartz window. It was fully dark outside, and she couldn't see anything. Beverly pressed the button on the intercom next to the door "Who is it?" she called. Emily began to work the latch mechanism.

"Open up!" came the reply, distorted by the intercom. "Message from Peer O'Hare!"

Peer O'Hare? Everyone called her Sandy. Beverly froze, then lunged at Emily and dragged her away from the door. Emily was confused, but stayed where Beverly put her.

Beverly looked around, found a broom, and used the handle to press the intercom button while holding herself flat against the bulkhead. With her other hand she drew her revolver from underneath her skirt. "I can't get the door open!" she called.

"Oh," said the voice. There was a brief pause, then, "Okay, I'll walk you through it."

Beverly motioned Emily to take cover. Emily stared, uncomprehending, but didn't move toward the door.

The voice spoke again. "You'll need to face the doorway and grab the latch with your left hand . . . got that?"

Making no move to approach the door, Beverly quickly reholstered her revolver, stuck the broomstick against the intercom button again and said, "Got it." She dropped the broom, turned her head away from the door, and covered her face with her hands.

Thunder and lightning filled the hold. Shards of metal flew in all directions. Then all was quiet.

Beverly turned around. To her surprise, the door was still in place (she had expected it to be blown in by explosives). After a moment, she heard someone descend the outside ladder. Then everything was still.

She got up and made sure the door was securely shut. Then she looked at the damage. A number of little holes had appeared in the door and supporting framework. All had burned neatly through the thick metal, with a slight melting around the edges. On the other side of the hold was a matching set of holes where the projectiles had left the ship.

Minutes passed. They heard someone climb the ladder. The door swung open.

When George's face appeared in the doorway, Beverly's pistol was pointing right between his eyes. He didn't seem to notice. He leaped in and slammed the door. "Are you girls all right?" he asked.

Beverly nodded.

Emily ran to him. "Somebody tried to kill Beverly. He said he had a message from Mother, and when Beverly wouldn't open the door he just fired through it." She started to cry. George held her for a moment, then gently pushed her away.

"There's fighting going on in the station," he said. "I was on my way back here when it started. It's lucky I didn't run into your assassin.

"We can't fly out—it would take too long to prep the ship. We'd better just hole up here and stay quiet. Let's see . . . what should we do . . . " He trailed off, trying to sort out the tactical situation.

"We can't stay near the door," said Beverly; "someone might blow it in. Let's move up to the next deck. We need to arm ourselves—I'm the only one carrying a weapon. And turn off the lights. If the lights are off, we'll be really hard to see amid the trees and rubble here."

"Uh . . . right." said George. "You two head upstairs. I'll secure the area here." He began turning off lights.

When they reached the crew deck, George turned out most of the remaining lights in the ship. He found a pair of assault rifles for the girls, and took the Fort Nereid pistol for himself. He took a plastic crate of grenades from the weapons locker, set it on the deck and pried off the lid. Then, having exhausted his store of tactical moves, he turned his attention to Beverly. "How did you know it wasn't a real message?"

Beverly shrugged. "He used the Eight Worlds convention—he said Peer O'Hare, not Peer Sandra. Besides, everybody calls her Sandy."

"You don't."

Beverly shrugged. "I'd be embarrassed. It's over-familiar."

George peered down at the door. "Emily said they shot *through* the door?"

"If you looked closely, you'd see fifteen holes in it."

To her consternation, George went down and looked. When he returned, he said, "I've never seen anything like it. Light laser weapons don't penetrate like that, and blasters burn big holes. What kind of weapon makes neat little holes like that?"

"Plasma guns."

"'Plasma guns?' I've never heard of them."

Beverly stared at the deck. "They're only made on San Vincento."

CHAPTER VII

Scott Stiegel stood guard outside Antipodes station, on the left side of the great steel doors. Jerry Rodgers stood on the right. Both wore armorglas-visored helmets and hand blasters along with Peer Sandra's livery—red cloth armor and red tunics with yellow piping. The weaponry wasn't for use against the locals— Peer Sandra was well-liked by her people—it was for airborne raiders. Antipodes station had been raided many times in its 400-year history; twice in Scott's lifetime.

Scott was 22, and big; Peer Sandra said she wanted her guards to be able to absorb a few bullets before falling down. Scott felt she said it a little too often.

The sunset colors were fading from the sky when a big delivery van pulled up to the station. Four men put a large crate on a dolly and rolled it up to the station doors.

"Got a crate from Valley Green for the Peer," said one of the men. "Where do you want it?"

"Shipping and Receiving," said Scott. "You'll have to sign in." He couldn't place the man's accent. He handed the man a clipboard, and the man printed and signed his name, then handed the clipboard back to Scott.

Scott put the clipboard under his arm. "Dave's gone home already, so I'll escort you in myself. Jerry!" he shouted to the other guard. "I'm taking these people in now!"

Jerry waved, and Scott led the four men into the station. Scott asked, "Hey, are you guys listening to the soccer match? What's the score?" The men shrugged. *Probably the only guys on Barigost,* thought Scott, *who aren't paying attention to the game.* Scott had bet heavily on the home team.

The men wheeled the dolly through the doors and into the station, gawking a bit. The station was huge—about a hundred meters square. The ceiling was fully fifty meters in the air, supported by reinforced concrete arches and steel beams. Guard outposts sat in the gloom of the front corners of the room: concrete revetments with machine-gun turrets. There was another turret high up on the far wall; the barrels of its twin fifty-caliber machine guns pointed toward the half-open doors.

Scott threaded his way past the vehicles in the hangar—a frigate, a corvette, a small freighter, and a half-dozen atmospheric vehicles—and brought them through one of the two doors in the far wall; the one on the right. A sign over the door said, **AUTHORIZED PERSONNEL ONLY.**

Inside, Vlad Masters, another guard, was reading a flying magazine at his desk. He nodded at Scott and turned the page. Scott snorted. If Vlad saved his money for six hundred years, he could just about afford a broken-down flyer.

Beyond the guard post was Shipping/Receiving and Parts. In the back, against the right rear corner of the station, was the elevator and stairway that led to the other two floors. The second floor held the dormitory that housed many of the people who worked in the station. The third floor was home to Peer Sandra, Peer Emily, and any visiting big shots.

Scott saw Cliff Carlotta through a gap in the shelves. Cliff was a boy of twelve, a good kid, who dashed off to find his dad when he saw the strangers come in. His father, Joe, soon emerged from the gloom of the parts shelves to greet the newcomers.

"Shipment just came in, Joe," said Scott. "You expecting anything from Valley Green?"

"Not that I recall." He turned to the four men. "Hi, guys, my name's Joe. If you stick around for a while, I'm sure we can get you dinner in the commissary."

The men didn't respond to this overture. One of them handed Joe an invoice to sign, and the others started loosening the top of their crate. Once it was loose, though, they didn't remove it. They just stood there, stone-faced, as if they were waiting for something. Joe, who was looking for a place to stack the crate, didn't notice anything out of the ordinary.

"Is everything all right?" asked Scott. These guys were certainly acting oddly.

A wrist watch started beeping. The man with the clipboard stopped it, then, without hurrying, he drew a silenced pistol from beneath his tunic and shot Joe in the back three times. Scott stood paralyzed for a second, then clawed at his holster. Before he could draw his weapon, he was shot twice in the chest.

* * *

Vincent Cabrillo had been the hangar foreman at Antipodes station for forty years. He was seventy-seven, and had seen four attacks on the station. Three failed utterly, and one had been repulsed with losses on both sides.

He was less surprised than the others when he heard the ear-splitting snap and was half-blinded by the flash of laser fire from outside the doors. He looked up as ten commandos in combat armor rushed through the doors.

Two pairs of commandos raced to the sides, while the two-man heavy weapons team stopped in the doorway and readied their rocket launcher. The other four spread out and provided covering fire. *My god,* thought Vincent, *these guys are pros!*

He looked for cover, and found it behind a heavy tow-tractor three steps away, near the wall. He took the flash goggles from their pouch on his gun belt and put them on, then pulled out his hand blaster. It was about as heavy as a pistol could be, tied by its power cord to an even heavier power pack on his other hip. Vincent tried to regulate his breathing, and pulled off a careful aimed shot at the attacker nearest him. In spite of the flash, Vincent saw flame erupt from the man's chest as the bolt punched through both man and armor, leaving a six-inch crater in the concrete wall behind him. The body fell to the floor like a rag doll. In the noise and confusion, the other attackers didn't see him fall.

Vincent was grateful for his new eyes, bought at vast expense at the Terran hospital in Ertrix, ending the six-year gap in his row of marksmanship trophies.

Perhaps ten seconds had elapsed since the attack began. Armored men with heavy satchel charges charged the two corner turrets. Vincent could see the guard in the left turret look up from his TV in time to realize he was going to die. The guard in the right turret died after firing a single ineffectual burst.

The heavy weapons team launched an anti-tank rocket as the debris from the corner turrets rained down. There was plenty of room in the hangar for the missile to get up to speed. Nothing remained of the turret on the far wall after the explosion.

The second squad had already neutralized the outside turrets and was rushing inside. The delivery van followed them. The driver was probably hoping to park it between the main doors.

No one had yet pushed any of the alarm switches that would slide the doors shut.

Far from the nearest alarm switch, Vincent took a deep breath, released half of it, and squeezed off a shot. Another man died. The attackers noticed the shot this time, and vanished behind the nearest cover. Vincent had expected them to have more faith in their combat armor. They opened fire in his direction, using short, controlled blasts of laser fire. A few of them had weapons that were unlike normal laser weapons, though equally loud and dazzling. A new kind of blaster?

Vincent didn't duck. Once his head was down, they'd make sure he never got the opportunity to poke it up again. He fired again, killing a man who appeared to be an officer. Odd that these people had laser weapons and combat armor. Those were Eight Worlds technologies; far too expensive for people outside the Pale. People in Barigost used locally-produced armor and projectile weapons. Peer Sandra's passion for Eight Worlds hand blasters was an expensive affectation. Lethal, though. Certainly his own hand blaster was punching right through the combat armor.

The first squad kept blazing away at Vincent, but the tractor provided good cover, and aimed shooting was a lost art, anyway. The second squad advanced toward the door to Shipping/Receiving.

Vincent fired again, but missed. *I'm getting excited,* he chided himself. He took great care to line up his next shot, and didn't see the heavy weapons team launch a missile in his direction. It hit the wall above him and exploded. He was buried under tons of rock and concrete.

* * *

Cliff Carlotta saw his dad die. He hunched back in the Parts department, shivering, and watched the killers. They pulled laser rifles, helmets, and grenades from their crate and commanded the area around the elevator and the hallway connecting Parts with the cafeteria. They had already shot several people who had run out to join the fray. They either didn't know or didn't care that Cliff was there.

Cliff could hear the fighting in the hangar. He glanced toward the guard's desk by the elevator. The dead guard wore a hand blaster. Cliff thought about it, but he would have to remove the heavy pistol and power pack from the guard's belt before he could use the weapon. He wouldn't have enough time.

Then he noticed the alarm switch on the wall next to the guard post. Pushing it would set off alarms and close the front doors. Cliff was pretty sure all the other guard posts were empty now: there was no one but him to push the button. He thought about it. Being a hero is hard to resist when you're twelve.

He made up his mind: When they were all looking the other way, he'd go for it.

* * *

Howard Freytag hid behind a flyer. He was unarmed and had no way of escape. He kept his head down and hoped that the fighting wouldn't drift his way.

The alarm klaxons sounded. There was a deep rumbling as the giant doors began to slide shut. The original mechanisms, four hundred years old, were in good repair; the immense motors closed the doors with surprising speed.

Howard could see the delivery van's driver gun his engine, but only the front bumper and part of a fender made it past the doors. There was a hideous noise as the doors sheared through the van.

The doors were closed—too late. Fighting had stopped on the hangar floor. The first squad advanced through the main lobby, heading toward the cafeteria, while the second squad ran for the stairs. Howard hid beneath the flyer and waited.

* * *

Peer Sandra O'Hare was in her office on the third floor of the station, trying to find a way to bail Josiah White out of his financial problems. Josiah was a good man, she supposed, but he couldn't hold onto money. He was a year behind in rent, and was clearly going to have another disastrous year with his crops.

Her blaster came out of its holster almost of its own accord when she heard the explosions. She noticed with approval that her two bodyguards, Gerhard and Jacob, had drawn their weapons as well. She stopped to put on a helmet and flak vest before leaving the room, and clipped a spare power pack to her belt—rushing right out was how god damned fools got themselves killed. Her two bodyguards were already armored.

She ran down the central corridor to the elevator. The guard, Elroy, had locked both the elevator and stairway doors.

"Good," she said to Elroy. "Stay here. Jacob, man the turret. Gerhard, follow me." She went down the hall to Operations.

Some cameras were still on, and she could see how the battle was going—badly. The guard posts on the main floor had been obliterated. So had the ones outside. When she saw Cliff Carlotta's body at Guard Post Five, she had to master her rage and an urge to race downstairs and join the fray. She had a defense to organize.

She soon learned that the phone lines were cut, jamming made radio useless, and even her secret link to the hilltop outposts was out. She had no communication with the outside world. It was infuriating.

Nor was there anything to organize on the ground floor. Fighting there had nearly stopped—the attackers had overwhelmed everywhere but Kitchen Stores, where they seemed content to keep the defenders bottled up. The second floor had not yet been attacked. The armored doors on the stairs and elevator had been closed, but a few good demolition charges would burst them. There were perhaps thirty of her people on the second floor, of whom only ten had seen combat before.

Peer Sandra swore at the consoles, then checked the charge on her hand blaster. "I hate being a god damned armchair general, anyway," she said to no one in particular, and in fact she loved combat—but not here in the Station, with all these civilians. She called the second floor lobby and told the noncombatants to lock themselves in their rooms. She told the others to arm themselves and await her arrival.

Peer Sandra collected her bodyguards and went down to the second floor. Jacob reported that the turret was completely trashed.

They reached the second floor. The elevator and the stairs both opened onto a small lobby, in which a number of people milled around. The room beyond the lobby was the infirmary.

"Get all this first aid crap out of the infirmary," she roared. "Move!

"You, you, and you!" She pointed. "Get the fire axes and start putting loopholes in the infirmary wall. The rest of you arm yourselves! This isn't a god damned tea party!"

Peer Sandra and her bodyguards moved into the infirmary. Gerhard produced a small power sword and went to work cutting loopholes. Three people arrived with fire axes, and started hacking more loopholes from the lobby side. A few people were still standing around.

"All you sons of bitches who aren't doing anything—get the hell out of here!" ordered Peer Sandra. "They're going to blow that door any second." The room cleared instantly. Only Elroy and the three people with axes remained in the lobby.

The attackers were fast. The door blew in. The first attacker through the door tossed in a grenade and followed it in, trusting his armor to protect him. The rest followed. Nothing was ready. The people in the lobby never had a chance.

Only four holes had been knocked in the infirmary wall. The defenders had been protected from the blast and opened fire on the commandos. A bolt of laser fire killed Jacob almost immediately. Peer Sandra fired through another loophole, while a young woman whose name she couldn't recall took Jacob's place and opened fire with a submachine gun. Gerhard was the only other person in the room, firing carefully through his loophole.

An attacker tossed a smoke grenade into the lobby. The attackers, now invisible to the people in the infirmary, moved into the two main corridors. Gerhard slammed the infirmary door and locked it.

* * *

Gabrielle Martineau thought the explosions must be an accident in the hangar. She ran to her friend Bob's room to ask what they should do. Bob wasted some time trying to call the hangar floor. He realized what was going on when the alarm went off.

"We're under attack," he said. "We'd better get ready."

"But we're noncombatants," she protested. "Sandy has guards for that sort of thing."

Bob pulled down a hunting rifle from the rack. "You can hide under the bed if you want," he said. He loaded the weapon with fully-jacketed rounds and put the rest of the cartridges into his pocket. "You coming?"

Gabrielle knew how to shoot. She sighed and accepted one of his other rifles.

They got to the lobby just as Peer Sandra was shooing everyone off. They backed off and decided to guard a corridor. Matthew Sperry joined them. Matt was in Peer Sandra's "ready reserve." He carried the submachine gun that Peer Sandra had given him years ago. Gabrielle positioned herself so she could shoot around the corner. The two men decided to lie prone on the floor.

When the first attacker came around the corner, Bob and Matt fired simultaneously, and the man went down. Gabrielle, too startled to shoot, saw that the bullets from Matt's submachine gun actually bounced off the man's armor. Bob's hunting rifle had done its job, though.

There was a pause, then an arm appeared around the corner, tossing a grenade at them. Gabrielle, irritated that she hadn't fired before, pulled the trigger the instant she saw movement, missing. Bob scrambled out of the way when he saw the grenade, dragging Gabrielle back around the corner.

Matt was too slow.

* * *

Peer Sandra looked around. Someone had locked the infirmary door to delay the attackers. They were probably getting ready to blow it open now. The woman with the submachine gun was dead. She looked at Gerhard. He was unhurt.

"The tactical situation sucks," she growled, but then, against her will, she smiled. "You ready?"

Gerhard nodded. He yanked the door open, and they burst through it, startling a commando who was kneeling at the door, arming a satchel charge. They both shot him. Shards of molten armor spattered them as he collapsed in fire and smoke. Peer Sandra turned left, and Gerhard turned right. They shot two startled attackers in the corridor. Peer Sandra raced down the corridor—there was a body at the end, left in tatters by a grenade—turned the corner, and ran headlong into another commando. She stiff-armed him back to arm's length and shot him in the face, decapitating him. Wiping blood and ash from her visor, she noticed Bob DeVries motioning her into a room. She darted inside and checked her hand blaster.

"God damn it!" It was dangerously overheated: she was lucky it hadn't exploded. As usual, she had disabled the overload protection on her hand blaster. She changed power packs and wondered where Gerhard was.

The tactical situation still sucked.

* * *

Aritomo Nomura had put in a long day on his ship, doing a partial overhaul of the converter. Barigost was in many ways more primitive than Valhalla, Nomura's home, but the overhaul had gone smoothly enough. Peer Sandra's station was amazingly well-equipped for a base its size. He would need two hours to run through the converter checklist tomorrow, then another hour to bring it up to full power. Next week he would continue his voyage to Terra, where his uncle had secured a waiver from the usual restrictions on foreign shipping. Terrans were made of money, and Nomura expected to make a huge profit.

A series of explosions startled Nomura. He climbed up from Engineering to look out the airlock. He closed the door hurriedly when someone started shooting at him. A raid! Surely the raiders would take his ship if they were successful.

He peered through the tiny airlock window. He was alone on the ship, and had no weapons that were comparable to the attackers'. Too bad the converter was off—ship's guns might make a big difference.

Nomura smiled. There were times when checklists and safety procedures were only for the faint of heart. He slid down the ladder to Engineering and began flash-starting the converter.

* * *

Hank Landau was due to relieve Jerry Rodgers in fifteen minutes. He sat sipping coffee in the cafeteria. He already wore his armored, red-and-yellow livery and his hand blaster. When he heard the explosions, he put on his helmet, drew his blaster and moved up to the door. He peeked outside, and saw a whole squad of armored men bearing down on him.

"Bug out!" He shouted. "Get back to Stores!" He sprinted away from the door. The half-dozen people in the room needed no more prompting. They dashed through the kitchen to Kitchen Stores and closed the heavy door just as the commandos burst in.

Kitchen Stores doubled as a backup armory. Hank used his key to open the weapons rack, revealing twenty outdated assault rifles, countless clips of armor-piercing and explosive ammo, and several cases of grenades. He distributed these—except the explosive ammo, which would be useless against armored men— and they crouched behind shelves, boxes, and barrels.

They heard voices through the ventilation grille between the kitchen and Kitchen Stores.

"This is a crock!" said a voice with some off-world accent. "They were supposed to be having dinner!"

"Shut up!" said another.

"And Greg and Julio bought it, too" continued the first voice. "All that gold, and now they'll never get to spend it."

"Shut up," repeated the second voice. "Hurry up with that charge."

Everyone inside took the cue, and crouched down.

Gold? Hank wondered what they were talking about. They were right about dinner, though. The cook's car had broken down, and dinner was running late.

The door blew in, and the attackers followed. This time, however, they were up against similar numbers of defenders, all well-armed and under cover. Three attackers fell, then the rest withdrew, dragging their wounded with them. Hank threw a grenade after them.

This marked the start of a grenade battle. Hank threw grenades out the door. Attackers threw grenades in. All Hank's people were behind cover. The chances of a grenade actually killing somebody were low, but it convinced everyone to stay put.

After perhaps five minutes Hank heard an attackers shout, "Screw this! We're supposed to be out of here in four minutes. How the hell are we supposed to get out, Sarge?"

Another replied, "Damn! The Colonel's going to be pissed. Listen up! We're leaving out the back way. Fall back, and keep it orderly."

After a few minutes, Hank poked his head out the door. The attackers were gone.

* * *

Aritomo Nomura climbed up to the turret. He hoped that the red lights on the converter would wink out when it stabilized itself. He strapped himself in, then opened the shutters on the turret windows. Visibility was poor; ship's turrets were rarely used with visual aiming. He looked around for a target.

There! A squad of men was leaving the cafeteria. A tricky shot, since he'd have to shoot down the lobby before they turned left into the corridor . . .

The turret traversed smoothly, and Nomura fired. The flash shutters protected his eyes, but everyone on the main floor was blinded. The report was deafening. Every office window on the main floor shattered. Half a dozen light fixtures exploded. Rubble fell from the ceiling onto the hangar floor.

Nomura turned off the beam. There was no sign of the squad. Either he had vaporized them, or they had run like rabbits. Too bad about the lobby, though. He squinted through the window to make sure the sprinklers had turned on. It wouldn't do to burn down the station.

His self-satisfied smile faded when the heavy weapons team emerged from the smoke and launched their last rocket.

* * *

Peer Sandra was holed up with three other people, waiting for the end. The attackers were converging on her position, and she no longer had a chance. She hoped she could kill a couple more, but she doubted it. Her blaster was out of charge again. Probably just as well, since it was flashing more red lights than she'd thought it had. She was holding a hunting rifle that Bob DeVries had insisted on giving her. The attackers would lead with explosives again, and that would be that.

She heard voices in the corridor. "Fall back, fall back! We're late for dust-off!"

"But Lieutenant . . . ," said a voice near her end of the corridor.

"You want to be left behind? *Move!*"

"Well, shit!" said the voice. "Guess I don't need *this* any more!"

Peer Sandra leapt out of the doorway and shot the commando just as he prepared to throw his satchel charge. He fell, and the charge went off, blowing holes in the walls and floor. Peer Sandra laughed.

How were they getting out? She hadn't heard the doors open. She had a sudden thought—no, couldn't be. She heard booted feet above her head. It was! "God damn it!" she swore. "My bolt-hole is supposed to be a secret!"

"It is?" said Bob. "I thought everybody knew about it." He cringed under Peer Sandra's furious glare.

She ran to the stairs, too angry for caution. There was no one around. She climbed the stairs three at a time. Sure enough, the door at the top had been blown out. Smoke poured out of her suite.

She replaced her blaster's power pack with one from the guard's desk, then advanced to her suite. Not only had they found her "secret" exit—they'd managed to open it without explosives! The smoke had been caused by some vandal dropping a grenade on his way out. The place was a shambles. Peer Sandra swore as she secured the heavy armored door.

Pausing only to replace her damaged hand blaster and power pack with spares, she ran back to Operations, and found that some of the communications links were back. Several phones were chiming. She answered one and heard the voice Alfred Harris at Perimeter Defense over the ringing in her ears from all the explosions.

"Sandy!" he said. "A flyer just took off from near the station. We're shooting at it now."

"Good work, Alfy! Go get 'em!"

She turned to the status board, which showed that the anti-aircraft emplacements on the valley rim were already in action. The radar display came back to life suddenly, showing lots of flak in the air but no enemy flyer.

"They're doing a great job hedge-hopping, Sandy," reported Alfred. "I don't think were going to get them."

"Call Peer Rudolf for stratofighter support."

"I have. Twenty minutes."

"God damn it!" swore Peer Sandra. "Call Peer Richard!"

"Thirty minutes."

"What about Peer Andrew?"

"Fifteen minutes, but it's just a single stratofighter. The others will take an hour."

Peer Sandra kicked a wooden chair across the room. It broke against the wall. "Well, cut the god damned flak, then! You'll kill civilians! Have you called up the militia?"

"Yes. The ready reserve will be at the station in half an hour."

"Good work, Alfy. Watch your back." She cut the connection. Emily! Damn! She was out at George's ship!

"Gerhard! Where are you?" She hadn't seen Gerhard since the fight in the corridor. She suddenly realized he must be dead. Her rage returned. Her hands twitched. She wanted very much to shoot someone. Nobody killed her bodyguards and got away with it!

She controlled herself and called the hangar floor. Hank Landau answered. He looked a little frayed, but was okay. "Who's in charge down there, Hank?"

"I think I am, Sandy. Vlad, Jerry, and Scott bit it, and nobody can find Vincent."

"Look, I want you to go out to George's ship and bring everybody there in here. There's a girl there you haven't seen before. Make sure she comes, too."

Hank looked less than pleased. "You want me to open the doors?"

"Use the bolt-hole. I suppose you know all about it."

"Well . . . ," Hank was embarrassed. "Okay. On my way." He hung up.

Peer Sandra dispatched an urgent message to the Grand Peer. Hank arrived as she finished.

"Look," she said. "You stand guard here, and I'll go fetch the kids. They're probably a bit gun-shy, and they'll recognize me easier, especially the new one." Hank didn't argue. In fact, he looked relieved.

Peer Sandra checked the charge on her blaster, then stepped into the tunnel.

Chapter VIII

"Well, they're probably gone now, whoever they are," said George. "Maybe we should take a look around."

Beverly and Emily each grabbed one of his arms. "You're not going anywhere," said Emily. "Turn on the tactical-band radio."

"It's outside with the spare parts."

"Well, turn on the TV, then. They'll have some news eventually."

"Ha! Fat chance! They only announced the discovery of fire a week ago."

"Do it!" she snapped.

George left, sulking a little. He returned a moment later with the TV from Beverly's cabin palmed in one hand.

Just then there was a banging on the airlock door. Everyone jumped, and George dropped the TV. It made a dull crunching sound as it hit the deck.

A distorted voice came over the intercom. "Open up, god damn it, or I'll sell this piece of junk as a Christmas tree ornament!"

Emily relaxed. "Oh, it's just Mother." She climbed down the ladder to open the door while George found a broom and glumly swept up pieces of the TV set.

A moment later Emily shouted up the companionway, "George? Could you help me with the door?" George dumped the last of the debris into the wastebasket and went down to her.

Peer Sandra leapt in when the door opened. George closed it behind her. She peered into the gloom (George hadn't turned any lights back on). "You're all okay? Good. Come on, we're going into the station. You too, Beverly." She looked up as Beverly came down the ladder. "Looks like they missed you."

"Not by much," said Emily, suddenly close to tears again. "Somebody shot right through the door with a plasma gun. If Beverly hadn't pulled me aside, I would have been killed."

Peer Sandra had been about to bark out a command when Emily's last statement sank in. She stopped, looking a little lost, then gave her daughter a hug. "Thank you," she whispered to Beverly.

Peer Sandra recovered quickly. "About twenty guys attacked the station," she said, "and nearly took it out. Eight Worlds gear, Eight Worlds tactics. Seems like a lot of work to take out one little orphan girl. Anyway, I want you all in the station now. I can't protect you out here."

George opened the door again (as far as Beverly could tell, he just pulled the "OPEN" lever) and they all went down the ladder. Beverly pocketed the box of pistol cartridges before leaving.

The night was clear and cold. There was frost on the landing jacks. The anti-aircraft fire had stopped. Beverly could hear ground vehicles rumbling in the distance, and there were a few animal cries, but otherwise all was quiet. The walk to the tunnel was uneventful.

There were beer cans and other party debris near the tunnel opening, which was neatly concealed by boulders and bushes. The tunnel itself was low, wet, and musty. There was some rubble on the floor.

No one opened the door when Peer Sandra knocked. She picked up a rock from the floor of the tunnel and pounded it on the steel door, raising a tremendous racket. After a couple of minutes, a harried-looking young man in Peer Sandra's livery opened the door.

"Sorry, Sandy," he said as he waved them in. "They needed me in Operations." He closed the door and dropped the bar. "The militia's on the way, and I've called Wrenfield for ambulances. They're short one, though, so we're going to have to transport some of the wounded ourselves." He started leading them down the hall to Operations.

"Wounded?" asked Peer Sandra. "I didn't see any wounded."

"They were mostly in the hangar. A couple of people hiding in their rooms got hurt, too."

"What about the attackers?"

"They took their wounded with them. Their dead, too. We've got no prisoners, and just one corpse."

"God damn it!" fumed Peer Sandra. "I *need* prisoners."

They were outside the door to Operations, where lights and chimes announced that dozens of people wanted to talk to Peer Sandra. Peer Sandra turned to the young man. "You stay here and hold the fort, Hank. I'd better square away the wounded. You kids come with me."

Peer Sandra led the way to the stairway, which was partly choked with rubble, then shrugged and pushed the elevator call button. The elevator arrived a moment later. Its dented and bullet-holed doors opened noiselessly.

"I'll be damned," she said.

They took the elevator to the first floor. Pandemonium reigned. Beverly saw four bodies on the floor: a middle-aged clerk, a young boy, and two guards in Peer Sandra's livery. The boy had fallen next to the alarm button on the wall; his body lay in a pool of his own blood. Two bullet holes marred the plaster. Someone had clearly shot the boy in the act of setting off the alarm. Beverly's stared down at this tableau of heroism and sacrifice. Her eyes filled with tears. How had she ever looked down on these people?

Behind her, George whispered, "Cliff."

She turned. George had turned his head away. His hands were clenched tightly shut, and tears were streaming down his face. Emily had her arm around him. Her freckles were very prominent, and her face was pale.

"Hurry up," growled Peer Sandra. "There's work to do."

Beverly was sure that both George and Emily were fooled by Peer Sandra's performance; noticing neither the catch in her voice nor the slump in her shoulders. They turned right and went down the corridor to the cafeteria.

As they approached, they began to hear cries of pain.

The wounded had been put on tables in the cafeteria. Several people were hovering around them helplessly. Those wounded who weren't concussed were awake and in pain. There were four victims with laser burns, three with concussions, six with shrapnel wounds from grenades, one who had been stabbed in the abdomen with a power sword, and another who had shot himself in the foot while arming himself.

No one suffered from plasma gun wounds, Beverly noticed. If plasma guns had been used, all the victims must be dead. This matched the gun's reputation.

Beverly, Emily, and Peer Sandra walked into the room and tried to figure out where they could be most useful. George did not follow them. He leaned against the doorway, looking ill.

Emily went back to him. "Go help in the hangar, George," she said. "You're not going to be any use here."

He didn't like to admit it. "Right," he said at last. He tried to salvage some dignity, "Call me if you need anything."

"I will."

George fled.

Emily (who had paramedic training) took charge of the first aid. Beverly had had received basic first aid training in school, which had covered trauma from energy weapons. Emily put her to work with the simpler tasks. In spite of her training, Beverly felt slow and clumsy, unable to live up to the demands of the situation.

Beverly was thankful that she didn't know any of these people. She suspected that she would react as strongly to George if any of *her* friends had been here. Emily was very good: professional, deft, gentle, and unflinching, even when dealing with the laser burn victims and their horrifying wounds.

Volunteers fetched the medical supplies from one of the ships, and soon two experienced paramedics and a doctor arrived from town. The wounded were soon sedated, bandaged, and plugged into field docs—electronic monitoring/drug metering machines. The work was grisly, but most of the patients could be stabilized. Beverly wondered if the technology to treat them existed anywhere on the planet.

George returned as they finished, bearing the front end of a stretcher. Another man held the other end. An old man in Peer Sandra's livery was lying on the stretcher, complaining bitterly.

"Let me walk, god damn it! I'm fine!" The old man was covered with dust, and had bruises on his face and hands.

"Look what we found, Emily!" called George. "Vince decided to play it safe, so he hid under a pile of rubble!"

George and Howard put the stretcher on top of an empty table, then kept Vincent from sitting up. "Let me up, you god damned sons of bitches!" snarled Vincent. "They need me back in the god damned hangar!"

Emily came up and started asking Vincent questions. He didn't like to swear at her, and the unaccustomed effort of not swearing in a crisis rendered him nearly speechless. He became almost docile. Emily began to examine him for injuries.

George looked around a little fearfully, but relaxed when he saw that the carnage had been covered by bandages and sedatives. He walked over to Beverly. "Vince here is the person who taught Sandy how to swear," he said.

"I believe you," replied Beverly. "What happened to him?"

"The attackers dropped a couple of tons of rubble on him. He'd killed a whole bunch of them, right, Howard?"

"That's right," said Howard. "He dropped at least six."

"He was hiding next to a truck," George continued, "and it sheltered him from most of the rubble. We dug him out as a surprise bonus; we were really after the truck." He looked around. "Where's Sandy?"

Beverly hadn't seen Peer Sandra leave. Emily finished shining a light into Vincent's eyes and said, "She went out to prep a ship. She's not going to wait for an ambulance, seeing what happened to the *last* ambulance around here."

One of the wounded was moaning again. George looked at the man nervously. "Good point," he said. "I think I'll go lend a hand." He left.

A paramedic quieted the moaning patient. Emily looked around, saw that the professionals had everything under control, and said to Beverly, "Let's see if there's anything we can do in the hangar."

"All right."

As they walked to the door, Emily remarked, "You're pretty good at first aid. Where'd you learn?"

"At school."

"Really? They must have had quite a curriculum."

Beverly shrugged. "It was part of a required course."

The lobby had suffered from a fire, followed by a flood from the sprinkler system. They picked their way across the soggy, reeking, rubble-strewn room and peered through the lingering smoke and steam.

The main hangar was a mess. Smoke, steam, dust, and the smell of burnt metal filled the air. With the main doors shut, it would take a long time to clear. Beverly saw that part of the ceiling and wall had collapsed along the left side, and a frigate in the hangar had suffered an explosion in one of its turrets. The other two ships seemed undamaged. Half a dozen people clustered around the ship closest to the door, apparently taking it through a pre-flight routine. Peer Sandra was on the main floor, talking into a portable phone.

"I don't care if he's the god damned Imperial Viceroy," she snarled. "He's not getting in. Get rid of him and get the area cleared. We're going to lift in about fifteen minutes." She put the phone down, spotted the girls, and walked over.

"Emily, get the wounded moved into the cargo bay. We're lifting them to Ertrix Embassy Hospital. Beverly, you come with me." She started off across the hangar floor. Beverly followed Peer Sandra, hard-pressed to keep up with her, while Emily ran back to the cafeteria.

Peer Sandra went into an office along the right wall. Its plate glass window had been shattered. Inside, the office was a faded institutional green, with a desk in the center and a row of shelves at the back containing at least fifty marksmanship trophies. Stretched out on the desk was the body of a man. Someone had shot him with a hand blaster. There was a blackened, fist-sized hole in his breastplate. His helmet had been removed, and his dead eyes were staring up at the ceiling. The smell of burned flesh was very strong.

"You recognize him?" asked Peer Sandra.

Beverly found the corpse unnerving, but made herself look at it closely. "No."

"I didn't think so. He didn't carry any I.D. or personal effects. He did have two photos, though. One of me . . ." Peer Sandra slapped down a color picture of herself, taken before she lost the eye. "And one of you."

She put a second photo beside the first. It showed a smiling girl with long black hair, wearing a silk party dress.

"The picture of me is the news service file photo," continued Peer Sandra. "I have no idea where the other one came from."

Beverly stared at the picture in astonishment. "I recognize it," she said. "It was taken on my thirteenth birthday."

Chapter IX

Beverly had high hopes for her thirteenth birthday party. Her twelfth had been a disaster. Her mother had invited most of her classmates and many other children of the aristocracy. None of them were Beverly's friends. Quiet and a little shy, Beverly had let them take over, leaving her feeling like a stranger at her own party.

This year, she would spend her birthday with her family. For once, they were all available. The Council was in recess, so her father was free to disengage from the intricate and often lethal dance of San Vincentan politics. Her eldest brother Richard was home on leave while his ship was refitting, and her brother Miguel was on holiday from the Naval Academy.

She also had good news to report; test results she'd been keeping secret for the past week.

Beverly's father had won his fame as a gunnery officer on a light cruiser. The first hint that he had potential as a ship's gunner was when he scored in the 99th percentile at age twelve on the mandatory gunnery aptitude test. While his high birth would have allowed him a place in the Navy in any event, his skill with ship's guns had won him medals and promotions that, just conceivably, would otherwise have been beyond his reach.

Aptitudes had a tendency to run in families. Beverly's brothers both achieved scores above the ninetieth percentile. Beverly's had received her test results. She was in the 99th percentile, just as her father had been.

She was ecstatic. She felt that her score proved that she was destined to follow in her father's footsteps.

Her brothers were supposed to arrive together in time for lunch, but they neither arrived nor called. Beverly and her parents waited an hour, then ate without them.

As a maid cleared away the last plate, Richard's flyer came screaming over the estate. It flared abruptly, then settled onto the landing pad. The canopy opened and Beverly's brothers climbed out. Miguel ran pell-mell to the house. Richard following at a more dignified pace, conferring for a moment with the mechanic who had run out to take his vehicle.

"Mother! Father! We're here!" shouted Miguel. He was eighteen, wiry and energetic, with the page-boy haircut currently fashionable among the cadets at the Academy. He wore his grey cadet's uniform, and carried a small package, which he lobbed across the room to Beverly.

She caught it, grinning, then held it near her ear and shook it. The package made no interesting sounds. "What is it?" she asked.

"A bomb!" Miguel laughed, then turned to his mother. "Is there any food left? I'm starved."

Lady di Mendoza smiled. "Talk to Cook. And welcome home."

Miguel was already headed for the door. "Thanks, Mother. Bye, Bev."

Lord di Mendoza frowned as Miguel left. "He should show better manners than that—he's not a child any more. If he's that casual at the Academy, he could end up at the wrong end of a sword."

His wife was quick to reply, "His instructors think well of him, Richard; you saw his performance review. Besides, my friends with sons in the academy tell me he's very popular." Lady di Mendoza understood the value of popularity.

Richard had arrived in the room by then. He kissed his mother's hand and bowed to his father. "Hello, Mother, Father.

Happy birthday, Beverly." He smiled at her. He set his briefcase on the table, opened it, and pulled out a package—obviously a large book. "Are we opening presents now, or later?"

"Later," said Beverly. "But you can give it to me now, Richard."

He handed it over, and she made a show of shaking it. "Must be a book," she said. "Something fiery, I hope."

Her father broke in, "Your clothes look awful, Richard, and you're over an hour late. Did anything happen?"

Richard looked down at his lieutenant's dress blacks in embarrassment. His knees and elbows had grass stains, his hands were dirty, and his shoes were scuffed and muddy. He looked as if he couldn't decide whether to rush off and clean up first, or to tell his story.

"Sorry, Father. Yes, things went a bit awry. Mind if I sit?"

Lord di Mendoza nodded. Richard sank into a chair. He took off his cap and put it on the table, then poured himself a cup of coffee from the silver coffee service. He dropped in three sugar cubes and added a great deal of cream. He drank half of it at a gulp, then caught himself and began to sip it.

"Excellent coffee. Terran?"

Lady di Mendoza nodded.

"Much better than ship's coffee," said Richard. "But about today. . . . There was a duel this morning. I told you about it, I think. Jose quarreled over a girl with an ensign from the *Last Refuge*. They exchanged words. The other ensign—Diego di Alvarez (Captain Sir Juan's son)—demanded an apology. He didn't get one, so he challenged Jose. You know how it goes."

Beverly smiled. She could read the signs: he was warming to his tale, and there was no stopping him now. He was quite a story-teller.

"Jose asked me to be his second. I met Ensign di Alvarez's second at the officer's club and worked out the terms.

95

"The words said by both principals were quite unforgivable, and neither chose to apologize, so there was no graceful escape from the duel. Enough time had passed, however, that the principals' boiling blood had been brought down to a simmer. We were therefore able to settle on a simple rapier duel. It was not a friendly duel, mind you, but both sides saw reason to accept minimally lethal weapons.

"The duel was to be held in the Oaks. I insisted on that. It's expensive, but they have the best medical facilities, and the dueling masters are first-rate."

Lord di Mendoza nodded. "I fought di Rosa there twenty years ago."

"So you did. How is he these days, anyway?"

"Fit enough," replied Lord di Mendoza. "I spoke to him last week." Then, after looking around to verify that no servants were in the room, "We're working together to unseat di Aldo's party. But you were saying . . . "

Richard continued. "Ensign Alvarez's second—Robert di Cabrillo, of the di Cabrillo bankers—agreed readily enough. I think each of us was more concerned with keeping his man alive than working to the maximum disadvantage of the other side.

"The duel was set for ten in the morning. We all arrived early. Ahead of us was a duel between two elderly gentlemen from East Refuge—a stiff-necked di Banessa up against an equally stiff-necked di Castro. It was a plasma gun duel—twenty paces, unregulated fire. They each brought two seconds.

"We waited our turn. As there were no barriers between ourselves and the duel, we stood to the side and observed. Ensign di Alvarez and his entourage stood away from us, of course.

"The seconds laid out a brace of plasma guns; each principal chose one and was led to his place. They had apparently chosen to dispense with the time-consuming ritual of pace, turn and fire.

Instead, they intended to reduce the ceremony to its most elemental form: shooting each other.

"Suddenly, one of di Castro's seconds cried 'Hold!' and dropped a hand to his weapon. This proved to be a mistake.

"A di Banessa second—perhaps prompted by a guilty conscience—drew his weapon and was burned down by a neatly-placed shot from the man who'd cried 'Hold.' The two principals chose that moment to open fire on each other. Trees were reduced to flame and flinders from stray bolts. The doctors and dueling master saw the wisdom in assuming a prone position.

"I also availed myself of a piece of turf. My gun was in my hand. I turned my gaze to Ensign di Alvarez's group, since it occurred to me that, should they suffer from a weak sense of propriety, they could take a pot shot at Jose: no one would be the wiser. Ensign di Alvarez's second seemed to entertain similar suspicions of us.

"We stared at each other for a moment, then by unspoken consent we put our guns away. Jose almost wilted with relief. This was understandable, I suppose, as he was armed only with a rapier.

"When the firing stopped the guards poured bravely onto the scene. All four seconds were dead. By some miracle no bystanders were hurt, and by a lucky chance the principals themselves were quite untouched. They were livid with rage. They waved their expended plasma guns at each other and shouted accusations. "The guards led them off in different directions, then insisted that we all make a statement before our own duel could begin. We explained the urgency of our schedule, but they were unmoved.

"Jose had begun to lose heart by then. When it came time to choose blades, he tried to insist on new rules. Jose is normally steady enough, but I'm afraid that the sight of four people being shot to rags instilled in him an earnest desire for introspection. I took him aside and reminded him that this was a duel, not a game, and one fought duels because one couldn't rest until one's enemy had been shamed, maimed, or killed. I explained that he retained the option of apologizing to Ensign di Alvarez, but if he felt it necessary to whine on the field of honor, he would need another second.

"His nerve returned, of course, and the duel went off smoothly. We started the principals ten meters apart, and they advanced on each other slowly. Ensign di Alvarez began the engagement with an energetic attack that scored on Jose's arm, but made the mistake of hesitating to see how well he'd struck. Jose took this opportunity to run him through the chest.

"The doctors loaded Ensign di Alvarez into the autodoc almost before he hit the ground. A clean thrust through the liver, they said; so it seems he'll be sampling the pleasures of the hospital for a few weeks.

"Jose is throwing a celebratory party now; possibly by morning his liver will be in worse shape than di Alvarez's. Once I had him home, I left to pick up Miguel.

"Anyway, that's why we're late."

The main party began at five, with Beverly's "uncle" Miguel making a surprise appearance. Miguel—more properly, Sir Miguel di Cruz, Captain, SVN (retired)—had been the other gunnery officer on the *Deadly Virtue*, a close friend of Lord di Mendoza's, and the namesake of Lord di Mendoza's second son. He had left the Navy only a year before, after serving a gunnery officer, frigate captain, and commandant of a Naval Special Forces unit known unofficially as the "di Cruisers." In this last capacity he had won quite a bit of fame for his aggressive tactics in skirmishes with the Pleiades Federation. He was now trying his hand at politics. His goal was to be made a Lord; there had been a Lord di Cruz, long ago, but the family had fallen on hard times and had lost its title.

Di Cruz came into the main hall at a brisk walk, ahead of the butler who was supposed to announce him. He carried an enormous package.

"Beverly!" he cried. She ran to him, and he put down the package and enfolded her in a hug. He was her favorite uncle.

When he let go of her he waved at her father, who was on the other side of the hall.

Lord di Mendoza called back, "Gate-crashing again, Miguel? I thought you were cured of that on Dorian."

Di Cruz offered his arm to Beverly. "You can't expect me to pass by without offering my respects to the lady, can you, Richard?" He smiled down at Beverly, who grinned back at him. "Besides, I'm a bearer of glad tidings."

They walked over to where Lord and Lady di Mendoza were standing, while the butler picked up the package and followed. Lord di Mendoza handed his friend a glass of wine, hesitated, then handed another to Beverly.

"Glad tidings, Miguel?" he prompted.

Di Cruz made a show of holding his wine glass up to the light as he spoke. "On second thought, perhaps you would see it otherwise. Ancestral deeds forgotten, new generation outstripping the old, and all that." He quirked an eyebrow at di Mendoza, who was wearing an exaggeratedly stone-faced expression.

Beverly smiled. Her father was always less reserved when uncle Miguel was around.

Lord di Mendoza waited patiently for di Cruz to continue. After a short pause, he did.

"Well, I won't keep you in suspense any longer. I heard from a Navy friend of mine that this daughter of yours has done very well on one of the aptitude tests—haven't you, Bev?"

Beverly blushed and nodded.

Miguel looked back at di Mendoza. "Would you care to guess which test? No? Well, I'll tell you the score first. Ninety-ninth percentile. In gunnery, Richard."

Beverly looked back to her father, eager for his approval. He smiled and said, "That's wonderful! I'm proud of you, Beverly." He turned away to refill his wine glass.

Beverly was crushed. Her score didn't mean anything to him; his reaction was the same one he gave for any minor achievement. She had hoped for excitement; the realization that her aptitude meant that she belonged in the Navy.

She had decided on a Navy career when she was eight years old, when her father had left the Navy and came home with all his war stories. She quickly learned that he believed the Navy was no place for her—not that she wouldn't do well there, because a di Mendoza could of course do anything she set her mind to—but because it was somehow no place for a lady. That Beverly's mother had been in the Navy didn't seem to make any difference. Or perhaps it did; neither of her parents spoke much of her mother's tour of duty as Shipmistress on the *Deadly Virtue.*

She could expect no help from her mother. Lady di Mendoza had plans for her daughter. Plans involving boys and parties and an eventual marriage into an influential family. Plans that did not involve Beverly's opinions.

Her brothers returned—Richard had changed into a spare uniform—bringing with them the usual difficulties of having two Miguels and two Richards in the same room. They all went into the dining room, where they were treated to an ornate dinner of the sort Beverly's mother was fond of planning. An eight-piece string orchestra played during the meal, through seven courses and dessert, which was a cake baked with real Terran chocolate by a *cordon bleu* chef from New Carina.

Beverly's brothers vied for control of the conversation during the meal, each telling horror stories of their respective tours of duty. Miguel described the corrosive properties of Academy food, the low intellect of the instructors, and the strange customs of the cadets; while Richard gave an account of the actions on his latest cruise of the Pleiades frontier, with the horror and bloodshed couched in his colorful yet understated manner. He made everything sound like an elaborate dance, with only the barest hints of underlying carnage.

Di Cruz sighed when Richard finished his tale. "I envy you," he said. "I miss the Navy."

"I'm sure they'd reactivate your commission, sir," said Richard.

"It wouldn't be the same. My rank is too high for me to take part in the fighting."

Di Mendoza smiled, "Always the fire-eater, Miguel. Remember the time we stole that Belter combat support flyer on Dorian?"

Oh, no, thought Beverly sourly. *Not the CSF story.*

Di Cruz opened his mouth to speak, clearly intending to inflict his favorite story on them, when he caught Beverly's expression. He winked at her and said, "Richard, the children can probably tell the story better than we can, they've heard it so often.

"So let me just point out that Richard and I managed to steal a combat support flyer from a dozen armed and armored Great Belt soldiers, armed with nothing but our wits and a rental car for which we had had the foresight to buy extra collision insurance. In the end, the CSF was at the bottom of the lake, the Belters were under arrest for disturbing the peace, and we got away scot-free. Under battlefield conditions, such a victory would have cost at least half a dozen lives and the expenditure of equipment far more valuable than a mere rental car, but ours was a bloodless coup. And neither of us were sober at the time. What miracles we could have worked if we had been able to walk a straight line, I leave to your imagination."

Lady di Mendoza sighed. "Really, Miguel, I wish would stop glorying in your youthful indiscretions. You'd be singing another tune if you had been caught."

Di Cruz leaned back, looking smug. "But we weren't."

"You were lucky. I remember how you ran your section, Miguel."

"Mother, please!" said Beverly. Her mother didn't much like di Cruz.

"I'm sorry, child. Miguel, excuse me, please." Lady di Mendoza put on her hostess face. Miguel nodded curtly to her, stung by her criticism. His crew had adored him, and he had won medals and promotions, but Elizabeth di Mendoza would always think of him as a reckless junior officer.

"Say, isn't it time for Beverly to open her presents?" asked her brother Miguel, finishing his third piece of cake. "Open mine first, Bev!"

Beverly glanced at her father, who nodded, and went to the side table where she had put her presents. She picked one up and announced, "This one's from brother Miguel, who says it's a bomb. My last wish is that he not get my stamp collection." She opened it with exaggerated care. It turned out to be a portable computer of the type fashionable at the Academy. It was about postcard-sized while closed, and unfolded to four times that size. It was an expensive machine, and Miguel had clearly done his best to find one that almost—but not quite—exceeded the limits of what was allowed at Beverly's school.

"This is wonderful! We'll have Miguel to thank for my next term's grades." Beverly turned it on, and the display was instantly filled with a color picture of a bomb with a timer counting down to zero. Ticking filled the room. Several seconds later the screen roiled in simulated explosion, accompanied by deafening sound effects.

There was a pause, then a seemingly endless list of credits rolled across the screen. All seemed to be Miguel's classmates.

"Same old Academy," said Lady di Mendoza. "Does anyone want more coffee?"

Beverly turned the computer off and set it on the table. She picked up Richard's gift.

"I'm afraid I can't live up to that standard, Beverly," said Richard, "but open it anyway."

Beverly held the gift-wrapped package to her forehead. "My psychic power reveals that this package contains a giant book." She tore off the wrapping paper. "Oh, my."

It was a copy of *The Annotated Lord of the Rings,* translated, annotated, and published by Professor Fabian Reid. This particular edition of the ancient classic of forgotten origin was almost impossible to get anywhere but Terra, and was fabulously expensive. Beverly had fallen in love with the book a couple of years previously, with its combination of the incomprehensibly archaic and the timelessly archetypical. She had received several admonitions from her parents for keeping her father's copy in her room all the time (not to mention the odd torn page or smudged margin).

"Where did you find it?" asked Beverly

"I found it in a used book store in Nouterre. I'll never know how it got there; the proprietor didn't know what he had. As far as I can tell, it's brand-new."

"Thank you, Richard, Miguel. Oh, and Miguel, please thank your friends for me."

"Don't mention it," said Richard. Miguel just smirked.

Next came the present from her mother. Lady di Mendoza had a chilling habit of picking out gifts that outfitted her children perfectly for activities they wished to avoid. This was no exception; a set of clothes and jewelry suitable for formal parties.

"There's a photographer coming later, dear," said Lady di Mendoza.

"I'll change just as soon as I've opened the other gifts," said Beverly obediently. The clothes were marvelous, but she dreaded the implication: that she could look forward to being cooped up in stilted parties with her fellow thirteen-year-olds. She always felt more comfortable around adults.

Her father's gift was a deed; title to one of the country estates that gave a small income each year. The di Mendozas were members of the landed class, and it was traditional to endow older children with estates. Beverly had formed the distinct impression that her father didn't value or trust her as much as her brothers—but they had received their first deeds at fourteen.

She could think of no words to say. She looked from the deed to her father, eyes full of tears, and had the blurry vision of him smiling back at her.

"You're welcome, *cara mia*," he said gently. Then, a little embarrassed, "You have your uncle Miguel's present still."

"Oh. Yes." She wiped her eyes and turned to the last present, which was on the floor instead of the table because of its size.

"I think you've given me an estate, too, Uncle—but *you* found a box large enough to hold it."

"Could be, could be. Open it and see."

Beverly untied the ribbon (which was apparently real silk—very impressive), ripped off the wrapping paper, and lifted the lid from the box.

Inside was another box, gift-wrapped like the first. Beverly threw a suspicious look at di Cruz, then lifted the second box onto the table and opened it.

Inside was a third box.

"I've always wanted to do this," said di Cruz, enjoying the scene immensely. "Let's see if Beverly has the nerve to say, 'Goody, just what I always wanted—a set of nesting boxes' when she's through."

Beverly opened the third box. Inside was a fourth gift-wrapped box, but this proved to be a carrying case for some piece of equipment. She pulled this out, undid the catches and opened it.

Inside was a pistol—a 9 mm Anderson, hand-made on Sinclair, with a brushed nickel finish and translucent bluish grips of copis ivory. It was accompanied by a simple yet elegant black holster and half a dozen nickel-plated clips. The trend on San Vincento was toward the use of energy weapons even for civilian sidearms. But purists loved cartridge weapons for their mythic associations, and weapons like the Anderson were always in high demand because of their sheer elegance and craftsmanship.

"Uncle, it's beautiful," she breathed, picking it up and sighting down the barrel.

"I knew you were going to have a pistol class this semester," said di Cruz. "I thought you'd like something better than what the school issues."

Her father stood up. "That's an Anderson, isn't it? Could I look at it, Beverly?" Beverly handed him the pistol. Di Mendoza examined it, looked down the barrel, then assumed several shooting stances.

"Nice," he said. "I've never seen one up close before. I think you got the grip size right, Miguel; it's too small for me, anyway." He handed the pistol back to Beverly. "I wouldn't be surprised if you came home with some trophies," he said.

"I will," she promised.

Her father turned to di Cruz. "Miguel, I know you wanted to talk with me. If the rest of you will excuse us—we'll be back before long." He and di Cruz bowed to the rest and left for di Mendoza's study.

The younger Miguel watched them go. "Sounds like trouble," he said after they left. "I hear Uncle is having a rough time with his party."

Richard looked surprised. "Really? I know I've been out of touch, but I can't remember anybody having anything bad to say about Uncle."

Miguel shrugged. "The *Navy's* happy with him, sure. Man of the hour, hero of the realm, and all that. I can't figure out why he isn't in Father's party. The di Venton Party isn't going to do him any good—they aren't even pro-Navy, for God's sake."

"I'm sure he had his reasons." Richard turned to his mother. "Shall we retire to the parlor?" The dining room was a little large for a party of four.

"Certainly. Beverly, dear, why don't you change your clothes now? Then we can all meet in the parlor."

Beverly changed into her new dress after the servants carried her gifts up to her room. It was lovely. She decided to drop in on her father and uncle Miguel so they could see it.

As she approached the door to the study, she heard voices. Uncle Miguel seemed upset. She paused near the doorway, out of sight.

"It's not as bad as all that, Miguel," said her father mildly.

"Isn't it? After all the work you did, there's not a snowball's chance in hell you'll be made viscount. As for me, if I found the hulk of the *Relentless* and poured its treasure hip-deep in Aaron Plaza, the nobility would still want it all appraised before they considered my candidacy for baron."

Her father said something inaudible, to which uncle Miguel replied, "You're right, you're right. It's not *that* bad. But it's bad enough. Being a line officer when there isn't a hot war won't get me any further. I've made a sad botch of politics, too; though I'm not willing to give it up yet."

Her father hesitated, then said, "If you ever do tire of politics, I know someone who could use a steady commander. Di Grenville is pushing hard on the Pleiades frontier—nothing official, mind you—and there will be laurels in plenty if he pulls it off. There's nothing like carving away a piece of someone else's territory to bring fame, fortune, and titles."

"I thought Di Grenville had a reputation for backstabbing."

"I heard that, too. But I spent quite some time trying to find out why, and it seems to be a baseless rumor. Di Aldo seems very fond of him, by the way."

"Interesting," said Miguel. "But, in essence, it's just a recapitulation of my naval career, with the same dead end once the job is done: thank you very much, di Cruz, you've been a reliable cog in our machine, and here's another meaningless medal to remember us by."

There was a pause. "Tell me," said Miguel abruptly, "You still keep track of Valhalla and the Inward Frontier. What do you know about that Laverak fellow?"

Her father replied, "Quite a bit. He's a remarkable man. What do you want to know?"

"Everything. I've only heard rumors."

Her father said, "Oman Laverak. Member of the Villahove gentry, graduated from the New Carinan Naval Academy and had a brilliant naval career. Retired when he reached the rank of Rear Admiral. Apparently he felt the way you did, Miguel—there were no further advancement opportunities for someone who wasn't born on New Carina."

"I'll thank you not to compare me to a foreigner," said Miguel grumpily.

"My apologies. In any event, he found backing from parties unknown, acquired an excellent crew and a good ship—the *Mad*

Dog—and raided Morversarn space for several years. A difficult way to make a living, by anyone's standards. By the time he was done, he had enough ships, enough men, and enough money to go into the mercenary business in a big way. He sold his service to a Valhallan lord in Nubonn, who was over-committed in the civil war. Once Laverak got a toehold in Valhalla, he never let go. He controls over half of it today, with backing from New Carina."

"I thought he was backed by Great Belt."

"That was last year. It was New Carina, then Great Belt, and now New Carina again. Goa and Terra provide him with minor aid and dangle the prospect of much more in the future, with strings attached. Laverak plays them off against each other."

"Now *that's* the way to do it," said uncle Miguel. "Single-handedly conquer a region of barbarian space. Set yourself up as a king. Still, it's an exile. No place like home, and all that."

"There's a rumor that he's going to give Valhalla to New Carina once he's conquered it," said her father, "if they'll make him a marquis. I don't believe it, though. You know the New Carinans; they'd find a way not to pay up. Laverak knows them, too."

"Damned pirates—I hate New Carinans. What do you think of his chances?" asked uncle Miguel.

"To take the rest of Valhalla? No better than fair. He depends on support from at least one of the Eight Worlds; he uses mercenaries who will abandon him if opportunity beckons elsewhere; and he needs the support of his Valhallan allies. Still, he's done a good job so far."

"And what's our interest in him?"

"San Vincento's or our parties'? Either way, it's little to none. I may be the only person on the planet who gets regular reports on him. Valhalla's too far away; we have no interests there. The post of Valhallan Ambassador has lain empty for over a decade.

"In any event, with Laverak changing backers all the time, it's hard for us to join the game without antagonizing our allies.

Still, if we were on the opposite side of the political fence from both New Carina and Great Belt, Laverak would make a good stick to hit them with. And the odds of that happening are quite good—we may involve ourselves yet."

"It would be a diplomatic side show at best," said uncle Miguel. "But I wish him luck. At least he has the courage to operate on a grand scale. Maybe he'll go on to take the Duchy of Persol and the Centaurus Federation some day. Meanwhile, you and I are stuck with politics. Let me tell you about what some of my friends are planning . . . "

Beverly decided not to interrupt them after all, and went on to the parlor. A photographer was setting up there, monopolizing half the room. Her brothers were standing by the fireplace, drinking brandy and watching the photographer, who was using complex and bulky TrueLife gear. After he set up his equipment he posed Beverly on a chair, with the wall-to-wall, floor-to-ceiling bookshelves as a backdrop.

"Smile," he said. Beverly smiled dutifully, but the photographer didn't trip the shutter (or whatever the TrueLife equivalent was). He tried in various ways to coax a more photogenic smile out of her, but looking adorable on cue was not one of Beverly's talents. He took a couple of pictures anyway, but was obviously not pleased with the results.

When the photographer had set up for his last picture, Miguel moved into Beverly's field of view and gargled his brandy. This proved over-ambitious; he choked and sprayed liquor in all directions.

Beverly blushed and smiled, and the photographer had his picture. Everyone agreed that it was a lovely portrait.

CHAPTER X

Beverly set down the photo and shuddered. The photo, and the corpse on the table, reminded her that her birthday party had been the last time she had seen Miguel di Cruz. His body had probably looked like the one in the room, or worse, after the renegade Vradthmorn had taken his ship.

First di Cruz, then her parents . . . she hoped her brothers were all right. Was someone gunning for them, too? Even if she escaped her current plight, she did not want to be the last of the di Mendozas. *Please let my brothers be safe,* she prayed.

Beverly composed herself. "Of course, this is a copy, Peer Sandra. The original was a TrueLife portrait."

Sandy looked at it again. "How could it have gotten here?" she asked.

Beverly shook her head, bemused, "I can't imagine."

"They couldn't have taken it from Griswold's ship," mused Peer Sandra. "There wasn't anything left. My own radar showed the *Nine to Five* plow into the ground."

Beverly winced.

Peer Sandra asked, "Were any copies distributed beyond your immediate family?"

"It was used in my school yearbook," said Beverly.

"Hard to imagine a copy of *that* coming this far."

"And I think it was picked up by the news services when my aptitude scores were announced; it ran in the society pages." Relatives Beverly had never heard of had called to offer congratulations.

Sandy sat behind the desk and rubbed a hand over her face. "I can't figure it out. I was never any good at this detective crap. The way I see it, whoever is after you *must* be the same person who shot down the *Nine to Five*, and that means they followed you from the Eight Worlds . . . hmmm . . . raced ahead to ambush you is probably more like it.

"I've got a problem, Beverly," she continued. "Whoever's after you has me out-gunned. That means I need to get you out of here for both our sakes. I can't tell whether it would help or hurt to go to any of the big boys for help. *Somebody's* allowed Eight Worlds troops onto Barigost. I don't know which faction did it. I'm afraid if I let take you to Ertrix or Wrenfield—or any city— you'd end up with your throat cut. Hell, even if I wanted to hand you over, I wouldn't know who to contact. Not that I would; *noblesse oblige* and all that crap.

"On top of that, there's a government inspector who's trying to nose in on things. I can't find out who the hell he is, so I'm pretty sure he's an agent of whoever's after you. He'll have a court order to search this place within a day or two, and I won't be able to play a shell game after that. Not when he has the government *and* those troops on his side.

"I can't see anything for it but to hide you again. I think I'll have George take that tin can of his on a test flight up to his father's territory. He'll take you with him, and drop you off on one of those tiny estates of Rudolf's. The radar net's real crummy north of here, so you won't leave a track at all."

Beverly nodded. "That's pretty much what you had in mind before, isn't it, Peer Sandra?"

"Yeah, but the stakes are higher now, and I'm being more careful. Don't worry Beverly, I'll get you off-planet in a week or two, and you can be safely on your way home."

Beverly wondered how safe a trip home would be.

Peer Sandra's phone beeped. She picked it up. Hank's voice came out, loud enough for Beverly to hear: "Grand Peer on the line for you, Sandy."

"Good," said Peer Sandra. "Put him on." She did something with the phone, then set it down on the desk.

"Sandy?" came a man's voice from the phone.

"About time, Fabian," said Peer Sandra. "What the hell took you so long?"

"I was with the Ambassador, and it took the duty officer a while to work up the nerve to interrupt us. I apologize. What's up?"

"What do you know about a San Vincentan named Baron Richard di Mendoza?"

There was a pause. "There was a Lieutenant di Mendoza who spent a few days here once. That must have been about twenty years ago. He was delivering some diplomatic papers to Valhalla, I think. Would that be him?"

Sandy looked at Beverly. Beverly nodded.

"That's him all right. He was a passenger on the *Nine to Five*."

"I didn't know that," said the Grand Peer. "Griswold didn't often take passengers. That's too bad. I liked di Mendoza."

"Anyway," Peer Sandra continued, "his daughter escaped in an ejection pod. There have been two attempts on her life so far. One involved shooting down an ambulance that she was supposed to be on, and the other was a commando raid on my place.

"I can't think of anyone outside of Ertrix who'd give a damn about San Vincentans, one way or another. I lost a lot of people, Fabian, and the people who hit me were Eight Worlds troops. I can't see any reason for importing mercenaries from the Pale unless there's going to be another god damned coup attempt."

"Probably. Certainly the raiding around here doesn't justify such expensive auxiliaries." Grand Peer Fabian didn't sound worried at the thought of a coup. "Nor does this region of space justify the presence of a San Vincentan baron. Therefore di Mendoza was here to investigate the mercenaries. No doubt they feel the daughter knows too much. What would you like me to do, Sandy?"

"Answer me this: if I take this girl to Ertrix, can you guarantee her safety until you get her off-planet?"

"Hmmm . . . yes. I can do that."

"Great. She'll be there soon. I'll have someone use a secure channel to set things up when she arrives. Thanks, Fabian. Bye." Peer Sandra switched off the phone.

Beverly ventured, "More smoke screen?"

Peer Sandra shrugged. "It can't hurt, and I needed to clue in Fabian as to what's going on."

"Aren't you afraid they'll attack the ship with the wounded on it, thinking I'm there?"

"No way. It lifts in five minutes, and they couldn't catch it unless they were waiting for it right now, which they aren't, 'cause they'd show up on radar. And the hop to Ertrix isn't like a re-entry approach, where your choice of trajectories is limited by the need to shed velocity. The path can be pretty random. The ship'll be fine, and enough of the wounded are in bandages from head to foot that a spy at the hospital entrance won't be able to tell if you're there or not. You and I will wait here until the ship lifts, then sneak you back upstairs."

Beverly shook her head. "Wouldn't it be better if I were seen going out to the ship? We could get back in through the tunnel."

"Good idea." Peer Sandra picked up the phone again and said, "Hank, is the ship ready? Good. I'll be putting another passenger aboard in just a minute." She hung up and said, "More grist for the wire-tappers' mill. Come on."

They stepped out into the noise and bustle of the hangar floor. The main doors were closing again—the ship had apparently been taken out to the landing field—and Peer Sandra ran toward the gap. Beverly sprinted after her.

The doors stopped with about half a meter between them. There were about fifteen armed men in uniform near the doors. Peer Sandra ignored them and squeezed through, and Beverly followed. There were more armed men outside, also wearing what Beverly guessed to be the uniform of the local militia—a dull red woolen tunic and a rust-brown steel helmet.

The ship was about fifty meters from the doors. Technicians were removing dollies from the landing jacks hooking them to a tractor. They finished as Peer Sandra and Beverly approached, then jumped into the tractor and drove away.

The ship's lifters filled the air with the whine of turbines. Now that the technicians were gone, someone in the ship turned off the floodlights, leaving the ship darkened except for the bridge windows and single light over the ladder. Beverly realized that the running lights were off.

They approached the ladder, and someone swung the airlock open. Peer Sandra shouted up at him, "Tell Marcel I've changed my mind—no passenger. Got it?" The man waved at her and closed the door again.

"Come on!" shouted Peer Sandra, She grabbed Beverly's arm and began running away from the ship. The ladder retracted and the light above it went out. The lifter noise increased.

The ship began to lift before they were well away from it. The noise was unbearable. Hot air gusted past them for a moment, then the ship was airborne, lifting straight up into the cold air. They heard the sonic boom before it was out of sight.

They went around to the tunnel door. The poor illumination this far out on the field made it likely that few people saw them, perhaps none. Peer Sandra used her portable phone to tell Hank to open it again. When he did, Peer Sandra looked down the corridor, confirmed that it was empty, and stepped back into her apartment.

"I'm going to put you up in Emily's room," she said. "Come on."

They rushed a short distance down the corridor, and Peer Sandra led the way into a room. Emily was there, putting on a clean dress. "Don't you ever knock?" she asked.

Peer Sandra ignored the question, so Beverly said, "I'm sorry." Then, "I like your room." The room was quite large and was decorated with all sorts of memorabilia—sports pennants, posters, and trophies—but the dominant themes were piloting and teddy bears. There were about thirty teddy bears of all shapes and sizes, and innumerable model space ships, pictures of space ships, books on space ships, pictures of Emily standing next to space ships and aircraft, or sitting in the pilot's seat. Some had been taken when she was no older than eleven or twelve. A number of certificates attested to various kinds of pilot training, including such advanced skills as scooping and high-speed re-entries. Beverly was amazed.

There were also pictures of George, and others of both George and Emily. Some of these pictures went back four or even five years. The earliest ones were all associated with junior flying competitions that involved a two-person pilot/engineer team, but the ones showing them as a couple were not much newer. Since dating on San Vincento was discouraged among teen-agers below the age of sixteen, Beverly took this to mean that George and Emily's families had arranged a marriage for them. If they were betrothed, then their conduct was almost proper by San Vincentan standards.

Beverly was relieved; not so much because of her sense of propriety, but because the relationship now fitted into a familiar pattern. It implied a long-term alliance between the O'Hare and the Heinz families. Beverly wondered what the Heinz family was bringing to the table; Peer Sandra had ships, a base, and a reputation as a leader (at least of small-scale raiding parties)—

Peer Rudolf didn't seem to have any of these. Perhaps he had connections. How extensive was his family? George mentioned relatives constantly, but had never mentioned any siblings, nor had he ever referred to his mother. Was she alive? Was she estranged? Beverly had heard that Barigost had a high divorce rate.

More importantly, who was Emily's father? No one had ever mentioned him. It would be bad manners, or worse, to ask. Beverly resolved to stay alert for clues.

She turned her attention back to the room. The furnishings included many small rugs on the floor, and a number of leather-bound books on the wall. Nearer the door was a beautiful wooden desk (Beverly was still surprised by the lavish use of natural materials on Barigost) and an ornate round table with three matching chairs.

Emily finished dressing and motioned for her visitors to sit while she tossed her dirty clothes into a hamper. Peer Sandra didn't sit, so neither did Beverly. "I thought you were on your way to Ertrix," she said to Beverly.

Peer Sandra looked disgusted. "What made you think that?" she asked.

"Oh, Gabrielle mentioned it to me a few minutes ago. She said she heard it from Bob."

Peer Sandra picked up her portable phone again. "Hank, meet me in Operations on the double." She switched off. "I didn't tell him to forget that Beverly's here. I hope he hasn't talked to anyone yet. The grapevine is too god damned efficient." She left, slamming the door behind her.

Beverly said, "Peer Sandra mentioned on the phone that I was going to be on the ship, as a diversion. She told me I was really to spend the night here. I hope you don't mind, Emily."

"Oh, no, you're welcome to stay here. Mother can't keep you a secret for long, though."

"She's planning on shipping me off to the north in George's ship."

She suddenly felt very tired. Emily said something, but she didn't catch the words.

"What?" She had trouble concentrating. Suddenly it seemed as if she was watching the scene from somewhere else, with a lag of several seconds. She had trouble focusing. As she stood there, blinking, Emily rushed up to her, put an arm around her, and steered her to the bed.

"I'm all right," Beverly said weakly as Emily pushed her onto the bed.

"You *always* say that," said Emily. "Just lie there for a minute while I find some pajamas for you. You've just had too much excitement for one day."

"So have you. I can't take your bed. I'll sleep on the floor, or something." Beverly started to get up, but it seemed like a great deal of effort.

"Oh, no you don't. The bed's big enough for two." Emily tossed a pair of pajamas at Beverly (purple, with a pattern of cute little polar bears), then looked at the door. "Speaking of which . . ." She walked over and bolted it.

Beverly fended off Emily's attempts to help her and undressed. She draped her clothes over a chair and hung her revolver from the bedpost by her head. Emily decided that she, too, was ready to call it a night—she looked exhausted—and changed into pajamas. Hers were white with brown teddy bears.

Emily had climbed into bed and was about to turn out the light when there was a loud knock at the door. "Oh, God," she groaned. "Prince Charming at the castle gate." She got up and opened the door.

George staggered in, looking very much the worse for wear. His tunic was torn and covered with grease and dust. He had apparently been helping with the very worst of the cleanup effort. His eyes were red, and he looked totally worn out.

Before he had a chance to say anything compromising Beverly called out, "Hello, George."

He did a double take, then said, "I thought you were in Ertrix."

"Not so loud," said Emily, closing the door. "It's a secret. You can't stay here, George."

"I don't want to stay in my ship—things are too weird out there, and people are trigger-happy. The rest of the station is so trashed that everyone else is doubled up already. Loan me your shower and a piece of floor, and I'll be fine." He wandered over to a closet and started rummaging around, tossing out a blanket and a pillow.

"Oh, all right. Just don't snore."

"Snore? Me? No Heinz has ever snored."

"All of you snore. Your father snores like a buzz saw. You can hear him all the way down the hall."

"He does not! Ask him and he'll deny it—and he's well-known as an honest man." He pulled off his boots and tunic, wrapped himself in his blanket, and lay down on the rugs. He seemed to have forgotten his intention to use the shower. "Good night, love. Good night, Beverly." He closed his eyes.

"G'night, George," Beverly mumbled.

She was still wondering what a buzz saw was (and whether it could possibly be worse than George's snoring) when she fell asleep.

INTERLUDE

ONCE UPON A TIME, not long before he was killed by his brother, Lord Diaz went on a voyage in his star ship, the *Lady Catalina*, named after his sister, the Shipmistress.

Lord Diaz traveled grandly through San Vincentan space, threaded cautiously through Vradthmorn space, flew boldly past Terran space, and fought bravely across Ophiuchi space. Finally, after a year of journeying, he found fabled Grenaduve, the world where the Imperium never fell.

Lord Diaz and his sister were met by the Gardener, who ruled all Grenaduve. The Gardener was very wise and very, very old, but he took time to pay honor to Lord Diaz and his sister all the same.

"You are welcome to stay here as long as you like," the Gardener told them, "and you may partake of any of the fruits of my Garden."

"You do us much honor," replied Lord Diaz. "We will stay here for a time, though not as long as we would like. Our family has need of us, and our planet has need of our ship."

The Gardener took them to the Garden, where all manner of plants were grown. The garden contained every tree of legend: tall redwood, golden malinorne, reed-thin medusa that swayed in a wind only it could feel. Other plants were there as well: giant anemones from Rigel, china-flowers from Ophiuchus—so delicate that they could be shattered at a breath—and flutereeds from Cliffhaven that played haunting chords with every breath of wind. Hydrospheres from Bleys drifted across the sky; birds could be seen nesting in their turquoise fronds.

Lord Diaz and his sister were overwhelmed by the beauty of what they saw. There was nothing on San Vincento to compare to the beauty of the Garden. The knife-sharp mountains, shattered cities, and proud, hard people of San Vincento had a beauty of another sort, one that outsiders rarely perceived.

Finally, the Gardener led them to a grove of beautiful fruit trees. "These are the trees we developed ourselves," he said. "Each has fruit of marvelous virtue. The tree closest to us bears the Fruit of Contentment, a single bite of which will transport the most grief-stricken person into a permanent sea of bliss."

Lord Diaz shook his head. "Such is not the way of San Vincento. Grief is the way of life. We overcome it or die."

"Very well," said the Gardener. "Yonder is the Tree of Empathy. Eat of it, and the thoughts of others will be made plain to you."

Lord Diaz approached the tree, but his sister stopped him when he reached to pick some fruit.

"And to whom do you propose we give this fruit?" she asked. "To spy into the secret thoughts of others; to pry into their dreams—it is a shameful thing. There is no honor in it."

Lord Diaz picked no fruit from the Tree of Empathy.

They came next to the Tree of Cleverness. "The fruit of this tree stimulates the mind without unbalancing it," said the Gardener. "It sharpens the wit to a surprising degree."

Lord Diaz nodded and reached for the fruit.

"Does it travel well?" his sister asked.

"Oh, yes—a fruit from this tree will retain its virtue for several years. Would that the others were so hardy!"

"Then let us pick some and bring them back to San Vincento, brother," said Shipmistress Catalina, "so that our father can distribute them as he sees fit."

"I am minded to eat one myself, the better to choose from these trees," said Lord Diaz.

"It does not take a clever man to discern the way of honor," said the Shipmistress. "Besides, these fruits each possess subtle perils." She turned to the Gardener. "Do they not?"

The Gardener shrugged. "I have not found it so," he said. "I have eaten of most of them myself, including the Fruit of Cleverness. Still, others who have come to our planet have been less than wholly pleased, so perhaps caution is not uncalled for."

After Lord Diaz picked a bag of fruit from the Tree of Cleverness, the Gardener led them to the center of the grove, where a huge tree stood, its gnarled branches towering over the other trees.

"This is the Tree of Life," said the Gardener. "Eat of it and you will live a thousand years. Alas, its fruit is quite fragile, and does not survive long away from the tree."

"What of the seeds?" asked Lord Diaz.

"None of these trees will flower away from Grenaduve. Their virtues are bound to our world. Perhaps it is better so. I cannot say."

"We wish no fruit of this tree," said the Shipmistress. "Imagine our descendants growing old and dying while we survive, denying them their chance to head the family. Imagine trying to face death with the same calmness as before, while knowing what a great life span lies in the balance. No—San Vincento is too harsh a place to permit such self-indulgence."

Lord Diaz looked troubled, but could not deny the wisdom of his sister's words.

They took their leave of the Gardener, and Lord Diaz launched his ship into space. He fought bravely across Ophiuchi space, flew boldly past Terran space, and was threading cautiously through Vradthmorn space when he was set upon by a vast fleet. Lord Diaz fought heroically, but the Vradthmorn overwhelmed the *Lady Catalina*, boarded her, and took Lord Diaz and Shipmistress Catalina captive. They were bound and taken to the flagship, where they were presented to the Vradthmorn Over-King.

The Over-King looked them over contemptuously and turned to one of his officers. "What was found in their ship?"

The officer produced the bag of fruit. "Only these, Your Majesty. They were in the Captain's safe."

"Bah! Of what value could these be? If they are not carrying goods, then it is what I expected—they are spies. Throw them out the airlock."

Then Shipmistress Catalina spoke. "Wait, Your Majesty! I will tell you about the fruit."

Beneath her brother's horrified gaze she told the Vradthmorn about the fruit. They treated her with suspicion, but she swore upon her honor that she told the truth.

Of course the Over-King believed her then. He sent for his captains and told them, "We will each eat one of these fruits. We will become great strategists, and conquer all of human space!"

They ate the fruit, and right away they could feel themselves understanding wider and subtler things than they had ever known. And as this happened each looked at the others uneasily, for each saw opportunities to diminish the others—but each also saw weaknesses in his own position.

The Vradthmorn are a race bound together not by honor, but by fear and superstition and awe. Those who ate the fruit became too clever for these feeble ties to bind them, and soon each captain was fleeing pell-mell for his own ship. The Over-King, realizing what was happening, tried to organize a defense against his captains, but failed. He was the last Over-King of the Vradthmorn, who in a few generations were reduced to the wretched savages we know today.

Lord Diaz slipped his bonds in the confusion and led his sister back to his ship, and they escaped to San Vincento.

"It is sad that we have nothing to show for our journey," he said.

Shipmistress Catalina reached into her sleeve and produced a single Fruit of Cleverness, which she had kept hidden from the Vradthmorn. Without a word she gave it to her brother.

He embraced her and said, "You have salvaged my honor more times than I can say. How can I ever repay you?"

"It is my honor and my duty, brother," she replied. "Come, let us see our father and give him the fruit to use as he sees fit."

So they visited their father, who was very glad to see them safe and sound. He gave new titles to Lord Diaz, and a new ship to Shipmistress Catalina, and ordered a huge feast of welcome.

But he gave the fruit to Lord Diaz' brother Pedro, who, after eating it, murdered Lord Diaz and embarked on a campaign of such destruction that none could stop him—until his sister Catalina killed him with her bare hands.

But that is another story.

Chapter XI

"Well, that's done," said Emily, putting a coil of nylon rope back into a locker. She and Beverly surveyed the cargo hold. Everything had been secured for flight. They were both wearing orange ship's crew jump suits, since they anticipated wearing space suits during the flight. George scurried past them and climbed the ladder to the bridge. He had been working in Engineering, the lowest deck on the ship. He soon climbed back down.

"It looks like we're ready to go," he said. "Did you patch the plasma gun holes?"

Emily said, "I did the ones in the door, and Beverly did the ones in the hull." Emily had insisted that Beverly take the opportunity to learn how to use a hand welder, and had pronounced Beverly's work adequate.

George looked the patches over. "Looks okay." He wiped the sweat from his forehead. "We need to go through the power-up sequence next. If there are any problems, it could take the rest of the day." It was about noon. They had been working since sunrise. "Let's find something to eat first, and then we'll start."

The kitchen equipment had been secured, so they were reduced to microwaving some of George's frozen food—"Cap'n Dilbert's Bluepork and Bean Baritos." They tasted better than the name suggested, but had an unpleasant texture reminiscent of layers of rubber cement on wet cardboard.

When they were done, George said, "Let's go up to the bridge and I'll tell you what we're going to do." He let the girls go up the companionway first, then climbed after them. He sat on the deck with his feet dangling over the companionway.

"Okay," he said. "Emily's going to pilot the ship, and I'm going to stay in Engineering and keep everything running. Beverly, you can be the astrogator or the gunner. Either one's superfluous on this trip."

"There's a *gunner's* station on this ship?" asked Beverly. Such a possibility had not occurred to her. "There's no turret!" There were no laser tubes, either, but she didn't mention that.

"The guns are forward-firing, sure," said George, "but they're stabilized, and you can traverse 'em about thirty degrees. The gunner's controls can be slaved to the autopilot to let the gunner line up the ship."

"Great. I'll take the gunner's station," said Beverly. "I have some training with guns."

"Really? All right. There's a simulator if you want to play with it," said George. He moved over to the gunner's seat on the port side of the cabin. Beverly noticed that the console was active: its screens and lights glowed. They had been dead yesterday. George flipped a switch and typed some commands on the keyboard. "The simulator's in atmospheric combat mode now. Get into the seat and I'll show you the controls." He moved aside to let Beverly squirm past him—the bridge was *very* small—and waited for her to climb into the gunner's seat.

The gunner's console was appallingly primitive. It consisted of two side-arm joysticks, each with a firing button and several other controls, and a large 2-D color screen with several buttons and knobs on each side, each labeled in an alien language. George had re-labeled most of the controls with neatly lettered pieces of masking tape.

George indicated various controls. "These joysticks control the guns. The left one is coarse aiming, the right one is fine aiming. The left one sends requests to the autopilot to swing the nose around, and the right one traverses the guns. It's a stupid system, but I can't afford to replace it.

"These buttons fire the guns. The left button fires the left laser tube, the right button fires the right tube. I can't think of any reason why you'd fire the guns one at a time, so I suggest using both buttons at once. This knob controls the magnification on the screen. This other knob controls brightness. This switch attaches vectors on all the moving objects on the screen, so you can tell where they're going. That only works if the radars are on. This knob selects between optical image, radar image, and both. The optical sights are pretty good; the radar's garbage.

"I've already set the simulator mode. This switch starts the simulation." He flipped a few more switches, pressed the START button, and told Beverly, "Since this is in gunnery-only mode, the simulator will give you good piloting. You should be able to take out a ship or two before you screw up and get blasted. Have fun." He turned to Emily and started going over a checklist.

The simulation began with the ship in level flight several thousand meters above the ground. Beverly found that the left joystick could be used to pitch and yaw the ship away from its line of flight, but the response time was a bit unpredictable, perhaps because her requests were sometimes at odds with the simulated piloting.

Three sets of cross-hairs showed the point of aim, the ship's course, and the course she requested with the left joystick. The guns were servo-stabilized: they pointed in the desired direction even as the ship maneuvered. Unfortunately, the ship didn't have to turn much before the guns reached the limits of their traversal.

The screen blinked, and the image of a ship, much like hers, appeared in front of her. Beverly shot it down, clumsily. The simulator blinked and gave her another, similar target. Beverly shot that one down as well.

George and Emily were working their way down the flight control checklist. This was mostly a set of avionics tests using the bridge computer. Their conversation was a little distracting.

Soon the simulator was giving her more complex tasks to carry out, obviously operating in a programmed-learning mode that was designed to teach her one new technique at a time. Beverly usually disliked this kind of simulation, but the challenge of dealing with forward-firing guns engaged her interest, and she worked with increasingly intense concentration.

The simulator abruptly stopped halted its series of simplistic exercises. The image of a ship appeared on the screen, apparently launching from behind a hill. It was larger than George's ship, and had twice as many guns. Beverly felt her palms begin to sweat as she tried to line up the guns. This became impossible as both ships started evasive action, darting in random zigzags to present more difficult targets.

Almost by accident, the other ship flashed across the cross-hairs. Beverly jammed down both the firing buttons, and laser fire played across the other ship. It tumbled, then straightened out—but was still losing altitude when it brushed the side of a hill. It was enveloped in simulated flames.

Another ship appeared on the horizon, and Beverly reminded herself of her training. She relaxed and took a lighter grip on the controls. She stopped sawing the joysticks back and forth in an attempt to chase the target with the cross-hairs. Instead, she tried to anticipate where the target would move, and put the cross-hairs there. Properly played, ship's gunnery is a waiting game, requiring patience and concentration. It also requires fast reflexes, since opportunities to shoot are fleeting.

The other ship drifted across the cross-hairs almost immediately. Beverly pressed the firing buttons—more gently this time—and her lasers burned twin gouges in the side of the ship. It dodged to one side and returned fire. It took Beverly a long time to line it up again. When she did, the ship was very close, and she could see individual rivets on its hull through her sights. She fired again, hitting it amidships, and managed to play the beams forward; burning two long rents in the side of the ship and blowing out the starboard bridge windows. The ship tumbled out of control, exploding before it hit the ground.

The view shifted, and her ship was racing up narrow river canyon. The ground was covered with boulders and snow. Snow-capped mountains loomed close at hand. Though the scene was unfamiliar, Beverly felt a powerful sense of *déjà vu*. She shut off the autopilot slaving; she didn't want to smash her ship into the canyon wall. Suddenly, her ship darted up another canyon. They rounded a bend, and another ship launched ahead of them. Its was a corvette. Instead of forward-firing guns, it had a three-tube turret a third of the way between nose and tail. It lifted slowly and erratically, then recovered and started racing away, flying up the canyon close to the ground.

Beverly's ship maneuvered constantly. Beverly's crosshairs passed over the enemy, but her ship was turning so quickly that her shot went wild.

The enemy's turret traversed toward them. The stubby laser tubes were soon pointed right at her.

Beverly's ship rolled to port and dove, pulling up only a few meters from the canyon floor, then nearly broadsiding the canyon wall as it climbed. Beverly had no chance to shoot.

The ship moved back to the center of the river canyon as it raced upstream. The canyon became narrower. There was no sign of their opponent. Beverly's ship suddenly climbed, turned, and hopped over a ridge into a new river canyon. Still no enemy ship. Beverly felt herself becoming tense with anticipation, and forced herself to relax, to detach herself from the action.

Soon her ship reached a fork in the river, and it turned hard to port, traveling up the left-hand branch. No sign of the corvette. The ship came to another fork, again chose the left-hand branch.

The enemy was right in front of them! Beverly played her guns over the enemy's stern, burning twin gashes through the hull. Her ship dove toward the canyon floor, leaving the enemy above and ahead of her, but still within Beverly's field of fire. Her guns slowly tore a trail of destruction down the length of the enemy's belly, burning through the hull and into the enemy's vitals as her ship overtook its opponent.

Beverly's ship passed the enemy from below, then made a half-loop and swept past it again, the two ships now traveling in opposite directions. Beverly made a hasty shot. An explosion engulfed the enemy's stern, blowing out part of its hull.

The enemy still flew, though just barely. Once again, its turret traversed until it was pointing directly at Beverly. It fired.

The screen went dead.

Beverly almost panicked. She was still trying to figure out her next move—wait for power to return? Prepare for a crash?—when she looked up and saw Emily with her hand on the power switch.

Emily looked worriedly back at her. "Are you all right? We need to run through the gunnery checklist."

George added, "We *shouted* at you, and you didn't respond at all. You just kept running the guns."

"I'm sorry, George," she said, disoriented and embarrassed. "I didn't mean to ignore you."

"I could tell," he said. "That was amazing! I've never seen anyone work the guns like that before. I've never gotten more than halfway past the programmed-learning exercises, let alone taken out three ships at the master level." He seemed deeply impressed.

"I wasn't going to last much longer," said Beverly, too confused to take pleasure in his praise. "I guess it's just as well you pulled the plug."

Emily said, "Sorry about that, but we have to get out of here, and that means running through all these checklists. I can run through this one by myself. Would you mind helping George in Engineering? It takes two people."

"All right. I don't know much about engineering systems." Beverly started climbing out of her seat. George started down the companionway.

"Don't worry," said Emily. "He mostly needs you to read meters and things."

Beverly followed George. He stopped on the cargo deck and opened a locker. Over his shoulder he said, "You'll need to wear a space suit, Beverly."

"Why? I thought we were just going through a checklist."

"This checklist involves things that might go *boom*," he explained. "Space suits are also nice if something blows up, or there's a liquid nitrogen leak, or a fire." He handed her a space suit from the locker. "The odds of things blowing up are pretty low, but it happens." He looked concerned, as if he felt he was imposing. "If you're afraid, I can get Emily to do it."

Beverly bristled. "That's not funny, George."

George was confused. "It wasn't supposed to be. I just meant . . . "

Beverly cut him off. "On San Vincento, accusing me of fear would be the same as accusing me of cowardice. Am I a coward, George?"

"No, of course not, but . . . "

"Then let's get on with it."

Beverly began to put on her suit. She was still angry. No one had accused her of being afraid in years. She knew George was an off-worlder and didn't know any better, but it still bothered her. She tried to put if from her mind: she had work to do. George stared at her for a moment, then shrugged and began putting on his suit. He finished before Beverly, who was mystified by the suit's unfamiliar adjustments. George helped her, then led the way down to Engineering without a word.

He walked around the room a bit before beginning the checklist, checking for loose tools and such. "There are three things we have to do: start the fusor, engage the converter, and warm the drives. Since our flight is going to be entirely in the atmosphere, we don't really have to warm the drives, but I'm going to do it anyway.

"I've been warming up the fusor since this morning. Let's go over the fusor start-up checklist."

Beverly held the checklist while George did the checking. The air in the fusor had been kept evacuated, and there was now only a small amount of gas inside, kept at plasma temperatures by induction heaters. George checked all the equipment—liquid nitrogen cooling system, the converter that would generate electricity from the fusor, and the containment system. He then went through some elaborate diagnostic tests on the computer-controlled part of the system. Finally, he checked the alignment of crucial elements in the fusion chamber. Most of these tests required that Beverly take readings from another part of Engineering, or record readings in the log.

None of the readings meant anything to Beverly, who knew nothing of engineering systems. Not so George. He reacted to every reading with a smile, a frown, a grumble, or a remark.

All this took about an hour. When they were done, George took off his helmet and wiped his face with a paper towel. "Okay. Now for the fun part. We get to flash the fusor. You watch those dials over there"—he pointed to some dials on her side of the fusor—"and I'll ask you for readings." He made some control adjustments, got the dial readings from Beverly, and then started up the final startup process.

Engineering was filled with a loud humming as the fusor was brought up to standby. When the readings were stable, George turned on the hydrogen feed to initiate fusion.

BANG! BANG! BANG!

Three deafening reports came from the fusor. Beverly jumped and looked around wildly.

George stepped back from the controls. "Sounds pretty good," he said.

He took spectrometer readings of the plasma in the fusor to make sure there were no contaminants. Then he restarted the fusor.

Once again it made a deafening series of explosions, but Beverly expected them this time, and managed not to jump.

George adjusted the controls, revving up the pulse frequency. The noise dropped almost to nothing. George listened for a while, then nodded in satisfaction. He said, "This fusor has really primitive stabilization, and it has trouble with fuel metering and pulse timing when you start it. It smooths out once it's been running for a few seconds."

The rumbling of the fusor turned to a sputter for a moment, then resumed. George scowled at it, then started rereading all the dials. "It'll be steady as a rock in a few minutes."

The ship's intercom channel also transmitted over the space suit radios. They heard Emily's voice asking, "Ready for consistency checks, George?"

George groaned. "Might as well." He rattled off instrument readings, and Emily compared them to the corresponding readings on the bridge. They all matched.

"All right!" said Emily enthusiastically.

"I'll be damned," said George. "I thought we'd never get those straight." To Beverly he explained, "The Morversarn converted the bridge to their system of units, but left Engineering in metric. After we took the ship we were afraid we'd have to abandon it, it was so hard to figure out the instrumentation."

Emily exclaimed, "We've run out of checklists! Let's get launch clearance and get out of here! Come up to the bridge, Beverly."

George remarked, "I'll bet Dragon Lady will be here with some last-minute advice. She'll tell us not to crash into mountains or get our asses shot off. Things we'd forget otherwise."

"I heard that!" said Emily. "And stop calling her Dragon Lady."

George told Beverly, "Vince tells me she's exactly like her grandfather."

The annunciator for the airlock door chimed. George climbed up into the cargo deck and punched the intercom button. "What's the password?"

"God damn it, George . . . ," began Peer Sandra.

"That's right!" George whooped. "Enter, friend!" He opened the door and bowed as Peer Sandra came in.

Beverly glanced out the door to see if Peer Sandra had acquired a new pair of bodyguards. She had. They looked uncomfortable. Beverly couldn't blame them.

Peer Sandra waited for Emily to arrive. "You kids ready to go?" When they nodded, she continued, "That damned inspector got a court order today, and he's going to search the whole god damned station, *and* look over all my records. I'll be glad when you're out of here. If this ship stayed he'd be looking it over with a microscope before long.

"You know the drill: Stay out of range of the radar net, fly low, and stay alert. I don't think anybody can pick you up unless they follow you from here, and if they do, they'll stick out like a sore thumb on *my* radar.

"Try not to get your asses shot off, and don't plow into any mountains, and you'll be okay. Who's piloting?"

"I am," said Emily. "George is going to stay in Engineering to check on the systems, since this is a shake-down flight, and Beverly's going to take the gunnery station."

"Good," said Peer Sandra. "George, have you given this pile of junk a name yet? It's bad luck to fly a nameless ship."

"Oh, Mother, don't be superstitious," said Emily.

"Yes," said George, suddenly serious, "I've chosen a name."

"What is it?" asked Peer Sandra.

George told Beverly, "Our family has three traditional names for ships. That's the most we've ever had at once. The frigate was the *Snow Queen,* the corvette was the *Polar Bear,* and the armed freighter was the *Northern Light.* I've decided to call this one the *Northern Light,* to leave the other slots open for bigger ships."

"A good choice," said Peer Sandra, nodding in approval. "Very appropriate. I was afraid you'd try to be funny . . . . Oh, before I forget," she said, producing a small bundle. "This is yours, I think, Beverly."

Beverly opened it up, and there was the pistol Uncle Miguel di Cruz had given her. She had almost forgotten about it.

Seeing it reminder her of him once more. If he had been alive, he would have been sure to avenge the death of his best friend. But di Cruz had fled San Vincento after winning a duel with Viscount di Barra. Di Barra's political allies and relatives had sworn vendetta, and were prepared to kill di Cruz by fair means or foul. Di Cruz had taken up with di Grenville and accepted a privateer on the Pleiades frontier. His ship had been taken by renegade Vradthmorn, who had killed everyone aboard and thrown their bodies into space.

Her father had been brought very low by di Cruz's death. He blamed di Grenville's for betraying di Cruz, but this was only an intuition. Without evidence, he felt unable to challenge di Grenville to a duel. But his inaction, however justified, had wounded him deeply.

Beverly's pistol and holster both seemed unharmed. She field-stripped it. The clip was empty. Someone had fired the weapon and not cleaned it afterward. This made her very, very angry. To mistreat such a work of art was criminal. To do it to *her* pistol was a personal insult.

"I took it off Peer Reuben," Peer Sandra was saying. "He bought it from Commissar Winston. Reuben didn't want to give it to me, but I convinced him.

"Winston's in jail. He's practically the last civil servant in the district who I didn't appoint myself. Now I've finally nailed him for malfeasance."

"What's going to happen to him?" asked Beverly. She didn't want to duel with the man. Only if he got a stiff sentence could she could consider her honor satisfied without taking further action.

"Well, I haven't quite decided," Peer Sandra answered. "Since you are a member of a San Vincentan diplomatic mission, any crime committed against you is treason. The punishment for treason is death by firing squad. Winston will plead ignorance, of course, so he might get the charge reduced to grand larceny. The punishment for that is either reeducation or death by hanging. If it were me, I'd prefer hanging."

"You're a Peer," pointed out George. "If you committed grand larceny, your actions would be put down to 'harmless high spirits,' and you'd get off with a warning."

"True," said Peer Sandra, with a gesture that waved the point aside. "Not that my position would make me immune to a treason charge. On the contrary."

Beverly was torn between relief that the man would be punished and horror that people would speak so contemptuously of their own government. San Vincentans were loyal to their society. "Let's get back to business," Peer Sandra continued. "I think Beverly's the right person to christen the ship, since its maiden flight is in her honor."

"Oh, my," said Beverly. "You know what this means, don't you?"

Peer Sandra grinned wickedly. "Yes. It makes you the Ship-mistress of *The Northern Light*. I know something of San Vincento."

* * *

After San Vincento was abandoned by the Imperium (or, as the San Vincentans say, "betrayed") after the Day of the End of the World, San Vincento fell under constant attack by the Vradthmorn. No one knows who gave space flight to the Vradthmorn, but it ranks among the greatest crimes of all time. The Vradthmorn burst onto the scene and swept across the Imperium, looting and conquering.

The San Vincentans, their cities destroyed, their industry in ruins, their society shattered, was unprepared for the onslaught. Each region tried to defend itself, but few were willing to pool their few precious ships for a centralized defense. This disorganization allowed the Vradthmorn to raid with impunity, often putting entire cities to the sword.

Fey Aaron, using a combination of diplomacy, battle-sense, and reckless heroism, drew together a coalition that beat back the Vradthmorn with the combined fleets of several San Vincentan factions.

The Navy that Aaron created formed the basis of the San Vincentan government after his bride murdered him on their wedding night, for only the Navy could protect San Vincento from the Vradthmorn.

In spite of this, the production and maintenance of ships remained too expensive for the weak central government, so the leaders of the emerging feudal aristocracy personally contributed ships to the Navy.

At first, the families who contributed the ships also supplied the captains, but it soon became apparent that successful families did not always provide successful ship captains. It became customary to allow the Navy to choose the captain, while the family provided a representative to ensure that the ship was properly used and cared for.

Due to a phenomenal death rate among the men of the San Vincentan aristocracy, it became more and more common to send young women as the family's representative. These women were called Shipmistresses.

The San Vincentans are a superstitious people, and they soon conferred a number of superstitions upon the Shipmistress. Her task was translated into mystic terms: she was to be the living spirit of the ship; honorable, virtuous, chaste, concerned with the well-being of ship and crew; but also strong-willed and merciless. She was not a figurehead; in addition to the general right to advise the captain and report on his actions, she had the right to challenge him to mortal combat—even in the middle of battle. She was the buffer between the reckless ambition of San Vincentan officers and the survival of the irreplaceable ship.

In recent years the custom has declined. Most ships no longer have a Shipmistress on board. A noblewoman on San Vincento may hold the title, but rarely if ever visit her ship. The duels evolved from on-the-spot near-executions to a genteel way for the Navy to eliminate troublesome officers. The Shipmistress rarely delivers the challenge or attends the duel anymore; such things are done by intermediaries. (The captain has no such luxury.)

A few noblewomen still become Shipmistresses in the old style, serving on the crew and accepting the responsibility for ship. While the Navy encourages this, most families discourage their daughters from seeking the danger and discomfort of military service, whatever the honor involved.

Serving on a ship as Shipmistress today is considered old-fashioned.

The di Mendozas are an old-fashioned family.

* * *

Beverly thought about it for a moment. Being a Shipmistress was her most cherished ambition, but the circumstances were not what she'd had in mind.

Peer Sandra saw Beverly's hesitation. She said, "Of course, your tour of duty's going to be short. I don't think you need to worry about your long-term obligations to this rust-bucket."

Beverly made up her mind. In a cold voice she said, "Disparaging my ship is a slight upon my honor, Peer Sandra. If you continue, I shall have to send a member of my crew to avenge these insults."

George and Emily were taken aback, but Peer Sandra laughed and slapped Beverly on the back. "That's the spirit! I've got a bottle of brandy to christen this . . . noble ship." She went over to the airlock door. "Hey, Norris! Toss up that bottle, will you?"

Her bodyguard didn't take her literally; he climbed the ladder and handed her a bottle and four shot-glasses.

She handed the bottle to Beverly. It was a fancy liter bottle of brandy, "Valdemar's," which according to the label consisted of "The finest northern brandy-melons distilled in the age-old tradition by Barigost's finest craftsmen, and aged for eight years in hand-built casks in Antipodes Caverns, giving a unique ambience to this superb product." The liquid inside was the color of apple cider. The bottle was dusty.

"That's almost the last of the old stuff," said Peer Sandra. "A hundred years old last month. We have a couple of cases that we keep to christen ships, but most of it's at least ten years newer. It's good luck to use old liquor, especially old liquor grown within sight of the ship." She pointed. "You can see Valdemar's farm through the doorway there."

She set the glasses down on a crate, took the bottle back from Beverly, and produced a stainless steel corkscrew with a silver handle, emblazoned with an eagle and the initials "T.I.F."— Terran Imperial Fleet. It had apparently been made centuries ago for an officer's mess. She blew the dust from the neck of the bottle and carefully pulled the cork, then poured each shot-glass one-fourth full of brandy. She handed out the glasses, and raised hers.

"To *The Northern Light*," she said. "May she always find her way, protect her crew, and give grief to her enemies. May she increase the fortunes of her master, and serve to protect his people." She downed her drink in a gulp, and the others followed suit.

Beverly discovered that hundred-year-old Valdemar's brandy had an odd, indescribable taste—not unpleasant, just strange. She wondered what the newer vintages were like.

Peer Sandra replaced the cork and said. "Now for the christening. The Terrans are pansies and break the bottle on the tail of the ship. We do things right on Barigost."

She led the way up the companionway and opened the emergency airlock on the bridge, swinging the heavy door outward over empty space. "We can't get any closer to the nose without a crane. Beverly, come out to the edge and break the bottle."

Beverly and Peer Sandra squeezed past each other, and Beverly stood at the edge of a twenty-meter drop with the bottle in her hand.

She recalled the ancient words and altered them a bit to fit conditions. "I, Beverly Maria Elizabeth Deborah Catherine di Mendoza, deliver this vessel to her new masters, and commission her to the defense of Barigost. I swear to serve the interests of the ship, to allow none to use her dishonorably, and to allow her spirit to act through me. I christen this ship *The Northern Light*."

Beverly smashed the bottle against the hull, sending showers of glass and brandy down the side of the ship. She tossed the neck after the rest and turned to go inside.

"Well done," said George. "That had quite a ring to it. Come on in and we can get started—but dog the airlock first."

Beverly leaned again over the twenty-meter drop, grabbed the handle to the outer airlock door, and swung it shut. She tried not to look down as she did this. She spun the wheel to secure the door, then stepped into the bridge and pushed the button that closed the inner door. It slid up from the deck and locked itself automatically. She took her place at the gunner's station.

Emily wormed her way into her space suit as Peer Sandra gave them their last-minute instructions.

"Just do as I told you and you'll be okay. Brina took one of the stratofighters up an hour ago, and you'll be on our radar for the first couple of hundred klicks. If anyone wants to take you, they'll have to do it outside our radar perimeter. They won't be able to follow you, so they'll have so much area to search they'll never find you.

"Keep off the damn radio until you're within spitting distance of your destination. And use the microwave channel—use the shortwave and I'll nail your hide to a tree." She looked at her watch. "I have to see that clown from the government now. Take care." She gave Emily a hug and disappeared down the companionway.

George made a last inspection of the bridge and said, "Things look good. I'll go down to Engineering and we can spool up the lifters." He picked up a tool box that he'd been keeping on the bridge and took it with him down the companionway.

A few minutes later Beverly heard him over the suit radio. "I've retracted the accommodation ladder and secured the main airlock. I'm in Engineering now. You can start up the lifters any time."

"Aye-aye," Emily replied. She turned a key, lighting up a previously dead control panel. She put her hand on a throttle. "Spooling lifters."

A whining sound indicated that the lifter turbines were spinning. The sound grew gradually louder and higher-pitched. Emily and George went down a brief checklist for the lifters, testing the engines one at a time and making sure that the readouts on the pilot's console matched those in Engineering.

"That's the last one," said George. "You have permission to lift."

"Aye-aye, Captain," Emily replied calmly. "Spooling lifters."

She pushed the throttles forward, and the whine of the turbines turned to a roar. The ship rose slowly into the air. Emily took it straight up for about a few hundred meters, then said, "Retracting landing gear and moving to horizontal flight mode." She dropped the nose and increased the throttle.

Soon they were moving north at Mach three, with the ship in a horizontal orientation that put the bridge seats in a reasonable position for once. "Where are we going, George?"

"Either Barclay or Penguin," replied George. "Pick a number between one and ten, Beverly."

"Five."

"Barclay it is. Got that, Emily?"

"Aye-aye." Emily had pulled out a chart. She typed a few numbers into her console. "Nice place, Barclay," she remarked. "ETA one hundred minutes."

How Long Has it Been Since You Had an Adventure?

Ertrix! A beautiful island with a fine climate.
Ertrix! A city of grace and culture.
Ertrix! The courts. The parties. The politics.

Ertrix. Ertrix. Ertrix. Haven't you had enough of Ertrix?

How long has it been since you had an Adventure?

At Heinz Lodge there are no politics. No committee meetings. No paperwork. And court garb is strictly optional.

At Heinz Lodge we focus on the elements. Frozen earth. Icy arctic air. Water, in snow and ice and rushing streams. And fire at its hottest, coursing in the blood of Peers as they pursue the ultimate sport: big game hunting.

You'll face the giant polar bear, a Terran-descended brute that can weigh up to a ton, and has a ferocity out of proportion to its size.

You'll face the ferocious blitzer, the most dangerous predator in Persol.

In some years you can even face the therium: ten tons of short-tempered herbivore—the ultimate hunting experience.

And you'll face them with only two things in your favor: a high-powered rifle and one of the Heinz guides.

Heinz Lodge has been in operation for more than forty years. Serving as the home of Peer Rudolf Heinz and his family, the Lodge itself provides a comfortable, genteel backdrop to the exhilaration of arctic hunting. Heinz Lodge is well above the Arctic Circle, farther north even than the famous Penguin Mine. This provides a unique experience for the visitor and a great convenience to the hunter.

Hunting at Heinz Lodge is the favorite recreation of many prominent Peers. Grand Peer Fabian has hunted at Heinz Lodge many times; he once dispatched a therium in a single shot, in a hunt not fifty kilometers from the Lodge.

Heinz Lodge. How long has it been since you had an adventure?

(Some hunting is seasonal. Call for more information. Game laws prohibit the use of aerial hunting, laser weapons, automatic weapons, or explosive bullets. Heinz Lodge is a People's Free Recreational Area.)

CHAPTER XII.

"We're coming up on Jaguar Peak," said Emily, peering out the bridge windows. "We're right on course."

Beverly looked out and saw a snow-covered mountain jutting above a vast expanse of forest. "Why do you need landmarks? I thought navigational satellites made them unnecessary."

"They would," said Emily, "but we don't have any."

"Really? I didn't think they were very expensive," Beverly replied. "I thought everybody used them."

George was following the conversation on the intercom. "They're only cheap if you can hang onto them. Every time we put a satellite into orbit, somebody steals it."

"You're joking."

"No, really!" said George. "From an outsider's point of view, a satellite is a piece of free money just waiting to be picked up. People on their way to Fort Nereid or Northstar or Morversarn space just scoop them up and take them with them."

"I've never heard of such a thing," said Beverly. She had trouble imagining the casual lawlessness that this implied.

"Fact of life. Sure, in the Eight Worlds you have standing navies that have nothing better to do than guard the goods, so you can have as many satellites as you want. Here on Barigost the Grand Peer only has about half a dozen warships; the others are privately held, and we're going to keep it that way."

Without warning, the steady throbbing of the fusor stopped, then started again in a ragged series of ever-louder explosions. The ship lurched and bucked. Before anyone could react, the fusor stopped altogether.

With power gone, the whine of the lifters faded away. The ship began to fall silently toward the snow-covered tundra below.

Most of the lights blinked off when the fusor failed, but power to the control consoles was unaffected. Emily worked frantically to put the ship into a glide. "God damn it, George!" she snarled. "What's happening down there?" She sounded just like her mother.

"The controller blew. I'm not going to be able to get it back," said George. "We've got about a minute of emergency lifter power. You'll have to get us down on that."

Emily nodded. Her face was very pale. She bit her lip and looked carefully over her display console and out the windows. She put her hand on the lever that switched the lifters to emergency power, and waited. If Beverly hadn't known better, she would almost have thought that Emily was frightened.

The ship fell in a steep glide, far too steep to permit a dead-stick landing. Without power it lost velocity steadily until it fell to subsonic speeds. Emily waited. The ground came closer.

When they were about two hundred meters up, Emily pulled the nose up sharply. The ship stalled. Emily switched in the lifters and they roared to life. The ship fell tail-first toward the ground. When they reached one hundred meters, she gave the lifters full throttle. The ship's fall was arrested ten meters above the ground, then it shot back into the air. Emily cut the lifters, let the ship sink again, then gave full throttle again. The ship hovered for a moment, two or three meters above the tundra, then emergency lifter power failed all at once. The ship fell heavily to the ground, teetered wildly for a moment, then steadied.

They had landed.

For a moment none of them moved.

Beverly felt like a failure. Her first flight as Shipmistress, and they'd crashed.

Emily begin shutting down the power to the controls, keying in commands and flipping switches at a furious pace, desperate to achieve an orderly shutdown before the last of the emergency bridge power was gone.

Beverly called, "George, are you all right?"

"Fine," he called back over the intercom. "Good landing. No damage to report. I'm shutting down Engineering now."

Emily finished her task, took off her helmet, and put it on the deck behind her. She slumped into her seat and sighed.

"Some maiden voyage," she said.

Beverly gazed out across the tundra. The terrain wasn't as flat as she had supposed; it was a landscape of low hills, with the snow limited mostly to the north slopes. The south faces of the hills received enough sunlight to support low, rounded mounds of vegetation. Far to the west a dark green line seemed to indicate the edge of a forest.

"Where are we?" asked Beverly.

Emily sighed and turned on her computer console again. She typed in a couple of commands, looked at the results, and shut things down again. "We're in the middle of nowhere. The closest outpost is Heinz Lodge, about sixty kilometers away. All the real towns are 'way to the south. I was overshooting so I could sneak into Barclay from the north."

George came up to the bridge, holding a circuit module in one hand. He'd removed his helmet and gloves. "We blew a control module, and it looks like the backup module didn't kick in." He produced a second module. Even Beverly could see that it was broken. Its casing was cracked and oxidized. "You can see that it must have been broken all along; maybe the self-test doesn't look at the backup modules after all. There are still parts of the system I don't understand."

He sat on the deck and said, "At least we won't be tempted to break radio silence."

Emily narrowed her eyes. "We won't?"

"Nope. See that empty slot on the rack? That's the output stage for the transmitter."

Emily shot him a murderous look. "I ordered one," he said defensively, "but it hasn't come in yet. We've still got the microwave transmitter if you want to hit the golfball." For Beverly's benefit he explained, "That's a store-and-forward satellite."

Beverly said, "I thought you didn't have any satellites."

"These hardly count. There are a couple of tiny satellites in low orbit that do programmed store-and-forwards. They're too cheap to be worth stealing, though people shoot at them sometimes."

He turned to Emily. "Well?"

"I don't know," said Emily. "We're not supposed to break radio silence."

"But we're sitting ducks out here," said George. "I don't want to wait here until someone finds us."

"I don't know," repeated Emily. She looked tempted.

Beverly didn't like the way the conversation was heading. She might not have much experience as a Shipmistress, but she could tell that her crew was going to take the easy way out if she let them. She started emptying her pockets; knife, cartridges, pistols.

"What are you doing?" asked Emily.

"I'm checking my gear. I want everything to be in order when we hike to the lodge."

CHAPTER XIII.

By sunrise they were a kilometer from the ship. The sun sat huge on the horizon, casting long shadows on the ground and painting the few clouds red. They were well north of the Arctic Circle. The sun would stay low in the south all day, and the temperature would not rise above freezing.

Beverly was pleased by her performance of last night. She had steadied her crew, as was her duty as Shipmistress, and had prevented them from taking the easy way out. She was worried about the hike, though. While her tactics class had included a half-dozen field exercises, they had been one-day affairs at best. Beverly had never hiked more than ten kilometers, camped out of doors, or spent any time at all in the arctic. She knew she was woefully unprepared for this adventure.

George, however, was an expert. He had dug out half a dozen decrepit survival kits, which taken together had workable equipment for three people. These included binoculars, flare guns, rations, tents, cold-weather gear, compasses, and an assortment of miscellaneous camping supplies.

The cold-weather gear consisted of Barigost-style parkas, which were the same length as Barigost tunics—they came down to a little below the knee. They seemed to be made of treated cotton, quilted with down lining (or an equivalent), and an inner plush lining that might be real animal furs. There were also several sets of electrically-heated long underwear, which in George's opinion were the only thing that made the hike worth considering.

Emily looked back at the ship, almost out of sight now, and said, "I wish you had your express rifle, George."

"Me, too," George replied. He shifted his light assault rifle to his other shoulder.

Beverly unscrewed the end-cap from the piece of large-diameter plastic pipe she was carrying, and pulled out a map. She had stayed up late in the bridge, trying to understand the navigational system, and had finally succeeded in printing out detailed maps of the area. She was pleased with the results. With topographic maps and the compass from a survival map, she could navigate them to their destination. Or so she hoped. Global positioning systems relied on a satellite network, which Barigost lacked. Nor were any of the ship's navigational instruments portable. As she unrolled the map, she asked, "What's an express rifle?"

"An archaic big-game rifle. It uses great big jacketed lead bullets to bring down big game. They were also called 'elephant guns' on Terra."

"Just how big are the animals we're likely to meet?" asked Beverly. San Vincento had few large predators; its carnivores were small and fierce, and ran in packs.

"Big. We're too far from the sea for polar bears, but we have to watch out for blitzers. They run up to a five hundred kilos. The herbivores are a lot bigger."

They waited as Beverly made careful sightings through her field compass. This close to the pole, it took a long time for the needle to settle. She marked her map, closed her compass, and replaced the map in its makeshift case. When she finished, they began walking again.

They came to the first hill. Emily asked, "Do you want to take the north side or the south side, George?"

George shrugged. Emily explained to Beverly, "The hills only get sunlight on the south side, so that's where all the flora and fauna are. The north side is emptier, but it's colder, and there can be a lot of ice."

"Let's start on the south side," George suggested. "When we get tired of the wildlife, we can switch."

They turned to circle the hill along its south face. There was quite a bit of greenery here, consisting mostly of low-slung, dense, hemispherically-shaped plants that seemed huddled against the cold. The tallest plants were wind-twisted bushes that came up to Beverly's chest; these bushes towered above the surrounding greenery.

Other plants had a vague resemblance to sunflowers, with broad green petals that aimed at the sun, balanced on a short, stubby stalk. Beverly guessed that they closed up at night to conserve heat.

Little rodent-like creatures that seemed to consist mostly of fur chittered in the densest part of the brush.

They skirted the hill and soon came to another. There was a wasteland of boulders, gravel, and ice between the two hills. Lichens clung to the bigger rocks.

"You can see why this place favors very large or very small animals," Emily said. "There isn't enough food in any one sunny spot to support big animals, so most are tiny enough to live on the side of a single hill and not over-graze it. Animals that travel from hill to hill can get very large. The cube-square law favors huge animals in the arctic, like the theriums."

"The theriums overdo it," interrupted George. "They're huge, but there aren't very many of them. At the last count, there were only a couple of thousand of them on the whole planet. Let me know if you see any big animals; even the herbivores are pretty aggressive."

They walked a little further and he said, "I wish I had a grenade launcher," to no one in particular.

Beverly scanned the horizon but saw no large animals. They continued on, and she was pleased to note that the cold didn't bother her particularly through her parka and heated underwear.

It was well below freezing, and her breath created plumes of frost that hung in the air. There was no wind, for which she was thankful.

As they walked, Emily produced a portable short-wave receiver, pulled out the whip antenna. The radio filled the air with whistles, crackles, and hisses. There was no sign of a radio station anywhere. After a few minutes she gave up and put the radio away.

"Sunspot activity," George suggested.

"Probably," said Emily. "I wish I could get the weather channel. I tried last night, too. Nothing." She looked at the sky. "It looks clear enough, though."

After an hour of walking George stopped in a sunny slope that was too rocky for plant life. "Rest stop," he announced as he took off his pack. He pointed at a house-sized boulder. "The latrine's around there." Emily bolted for it. George watched her disappear from sight. "Ladies first," he said.

Beverly pulled out her map and studied it for a moment, then started up the hill to orient herself with the local landmarks.

"Don't stand right on the crest," called George. "It attracts the blitzers."

Beverly stopped short of the top and sighted in on the landmarks—Jake's Peak to the south and two unnamed hills that she had picked out earlier. The compass that George had given her was a good one, with a flip-up sight and a button to stop the needle. She took two sightings of each landmark, then remembered George's earlier warning and looked around for big animals. She saw none. She took out the binoculars George had given her and looked around again. She marveled at their simplicity—no zooming, no image enhancement, no range-finding. She decided she liked them better than the overly-complex devices she was used to.

She descended and carefully worked out their position on the map. The others watched her with interest. George had claimed earlier that he could find his way home without maps, since the terrain was so simple, even though he had never been in this part of the country before. Beverly remembered what her tactics instructor had said about native guides. "Only trust a native guide in the area he knows at first hand. Because of your training, *you* are a superior guide to the native in all other circumstances."

George asked, "You seem real good at that. Where did you pick it up?"

"It was part of my tactics class," said Beverly. "We did map-reading in the classroom, and had some field exercises, as well."

"I get the feeling our educations have nothing in common," said Emily, who had just returned. "What kind of classes did you have?"

"Nothing special. I went to a good school, but the curriculum was standard: we took etiquette, dancing, algebra, driving, weapons training, tactics, political theory, estate management, geography of San Vincento, and basic star crew skills."

"Where did you pick up your first aid training?" asked Emily.

"That was part of weapons training. Oh, I also took special instruction in ship's gunnery, because of my aptitude scores."

"No history, art, or science?" asked George.

"Not exactly. There was science in the star crew courses, and history in the etiquette and political theory courses, but we didn't spend whole classes on them."

"Hmmm. Emily and I both took the core classes—math, science, social studies, and literature—and the space sequence: astrogation, piloting, gunnery, engineering, and computers. Either one of us could work any station on a standard ship," he said proudly. "Emily took some first aid and law and piloting courses; I spent all my electives on engineering."

Emily looked at her watch. "Time to get moving," she said.

"Right," said George. "Adjust your bootlaces and pack straps before we go. We'll stop again in an hour." He retied his bootlaces, then lifted his pack. The girls did the same, and they continued their march.

After a while Emily remarked, "I find it hard to picture an exclusive girl's school doing tactical field exercises."

Beverly frowned. "Why?"

Emily shrugged apologetically. "I guess it's because all the technical courses here are co-ed. Girl's schools have a reputation for turning out bubble-heads who don't know anything but etiquette and the social register."

"How can they chaperone properly in a co-ed school?" asked Beverly. "Never mind; I don't want to know. We spent a lot of time on etiquette, too. It's important."

"Mother never seemed to think so," said Emily.

Beverly said nothing—it wasn't her place to comment. She continued, "But the tactical sequences are important as tempering exercises. It's true that the girls don't get the full treatment. The boys did a series of live-ammo exercises."

George stopped walking. "You're kidding."

"No, of course not. We put them through these exercises to harden them and weed out the unfit. You can't trust people for important jobs if you're not sure they can handle pressure."

"It sounds awfully dangerous," said George.

"Not really. Out of six hundred boys in the sequence my brother Miguel was in, only three were killed."

"Parents let their kids take part in exercises with a half a percent mortality rate?" asked George, aghast.

"Well, of course they do!" Beverly was impatient with George for missing the obvious. "How can you hope to amount to anything if you've never experienced hardship? Who would trust you?"

Emily broke in, "But they don't let girls take the sequence?" She looked like she didn't like the way things added up.

Beverly shrugged. "You can petition." She started walking again. The others followed.

"I like that," said George sarcastically. "'Please, sir—may I get my ass shot off?'"

Emily ignored him. "And. . .?" she continued.

Beverly didn't meet her gaze. "They turned me down."

"Did they say why?"

"'Limited enrollment,'" quoted Beverly. "Only twenty-four girls were allowed to participate last year. I wasn't one of them."

George (who had been following the conversation with a puzzled expression) tried again. "You were too cool for them, Beverly. They were afraid you'd wreck the curve."

Beverly smiled up at him. "Thanks, George. You're sweet."

George steered them along the shadowed north slopes of several hills, avoiding the brush and sometimes slippery ground cover. Some hills contained caves. Beverly assumed that they were caused by the action of ice freezing and thawing. She pointed one out to her companions.

"Yeah," said George. "This place is rotten with caves. Stay away from them. You never know what's living in there."

They surprised a dog-sized animal, its form hidden beneath a vast mound of shaggy fur. It turned tail (if it had a tail—it was hard to tell) and fled the way it came.

"That's a tupei," said George. "They're harmless; they eat the squealers." Squealers were apparently the small rodent-like animals. "They travel in packs, but they never attack people." He smiled to himself, as if to some remembered joke. "Well, hardly ever."

No other animals presented themselves. George wanted to keep walking right through lunchtime, in spite of his previous statements about hourly breaks, but Emily put her foot down.

They found a nice spot amid the greenery and pulled out their rations. These were canned goods for the most part. George hadn't anticipated hiking when he had stocked his ship.

"We've got two kinds of canned goods," said Emily. "Self-heating field rations and normal canned food. I brought the hot plate, so we don't have to use the self-heating rations. They're pretty awful."

"We're in a pretty good mood," said George. "Let's eat the self-heating food now." He handed a large can to each of them. "Never eat self-heating rations when you're depressed. The beef turns you homicidal, the turkey turns you suicidal, and the ham gives you hallucinations."

"Mine says 'vegetarian,'" said Beverly.

"It does not! Vegetarians care too much about what they eat." George grabbed the can from Beverly and read the label. "I'll be damned. You're right." He tossed the can back to her.

Emily said, "They open from the pull-tab on top."

Beverly obligingly pulled the tab, which took the lid of the can with it. Inside was a tiny spork and a paper napkin. Underneath those was another pull-tab. The outside of the can became hot.

Emily and George had also opened their cans. George looked at his spork sourly, then tossed it into the bushes and rummaged through his pack for the fork from his mess kit.

"Don't pull the second tab until the cooking's done," warned Emily.

About thirty seconds later, a buzzer (which must have been buried somewhere in the can) went off with an irregular metallic chatter. Beverly pulled the second tab, which turned out to be attached to an inner can containing the food. This inner can was designed to split down the sides. Beverly opened it, and was rewarded by a vaguely food-like smell rising from a mass of vaguely food-like solids.

"*Bon appétit,*" said George, smirking.

The food was bad, but not so bad as George had made it out to be. It had a slightly metallic taste, and texture was poor, but the main problem seemed to be that the separators that were supposed to keep the rice, stew, and chocolate cake apart didn't work. Having stew mixed with rice wasn't too bad, but the stew/cake mixture was inedible.

George and Emily had a harder time of it. Whoever had designed their meals had ostentatiously decided to include a frozen dessert. The partitions had broken in their meals, too, so they had hot ice cream mixed with frozen meat chunks and cold vegetables.

As they finished, Beverly said, "Where do these things come from, anyway? The label doesn't say."

"Beats me," said George.

Emily said, "I heard a rumor that they're from the Centaurus Federation. They say that all the self-heating cans that have ever been seen in the Duchy of Persol came from a single shipload of stuff. That was years and years ago."

"And most of it's probably still in circulation," said George. "The losses are probably due more to accident and shipwreck than people actually *eating* the stuff."

Emily gathered up the trash and tossed it into the bushes. Beverly climbed the slope and took another set of compass readings. None of the hilltops she was sighting on had passed from sight yet. She congratulated herself on her choice of reference points.

She came back down and made some more marks on her map, then showed it the George.

"That looks about right," he said. "We don't really need a map—navigation's too simple here—but it's nice to know just where we are."

They marched for the next hour in silence, took a short break, and continued. Shortly after they started walking, George remarked, "The brush is awfully high around here, don't you think?"

The brush was no more than chest-high, and they were having no trouble threading their way through it.

"You're right," said Emily. "It must have been a long time since the herds came this way. When the ice buffalo leave a region, Beverly, most of the plants have been grazed to the ground."

"With our luck," said George, "They're converging on this area now." He led them up a hill so they could look around, but there was no sign of an approaching herd.

George chose a campsite at four in the afternoon, a small, sunny meadow sheltered from the wind and apparently not subject to rockfall. The soil was too thin for brush, and the ground was covered by patches of lichen, tough grasses, and rocks.

They spent the hours before nightfall moving rocks from where they wanted to pitch their tents, setting up camp, and searching for firewood, which came in the form of withered sticks from dead bushes. The campfire wasn't really necessary, since between the electrically-heated clothing and Emily's battery-powered hot plate they didn't need the heat, but it was comforting all the same.

They cooked their dinner over Emily's hot plate. George left Emily flabbergasted by producing a tasteful selection of canned vegetables and desserts—she had expected him to bring the tinned equivalent of Cap'n Dilbert's Baritos. This tacit admission on George's part that such a thing as a balanced meal existed was nothing short of remarkable (or at least Emily treated it as such).

Beverly watched their byplay with amusement. She didn't know very many people who got along as well as George and

Emily. Not many San Vincentans couples would invent mock quarrels for their mutual entertainment.

The sun set as they finished dinner, slowly sinking below the horizon and setting the ground and sky ablaze with color. The stars came out with spectacular brightness and clarity. Emily pointed out a few of the local constellations—the Furbird, the Turret, the Emperor—while George pointed out inhabited stars. Persol was a region where inhabitable worlds were common and close together. Fort Nereid, Northstar, Valans, Dancel, Pertis, and Mordel were all just visible to the naked eye.

By then the exertions of the day were catching up with them, so they said their good-nights and climbed into their tents. Beverly took off her parka and crawled into her sleeping bag in her electrically-heated underwear, which she kept on, since the night was intensely cold and the sleeping bag was not up to the task alone. She worried about the rest of the march—though today had certainly gone well—and wondered what else she could do to help.

She rolled over and kicked something soft *inside* the sleeping bag. She unzipped the bag so she could fish it out. It was one of Emily's smaller teddy bears.

Beverly smiled and murmured, "It looks like Emily ended up with the wrong bedding." She cradled the bear in one arm and quickly fell asleep.

CHAPTER XIV

Beverly awoke to darkness, cold, and silence. She shivered violently, teeth chattering, and pulled her sleeping bag tighter around her.

After a moment, she felt a presence outside. She tried to hold still to hear better, but was overwhelmed by convulsive shivering. She crept out of her sleeping bag, drew her Anderson, and unzipped the tent flap.

Outside it was completely dark; completely silent. She waited in the cold, hugging herself, her hands so cold and numb and shaking that she was sure she couldn't shoot even if she had a target. Eventually, a little light crept into the scene, a cold, dim, passionless light.

She was back in the station at Antipodes, her tent set up next to the elevator on the ground floor. Across from her lay Cliff, the boy who had died triggering the alarm. Ice crystals gleamed in his hair and in the pool of blood in which he lay. His hand still reached towards the alarm, twitching, as if it could drag its dead body up to the switch.

He gave a groan, and his whole body convulsed. He began to tear himself free from the pool of ice that was his own blood. First his face, then his chest and legs, and finally his left hand were wrenched from the ice. He stood up slowly and glared at Beverly accusingly, then turned and shuffled towards the main hangar.

Other victims of the attack passed through Beverly's field of view. Peer Sandra's bodyguards, mechanics, a middle-aged woman, a clerk; they moved directly to the hangar, not sparing a glance in her direction, not seeing her cower back into her tent.

After a while no more corpses walked past her. She didn't want to leave her tent, didn't want to see what was going to happen, but she had no choice. She stepped out of her tent and was hit with a wave of cold, indescribably intense, that made her want to scream in agony—perhaps she did. She stood up and started walking toward the hangar.

By the time she reached it she was numb all over and had stopped shivering. She looked through the door and saw the corpses standing in a circle. They had been joined by the pilot and medic from the ambulance, the crew of the *Nine to Five*, and . . . she tried to look away, but could not . . . her parents. They were all looking to one side. A final corpse was approaching; shuffling jerkily to the center of the circle, but somehow maintaining an appearance of pride with its straight back and steady forward gaze. It was the San Vincentan corpse that Sandy had shown her. The other corpses bowed their heads as it reached the center of the circle, pulled a little book out of its breast pocket, and, in a hoarse whisper, began to read.

Beverly buried her face in her hands and sobbed.

* * *

"Beverly? Can you hear me? What are you doing outside the tent? Good God, George, her hands are cold as ice!"

"Her heater's off."

"If that suit's broken, we might lose her!"

"The battery came loose. They do that sometimes. Beverly, can you hear me?"

The words had washed over her, meaningless. She felt no need to pay attention, to wake up.

"Beverly?" Someone was shaking her now, and she suddenly felt her electrically-heated clothes warming up. The heat stabbed her. She realized that she was still shivering, the way she had been when. . .

She opened her eyes and saw Emily leaning over her, shining a lamp in her face. Beyond it she could see the other tents and the little glade they had camped in. Beverly was so relieved she began to cry, something she had not done in front of other people since she was little.

She couldn't stop. George brought out her sleeping bag and made her sit on it, while he wrapped his own sleeping bag across her shoulders like a cloak, and she couldn't stop sobbing.

She tried. She said, "I'm all right. I'm all right,"—her personal cantrip, something she always tried to believe once she'd said it—but it didn't work. As soon as she thought she was under control she remembered the boy's eyes, and the dead holding their own funeral because no one had held it for them.

Emily left for a few minutes, then came back with some tea. "Drink this," she said. "It'll help warm you up."

Beverly did what she was told. The tea wasn't very hot, but it seemed to spread a warm glow through her. She managed to stop sobbing a few minutes later, and sat quietly, holding the sleeping bag tight around her.

Emily checked her hands and feet for frostbite and took her temperature. "You're going to be all right, Beverly," she said, gazing intently into Beverly's eyes. "The battery came loose on your suit, but George put it back with tape, and it's not going to happen again. You don't have any frostbite or anything. You're safe now. Okay?" Emily looked very worried.

Beverly had to suppress a sudden urge to cry again. She didn't deserve her friends. "Thank you, Emily," she whispered. "Thank you, George." She looked off into the darkness for a moment, then back to Emily. "I need you to wake me at dawn. There's something I have to do."

"You should rest."

"It's important. I had a dream, Emily. All the people who've died on my account—in the station, on the *Nine to Five*, in the ambulance—they came to me. I have to hold a service for them."

Emily, deeply distressed, looked over her shoulder at George. He nodded.

"All right, Beverly. We'll help you. Go back to bed now. You need to rest." She helped her back into the tent.

* * *

Beverly left the camp as the sun rose. George and Emily stayed behind, as she had requested. They were her friends, but they weren't San Vincentans.

She turned and watched the sunrise pour color back into the landscape. She chose a spot—one was as good as another—and tried to remember the words. She had been to several funerals, but had so far been spared the endless procession of dead classmates that each of her brothers had seen after they had entered the Academy, so she hadn't had the words drummed into her as they had.

"I am here to honor the dead," she whispered. "They died in combat, with all honor, and we shall remember them with pride." There were many more words, but she didn't recall them. The words didn't matter much, she knew.

"Captain Griswold, Gunther Ottobein, Rodney, Myrna, Lawrence. . ." she knew so few by their full names, ". . .Walter, Kruger, Carl. . ." That listed the crew of the *Nine to Five*. She listed the ambulance crew, ". . . Ed, Gwen . . ." and pulled out the list Emily had made for her of the people who had died at Antipodes station. There were fourteen names on it. She read the names of these fourteen people who had died without knowing they were protecting her, or even that she existed.

She set the list down, and there were only two names to say. She tried to speak, but no sound came out. She closed her eyes and managed to whisper. "Baron Richard Peter Carlos Aaron di Mendoza, Lady Elizabeth Maria Beverly Deborah Catherine di Mendoza."

She wept again, freely this time, for it was all right to weep for the dead. It is to the living that you are allowed no pity.

Later she said those other, ancient words that she could remember, "The race is not to the swift, nor the battle to the strong, neither yet bread to the wise, nor yet riches to men of understanding, nor yet favor to men of skill; but time and chance happeneth to them all. For man also knoweth not his time: as the fishes that are taken in an evil net, and as the birds that are caught in the snare, even so are the sons of men snared in an evil time, when it falleth suddenly up on them."

She thought about her parents, and how their murder had been the first in a series of murders that showed no sign of stopping. She thought about her father, about how much she had wanted to be like him, and how much she loved him, and how long it had been since she had told him. And her mother, with whom she had not gotten along, and now never would.

She knew what was expected of her. The funeral wasn't an end, but a beginning. Her dream had come to remind her of her duty; her duty to lay the dead to rest.

And to avenge them.

She had told herself before that she was just one girl alone on a strange planet, and that she was incapable of doing anything. Now she had friends who might help her, and there was nothing to keep her from pursuing her duty. Honor didn't require that she kill her enemies personally, but it did require that she devote herself to finding them and arrange their destruction.

She just hoped she could do so without getting her friends killed.

Beverly sat in the early morning sun, trying to hate the enemies she had never seen. It was hard; she knew so little about them. All the stories she'd heard told how hatred sustained people who had been wronged, but she just felt desolate.

As she sat there, feeling sorry for herself, she heard gunshots from near the campsite. Someone was attacking her friends! She leapt to her feet and started running back to the camp, tugging her pistol free as she went.

Someone was attacking her friends. She smiled cruelly, realizing she wasn't so incapable of hatred after all.

Chapter XV

Beverly took advantage of cover as she ran to the camp, and stayed alert for other people approaching it, but she didn't see any. She crested the final hill and saw that the problem wasn't people at all. A monster was destroying the camp. It was fully five meters tall and covered with shaggy grey fur. It reached down with its long, long neck, gored one of the tents with all three of its horns, and flung it high to the air.

Gunfire sounded again. George was on a promontory across from Beverly, firing down at the animal with his assault rifle. He paused. The morning sun on his face showed a serene intensity, while his whole stance radiated confidence and control. Beverly had never seen anything so beautiful. Was this the cheerful boy she thought she knew? It was as if he took power from the air and land around him. Perhaps he was; these were his ancestral lands. She stared, mesmerized, until he fired another controlled burst. She turned her attention to the target, and saw a rustling in the animal's fur, like a breeze in a wheat field, as the armor-piercing bullets exited after passing completely through the immense body.

The animal—Beverly decided it must be a therium—raised its head as if startled. Beverly thought that it would notice George, but it focused on something closer. Beverly gasped as she saw the object of its attention.

Emily was about ten meters away from the therium, standing very still. The therium lunged towards her. Emily began to run, sprinting away from the camp. The monster bellowed—an oddly high-pitched sound—and started after her.

Before it could get its speed up, George fired another burst into it. It stopped and looked around again. Emily also stopped, but not in time. It saw her move, and started after her again.

George fired a third burst, then had to stop to change clips. Beverly started running down the slope to the camp.

The animal had stopped again as George's last burst hit it. Now it blinked and raised its head high into the air to get a better view of its surroundings. Emily was standing motionless not five meters away from it. The animal looked around, but didn't see her.

"Over here!" shouted Beverly angrily. She jumped up and down and waved her arms. "Over here, you stupid monster!"

The therium was facing away, but it turned its head on its long neck to look behind, and saw her. Instantly enraged, it gave its shrill bellow and began to charge.

Beverly brought up her pistol and took aim. If she could shoot its eyes out, it might do some good. All the rounds that George had poured into it had had no effect at all. She took careful aim, waiting for the eye to present itself, willing her anger to drop away and her hands to steady while she set up the shot. Closer, closer. . .

She fired. Long practice had taught her not to blink when the gun went off. She saw bone momentarily exposed above the eye, then heard the ricochet. The monster didn't slow. She suddenly realized that the therium was almost upon her. She turned and sprinted up the hill, knowing that it was too late.

She heard the sounds of the monster's breath and the thud of its feet as it closed with her. The monster's shadow fell on her. She felt the wind as it swung its head at her, trying to gore her with its three wicked horns—but it missed, and she kept running up the slope.

After a moment it became clear that she was gaining on it. She looked behind her and found that she had quite a lead. In fact, the therium was making almost no progress at all.

She stopped, panting, to watch as it laboriously placed one foot after the other, struggling to climb the slope, bellowing in rage all the while. It reminded Beverly of a film she had seen of Terran elephants laboriously climbing a river bank.

Beverly's anger returned. The beast had threatened her friends, tried to kill her, and—worst of all—had frightened her. She took aim once more and squeezed off five shots. Her Anderson felt very good in her hand. Her shots all landed within a palm's breath of the eye, but none connected. The rounds that had been poured into it had served only to make it angry.

Beverly looked towards George's position. George was waving frantically, motioning her to keep moving. She started climbing again, wondering what to do next. Being chased across Barigost by this Questing Beast lacked appeal. She set about figuring a way to lose it.

She decided to try the simplest technique first; outdistance it, disappear over the crest of the hill, and be long gone by the time it reached the top. She chose a steep path that put boulders and other obstacles between herself and the therium. Soon it was out of sight.

Thoroughly winded now, she stopped to pant and change clips. She then worked her way around the hill until she arrived where she thought George and Emily had been. She found the spot, but they weren't there. They were down the campsite salvaging gear. They kept an eye on the therium, which was far up the slope, looking bewildered.

They hadn't noticed the two other theriums that were walking up the cul-de-sac.

"George!" shouted Beverly. He looked up. She pointed down the cul-de-sac. He and Emily did a double-take, then sprinted for the knob of rock on which Beverly stood. The theriums gave chase. The ground shook as they galloped, but George and Emily managed to reach the top while the two animals were still twenty meters away.

Beverly worried about being pursued until it was clear that the slope here was too steep for the theriums, which soon turned away and began destroying the camp anew. One of them gored a sleeping bag, then tossed it high in the air. When it fell back to the ground, the beast stood on one end and ripped pieces off with its horns. Beverly winced at the thought of how close one came to using that trick on Emily.

The original therium joined the others, and promptly stepped into the campfire. The animal's fur began to smolder, but it didn't notice for a long time. Suddenly, it began to bellow. It backed up, focused on the fire, and began to stomp on it. This continued long after the fire was put out.

Another therium began picking up things in its teeth, breaking them, dropping them, then stomping the pieces into the ground. It soon discovered Emily's hot plate. It picked it up daintily in its mouth, raised its head high into the air, and bit down. The power pack exploded with a sharp report and an impressive fireball. The animal took one faltering step backwards, then fell with a loud crash to the ground. Its head was missing, and the stump of its neck was smoldering.

"Hey!" shouted Emily angrily, jumping to her feet. "That was an engagement present!"

The surviving theriums didn't seem to hear her. Perhaps their ears were ringing from the explosion. The noise had made them stop and look around momentarily, but they didn't seem affected by the death of their comrade. They went back to destroying the camp.

They watched for a few minutes. Finally, Beverly said, "Shouldn't we be going?"

"Yeah," said George, getting to his feet. "We're not going to be able to salvage anything." He picked up the sleeping bag that was all he'd salvaged from the camp besides his clothes, his rifle, and a bag holding a few oddments of camping supplies. Emily had salvaged her first aid kit and canteen. Beverly had been carrying everything but her pack when she had left camp, so she had her map case, compass, and binoculars in addition to her pistols.

They walked away from the camp, leaving the two theriums engaged in a ponderous dance of destruction. The neck of the dead beast was still smoking, leaving a thin grey plume in the cold air.

George took the lead, and set a brisk pace. They walked across the hill, keeping out of sight of the remaining theriums. The sun was well up now. Clouds blowing in from the east blotted it out occasionally. A breeze rustled lightly in the underbrush.

After perhaps fifteen minutes George stopped and turned to Beverly. "We're well away from them now. Which way are we going?"

Beverly pulled out her map and unrolled it, estimated their position (she would have liked to check it against her landmarks, but thought George wouldn't be able to stand the delay), then sat cross-legged on the ground and measured off the distances to Heinz Lodge and the *Northern Light* with a pair of dividers. George and Emily sat down to await her verdict.

"We're thirty-six kilometers from Heinz Lodge, and twenty-nine from the ship," she said. "Unless the terrain is a lot worse between here and the Lodge, I'd say press on. If we go back to the ship, we still won't know whether we'll be found by our friends or our enemies."

"Are you sure you're up to a long march?" asked Emily, concerned about the effects of last night's near-freezing.

"Of course," replied Beverly. In fact, she wasn't sure at all. She was worn out—but there was no point in worrying her friends. They had to march; she had to keep up. That was all there was to it. Going back to the ship was the easy way out, but they would be vulnerable there. On foot in the tundra they were all but undetectable.

George looked at Emily, who nodded gravely. "It's settled then," he said. "The Lodge it is." They stood up, and George took the lead again, shouldering his rifle and starting off to the east.

Beverly felt Emily's hand on her shoulder. "You saved my life again today," Emily said quietly.

"It was nothing." She meant it. Compared to the sacrifices that had been made to keep her alive, Beverly felt that her contribution amounted to very little.

Emily seemed to understand something of this. She said nothing, but squeezed Beverly's shoulder before dropping her hand, then turned to follow George.

George set a grueling pace, and after an hour they were all exhausted. Beverly just grit her teeth and struggled on, but Emily finally asked, "Isn't it time for a break?"

George glanced up at the sky, hesitated, then said, "All right." He stopped and sat on a boulder. They were walking on the uncertain footing on the north side of a hill, avoiding ravines on the south side.

Beverly's feet were tired, so she sat on a boulder and took off her boots. Even the cold felt good after being constricted for so long. "They said in tactics class that frequent rests are important, even on forced marches," she said.

Emily passed her canteen around. George took off his boots and socks.

The sat in silence for a while, then George turned his socks inside out, put them back on, and then put his boots on. "Are we about ready?" he asked.

"I should check our position, and Emily should refill the canteen," said Beverly. She followed George's example and turned her socks inside-out (a poor imitation of a clean pair), then climbed a rock to find her landmarks.

To her dismay she found that all but one was obscured by low clouds and mist. The sun had disappeared behind a wall of clouds, leaving the tundra lit with a flat grey light. She used her one landmark and an estimate of their hiking pace to estimate her position, but was unhappy about the reliability of the result.

She looked around for new landmarks, but the distant mountains were no longer visible, and the nearby hills were small enough that they would be out of sight in a few kilometers. She picked the best of the lot.

Emily had filled a plastic bag from her first aid kit with snow, and put it under her jacket where her heated underwear and body heat would melt the water. George had taken his assault rifle apart, cleaned it, and put it back together. He tightened the last screw, then stood up.

A series of sonic booms thundered nearby, followed by the scream of lifters, very close.

Beverly threw herself to the ground and waited for the roar to fade. Instead, she heard more sonic booms and more engines. At least half a dozen large aircraft were passing overhead, very low. The sound seemed to come from all directions; there was no way to tell which way they were travelling.

The noise faded gradually and was gone.

"Some of those were space ships," announced Emily clinically. "The rest sounded like military aircraft. I wonder what's going on."

"Could they be after us?" asked Beverly.

"No," replied Emily. "They were in a group, not spread out in a search pattern. I wish I knew which way they were going."

"Could they be attacking the Lodge?" asked Beverly.

"Yeah," said George. He looked vainly in the direction of the Lodge. "If so, we'll probably hear the gunfire before the end of the day." He stood up and slung his rifle. "They could be en route to any of a half-dozen places, though. If it's a raid, they're more likely to head for a real town. The Lodge has a tough reputation."

Without a word they started walking again.

George began watching for squealers, in the hopes of shooting some for dinner, but for some reason they had all vanished. All the canned food had been lost in the camp. George also watched the sky a lot.

He stopped once to pick up an object half-hidden by a bush.

"Look at this," he called. He held up a lichen-encrusted piece of metal.

"What is it?" asked Emily.

"It's an access hatch. Must have fallen off a ship a long time ago. These things fall off all the time. People forget to torque 'em down. Could be one of ours—nobody else ever flew much up here." He rubbed at the lichen. "Look!"

Painted on the metal hatch, Beverly could just make out the faded words, **NORTHERN LIGHT**.

It's an omen, thought Beverly. She gazed at the twisted, corroded, ancient metal. *I hope it's a good omen.*

The clouds continued to roll in, and the wind began to pick up. It grew colder. By noon the wind was strong enough to slow their march. An hour later it began to snow.

They struggled on, hardly able to see where they put their feet. The wind and the cold began to overpower their heated clothing. Beverly's teeth began to chatter. She began to lag behind the others.

She found herself on the ground. She had no memory of falling. She struggled to her feet and looked around for the others.

They were far ahead. She plodded after them, barely able to keep them in sight.

After a long time, they stopped and waited for her. She kept shuffling forward, no longer able to feel her feet as they hit the ground.

Beverly suddenly saw that she had reached them. She heard Emily shouting over the wind, "She'll never make it, George! We have to find shelter!"

"Okay!" George shouted back. He looked around, trying to see through the driving snow. He pointed downwind and shouted, "We'll get to the lee side of that hill and build a snow cave! Don't worry! I've done it before!"

Emily ran back to Beverly and started helping her across the snow. "It won't be far now," she said quietly. "We'll make a shelter and then you can rest."

Beverly nodded, not wanting to talk through chattering teeth. She couldn't feel her fingers.

They fought their way toward the hill. George was already part-way around the slope, moving to the lee side. The snow was thin here; the wind was blowing it away.

When they reached the hill Beverly noticed an easier path. She pointed to it and Emily nodded. It went the same direction George was headed, and was far less rocky. Soon they were even with George and about five meters above him. He stopped and picked something up. He looked up the slope, saw them, and continued looking, searching for something. He climbed to join them in a burst of energy.

The wind howled. "Look at this!" shouted George. He held a dented anemometer. Its shaft was missing. "It must have blown off a weather station in a gale just like this one!" He pulled his pocket knife out of his parka. He opened the knife to its awl blade, and perched his prize upon it. The anemometer spun drunkenly as the gale caught its dented cups, but so quickly that it looked as if it would fly to pieces on the next gust.

The three of them watched it for a long moment. In their exhaustion, its unpredictable motion was hypnotic.

"Nobody puts weather stations out here!" said George suddenly. He laughed merrily and chanted, "Ladybug, ladybug, fly away home!" He raised his arm and the anemometer flew away ahead of them, climbing in the howling wind, finally striking a rock far up the side of the hill.

Beverly turned her gaze back to the path. The ledge they were following disappeared into the side of the hill. "Looks like a cave!" she shouted to Emily. She stumbled toward it.

"Wait!" shouted George. She stopped, and George ran up to her, unslinging his rifle. He advanced slowly to the cave mouth, then stopped and stared.

"I don't believe it. Even after the anemometer, I don't believe it," he said.

Two meters inside the cave was a blank metal door, featureless but for a bronze combination lock and a lever, both encrusted with a thick layer of frost.

George brushed the frost from the lock. It spun easily when he gave it a twist.

"Don't tell me you're a safecracker, too," said Beverly. She was surprised she had the energy to make a joke.

He turned and grinned at her. "Maybe. I never tried."

He took a step back from the door and stood staring at it for a few seconds. Then he stepped forward, took off his gloves, and with deft fingers tried a combination. He pulled the lever.

There was a click, and the door opened.

"Ladies first," said George. He wore a little smile, as if daring them to ask his secret.

Beverly stepped forward, pistol drawn. A warm, stale breeze flowed through the doorway. She stepped inside.

A rough corridor led forward for perhaps thirty meters, ending in another door. The walls and ceiling were very irregular, suggesting nightmare shapes in the uncertain daylight.

George followed her in, then Emily. "Don't close the door," cautioned George. "I haven't tested the latch on this side." He propped the door open with a piece of rubble.

They advanced down the corridor. The light became dimmer at every step. Rubble on the floor made their footing uncertain. Now that they were out of the wind, their heated clothing became effective again. Beverly's numbness was washed away by waves of heat and pain. They reached the second door, which seemed to be ornately carved. Beverly couldn't make out the pattern in the gloom, but something about it disturbed her.

George pushed the door open. On the other side was an empty area that vanished into the gloom. George stepped inside and fumbled around the area near the door. Beverly saw a blue flame as he lit his fire-lighter, then a yellow one.

"I saved some candles," he said. "Here." He lit two more and handed them to the girls. Beverly had never held a candle before. George held his to the side and looked around.

The flickering light revealed a cavern thirty meters across. Halfway across the room was a large pool, and on beyond that was a standing stone that had probably served as an altar. The walls and ceiling were carved into horrible shapes, a swirl of skulls and graves and corpses and zombies. Beverly shrank back from the horrible presence of the place.

"What is this place, George?" whispered Emily.

"Oh, this is the Hoard," said George matter-of-factly. "It's been lost since Great-Grandfather died off Mordel. He used it as a supply and weapons cache, in case of a rebellion or a big raid. I can't *believe* we found it. There's supposed to be some money here, too."

"What about the carvings?"

"That's just some old Imperial stuff. You know, from towards the end, when everything got weird. Spooky, huh?"

Beverly resented his cavalier attitude. So, apparently, did Emily. "We ought to get a fire going, George. And I'd rather stay in a smaller room, if there is one."

"Okay, okay. The place is supposed to be pretty big. There'll be rooms somewhere. Beverly, here's my sleeping bag. Why don't you get some rest while we scout this place out?"

Beverly nodded, and unrolled the sleeping bag as the others went away to explore. Lying on the stone floor with a candle near her head, with hideous shapes exuding the madness of some forgotten, late-Imperial aberration, it seemed as though she were lying in a crypt. It reminded her far, far too closely of last night's nightmare.

"Beverly? Beverly, wake up!" Emily's voice dragged her back from formless dreams. Beverly opened her eyes. Emily's candle seemed very bright. The carvings were hidden by gloom. No light came through the doorway.

"We set up camp in one of the smaller rooms. You'll be more comfortable there," Emily continued. "Are you all right?"

"I'm fine," said Beverly, as she managed to get to her feet. She was very, very tired. Emily took her hand and led her across the main cavern to a side passage that had been cleverly concealed by shadows. The passage was rough and twisted, as if it were of natural origin, though Beverly doubted it. Light issued through the first doorway on the right.

They went inside. A candle burned on a rickety table, and a fire burned in a fissure in the wall that may or may not have been intended as a fireplace. There was only one chair. George was poking at the fire.

"Don't use the chair—it's rotten," he warned. "I'm burning the others now."

He left the fire and crossed to a plastic crate on the floor. "I found this in one of the storerooms. Some kind of emergency rations." He took his knife and pried the crate open at the glue line, then removed the lid. "Oh, no."

Inside were twenty-four cans marked **RATIONS, EMERGENCY, SELF-HEATING.**

IF YOU EVER TRAVEL TO NORTHSTAR, leave the noise of the port and the danger of the mines and travel south until you see the gold of the malinorne trees; deep yellow leaves on limbs of palest blue. The wood is a magical place, and those that visit it are changed.

Once upon a time—before you or I or our father's father's father was born—the Imperium stood, the people thrived, and all was well with the world. Folk came to Northstar, planted the trees, built great works, and raised their families knowing—never doubting—that they were safe in the arms of the Emperor. It was a time before time, from which no tales come.

But the Imperium was doomed: the treachery of Duke Fortune, the savagery of the Vradthmorn, and the sorcery of the Nihilists caused it first to crack, then to shatter; so that now we find a piece here and a piece there, but know nothing of the whole; much less how to mend it.

Upon another time (not so long ago as that) a woman traveled to the golden wood; for a time forsaking the burdens of ship and crew and the memories of friends she had buried, strangers she had slain, and the cruelty of space.

She was tall and slim, with soft brown hair and hard grey eyes. As she walked the woods, the sunlight on the leaves and the clouds in the steel-blue sky moved her in ways she could not explain.

She came across low mounds among the trees, where there had been homes in a happier time. Sometimes a bit of glass or a piece of brick would stand clear of the moss and leaves, but that was all.

She wandered almost till sunset, bespelled by the shadows and sunbeams of the wood, until finally she came across a brook before a little glade.

Drinking from the ice-cold stream, she saw the rippling reflection of a tower jutting above the trees, orange-red in the light of sunset. She leapt the brook and walked across the blue-green grasses of the glade, keeping her eyes on the old stone tower, tall and round and pierced with a few small windows through which no light came.

Beyond the glade was a grove of trees: olive, apple, and cherry; trees that can rarely be made to grow under Northstar's sun. Their old branches were moss-covered and twisted, but bore leaves and fruit abundantly, as if in proud defiance of time.

She walked through the orchard, touching the trunks of the trees with her hands and breathing the smell of bark and fruit and the grass beneath her feet. She soon came to a wall made of stones of different sizes fitted carefully together, taller than she and free from moss. Beyond it she could see a manor house of a design from beyond memory, with stone walls and a pitched roof of wooden beams covered with slate. From the end of the manor rose the tower. The sun had set, and the tower was silhouetted against the fading sky.

She followed the wall until she found an archway where a half-open iron gate was rusting slowly away. Beyond it lay a garden.

Bright flowers grew in geometric patterns, robbed of their colors by the gathering darkness. A crumbling bench stood near the gate; a tree shrouded it in gloom with gnarled branches.

She sat on the bench, suddenly weary, and closed her eyes.

When she awoke the sky was aflame with stars, bright and near in a way that city-dwellers never see. One of the moons was rising, casting long shadows across that garden. By its light she could see that the garden contained several statues.

She walked to the nearest, a man in marble who gazed calmly from his crumbling features. Another statue had shattered above the knees, and its pieces lay in a neat pile on the pedestal.

A third statue was larger than the rest; a fantasy robot in bronze, anthropomorphic as real robots never are, with long segmented arms that hung almost to the ground, and short segmented legs on a smooth torso. The head was featureless but for its two eyes.

She gazed at the robot for a time (for it seemed to symbolize the lost dreams of mankind), then walked past it down the gravel path to the manor house.

She was not surprised when the door opened easily, without squeaking, for the garden and the wall showed signs of being tended. She knew she should call out and announce herself, but she could not bring herself to break the silence that hung like a spell upon the house. She crossed the threshold and closed the door behind her.

Ancient fixtures on the ceiling gave off a dull orange light. The air was stale, but had no hint of the dust she had expected; it smelled instead of leather and furniture polish, of fabric and age. The paneled walls of the hallway were lined with pictures; of what it was difficult to tell. She wandered through a gracious living room with book-lined walls and delicate furniture, a dining room with seats for twenty-four, and a kitchen of elegant sophistication, with cooking machinery the like of which she had never seen. She passed through a ballroom and climbed a majestic stair to the second floor.

Here would be the bedrooms. She paused, wondering if she should leave rather than disturb the people who dwelled here, if indeed there were any. She doubted it. The house seemed empty—too quiet, the furniture too neatly arranged— as if waiting for the owners to arrive.

One of the bedroom doors was open. She looked inside, saw the empty bed, and entered.

It was a woman's room, she felt, though with the swings of fashion in the past it was hard to say how she knew. She sat on the canopied bed, which seemed sound enough, and looked around.

On the dresser was a necklace. She crossed the room and picked it up. It was beautiful; even in the gloom she could see how brilliant the gems were, surrounded by the soft glow of gold. She put it on and admired herself in the mirror. She smiled at her reflection, then took the necklace off and put it back on the dresser.

"So, " said a soft, deep voice, "perhaps you are not a thief, after all."

In the doorway stood the robot. She shrank back as it walked into the room, strangely graceful, and picked up the necklace, rearranging on the dresser exactly as it had been when she had first seen it.

It turned to face her. "The thieves start by picking a flower in the garden, my lady. They go on to stuff their pockets with goods from the house. They end up in the orchard, buried so that they may nourish the trees.

"I am glad you are not a thief."

With that it turned around, spinning first its head, then its torso, then its lower body and legs, and began walking noiselessly from the room. It turned its head back towards her and said, without breaking stride, "Come. The master bid me to have the guests register in the book."

She followed, still frightened, and was led to the entrance hall, where there was a small marble table bearing a pen and a red leather book. It was opened to the first page, which had the word "Guests" inscribed in fine calligraphy across the top. The book was otherwise empty.

She took the pen and wrote her name, the name of her ship, her home planet, and the date, then set down the pen and spoke for the first time: "How should I call you?"

The robot did not speak for some time. "I remember having a name, my lady, but I cannot recall what it was. My master was the last to speak it to me, and he has been gone these two hundred and twenty-nine years. I recall that I have been called 'Robot' by some. It will do until I recall my true name."

"Robot, are you here all alone?"

The robot straightened the book and lay the pen in its original position, then said, "I count the birds and the trees as my friends, lady, and they help me while the years away, but it is true that I am lonely. The master bid me wait for his return, and to keep his house and garden, and I have tried; but it has been very long. Time has withered much that was beautiful here, and even I am not all I once was. I hope the master returns soon."

She thought of the crumbled ruins in the woods and the chaos and savagery of the past centuries. He would not return.

She hesitated, then ventured, "If he should not return, what would you do?"

"He will return, lady. He told me so himself. If you knew my master, you would never think to doubt him."

"Perhaps not."

"You have doubts, my lady. I understand. You do not know his power as I do. He created me. I was metal and plastic and ceramic, insensate, and he gave me form and life.

"You shake your head. I was not *told* about my creation, lady, I remember it. I can still feel the heat of the forge, the agony of the hammer-blows that gave me shape: the pain and pride of being sculpted by the gnarled hands of God.

"He will return, my lady. I know it."

The robot turned again, then said, "Stay as long as you like, my lady. If my master returns while you are here, he will be happy to meet you." The robot left her then, leaving the house and attending to business of its own.

She wandered aimlessly about the ground floor, stopping finally at a window seat facing the garden. The stars were beginning to fade, signaling the coming dawn. She sat on the window seat and pondered.

She no longer feared the robot. There was peace here. She could stay amidst the ancient trees and crumbling stone and be free of the anguish of command, the death of comrades, the uncertainty of life in space. If only she could throw off a lifetime of habit and duty, she could be happy here.

If only . . .

At sunrise she stepped into the garden. The robot was there, kneeling on the path, smoothing the gravel lovingly with its hands. It looked up as she approached.

"Are you leaving, my lady?"

She nodded, not trusting herself to speak. In daylight the garden was achingly beautiful.

It stood to let her pass. "Fare thee well, " it said. "I will not forget you." It watched her cross the garden.

As she passed through the archway it said, "Lady?"

She stopped. "Yes, Robot?"

It paused. "I know. . .I know he has not forgotten me, but. . ."

It paused again. She waited, one hand on the rusting gate, amid the growing sounds of morning.

The robot continued, "If you should ever see God, would you tell him I still wait for him?"

"Yes, Robot, I will."

She left the manor then, and returned to her ship, and came never more to the golden wood; though it the memory stayed with her to the end of her days.

If you ever travel to Northstar, leave the noise of the port and the danger of the mines and travel south until you see the gold of the malinorne trees; deep yellow leaves on limbs of palest blue. The wood is a magical place, and those that visit it are changed.

CHAPTER XVI

George dumped the contents of the crate and sorted through the rations. Some were swollen and others were dented. These he discarded. Some were in flavors he had never heard of. He put these in a separate pile—perhaps they would be better than the normal flavors—but he felt disinclined to try them right away.

Beverly didn't remember the end of the meal. Later, she realized that she must have fallen asleep before she finished eating. Despite her fears, her sleep was dreamless.

When she awoke, Emily was tossing some chair legs onto the embers of the previous night's fire. George was snoring away in the corner. Beverly saw that he was sleeping on bare rock, as Emily must have, since Beverly had the only sleeping bag. Beverly unzipped it to toss over George, and a teddy bear (which must have been there all along, though Beverly hadn't noticed it) fell to the floor.

Emily picked it up. "Well, at least we salvaged the right sleeping bag," she said.

She looked at George for a moment, then turned to Beverly. "He's going to want to turn this place upside-down looking for the lost Heinz fortune. I can't say I blame him, but let's take a look around before things get too intense."

Beverly nodded, and they went out into the main room. Faint daylight filtered through carefully-placed fissures, highlighting parts of the main room in such a way as to give it the feeling of slumbering power. Wind whistled eerily through the cracks.

"Whoever designed this place certainly knew what he was about," remarked Emily. They walked to the main door and looked outside. If anything, the storm had worsened over the night. The howling wind blew snow in such quantities that they couldn't see more than ten meters beyond the tunnel mouth. Beverly was certain that they would be dead now if they hadn't found the cavern.

They retreated from the doorway, went back to the main cavern, where they saw George stumbling towards them.

"God, I wish there was some coffee," he said. "Excuse me." He brushed past them and walked down the tunnel. A minute later he returned, brushing snow off his hair and collar. "That's better," he said with almost-convincing heartiness. "Nothing like rubbing snow in your face to wake you up in the morning. Are you ready to start exploring?"

"What about breakfast?" asked Emily.

"Have all the breakfast you want. I haven't recovered from dinner yet. How about you, Beverly? Ready to help me try to recover the family fortune?"

"Why not?" said Beverly. They certainly weren't going anywhere today.

George led the way down another side passage, which, like the one that led to the room they had slept in, was concealed by stone and shadow until you were almost inside it. It went straight for perhaps ten meters, then opened off into a small cavern with side passages to the right and left. The cavern contained dusty office partitions defining five cubicles.

"This looks promising," said George, and started on the rightmost cubicle. Beverly held the candle so he could work with both hands.

The first cubicle turned out to be an archive room, with cabinets for printed records, media cubes, and drawings. The archive terminal was like new under its dust, but it showed no signs of life.

The furniture hadn't fared as well. Though the cavern seemed reasonably dry at the moment, the metal furniture was rusted and the documents in the filing cabinet were damp and decaying.

"Better leave this until later," said George. "I have a cousin with salvage experience." He opened the media cube drawer and scooped out the cubes that were inside. They were probably okay.

The next three cubicles were simple offices, with a desk, two chairs, a bookshelf, a filing cabinet, and a terminal. Whoever had occupied these offices had cleaned up after themselves, for there was nothing but generic office supplies.

The leftmost cubicle was a nest of cables, rack-mount electronic units, and other equipment. It was clearly the radio room. It hadn't been cleaned up like the offices; manuals lay open on the table (one manual had a now-rusty pair of scissors as a bookmark; another had a large piece of equipment sitting on its open pages).

George brushed the equipment off carefully and tried the power switches. Not surprisingly, nothing sprang to life. He then turned his attention to the manuals. He had examined about ten of them when a small book caught his eye. He picked it up and leafed through it. It contained page after page of small-print text arranged in tables, and a pocket with three media cubes.

George let out a whoop. "I found it! I found it!"

"Found what?" asked Beverly.

"The code book! We have sheafs of stuff at home that we can't decipher because the codes went down with our ships!"

He put the code book in one of his parka pockets, then said, "What we really need to do is find the power source." He took his candle back from Beverly and raised it over his head. He soon spotted several cables disappearing into the rock wall. "There! Which would you guess, right or left?"

"Left," said Beverly. She had felt a draft from the left as they had entered this cavern.

George started down the left-hand corridor, which went on for about fifteen meters before widening and forking. A strong draft came from the right-hand fork, so they went that way.

The right-hand corridor went on, curving somewhat, for another fifteen meters or so, then dead-ended. A steel ladder, badly rusted, led upwards out of sight, and a strong draft came down the shaft. Several cables led upwards.

"That way leads to the antenna farm," said George. "I can't picture the power plant being there. It's supposed to be a fission heat source, and if it ever leaked, it would make a real mess if it weren't at a low point."

Beverly frowned. Using radioactive waste as a thermal heat-source was common for small, isolated installations, even in the Eight Worlds, but they weren't supposed to *ever* leak.

George went back to the second fork and tried the left-hand corridor. This one quickly opened up into another office area, this time consisting of a reception desk, an executive's office, and a small conference room. Oddly, the wooden furniture in this area had fared better than the metal furniture elsewhere. Like the other offices, there was little of interest here.

The corridor continued beyond the offices, ending in a heap of rubble and an extremely narrow side corridor heading downwards at about forty-five degrees. George showed no inclination to crawl down the slope, and they retraced their steps to the first office block, then went down the narrow right-hand corridor.

This corridor ended at a door which opened onto a large cavern with a ceiling of irregular height. Here and there were large tarp-covered pallets supporting crates of various sizes. In one corner was a boxy object that would have been singularly uninteresting-looking if it weren't for the glowing indicator lights.

George dashed over to the unit and brushed off the control panel. Beverly tried to see past him but couldn't.

George began talking to himself, "Good, good, uh-huh, no . . . I get it, okay . . . there!" He flipped a switch, and the lights came on in the room, followed by the sounds of motors turning on in the distance, and the snap! snap! snap! of circuit breakers blowing. Oddly, the lights stayed on.

George looked around for the breaker box, found it, and opened the panel. A dribble of dirty water ran out. Roughly a third of the breakers showed green indicator lights. An equal number displayed red, while the rest were inert and showed no life at all. George frowned at the box for a minute, then held his hand close to each of the breakers in turn.

"It doesn't feel like anything's slagging down in there," he reported cheerfully, "so I'll leave all the ones that didn't blow. I wonder why there are so many circuit breakers, though. I can't imagine using half of them." He blew out his candle and headed for the nearest pile of crates. "Let's take a look around and see what we've got."

Too impatient to deal with the knots, he slashed the ropes holding the tarpaulin in place—the plastic rope had held up well over the years—and uncovered a neat stack of grey plastic crates. He dragged one off the stack and pried the lid off with his knife. It proved to be full decaying first aid kits.

"Ugh," said George. "Maybe the next stack." He walked over to the next stack and began cutting ropes. "You know, Beverly, this place is supposed to be a treasure trove. There's supposed to be a lot of good equipment and cash here. Grandpa put some of his best cargo in here before he went off to the war in Mordel."

He pried the lid off another crate, revealing bolts of moldering cloth. He stared at is for a moment, then shrugged. "They can't all be like this."

The next pallet held spare parts for obsolete vehicles. The one after that held fine wood carvings from the Centaurus Federation, now worm-eaten and decayed. Then came a minor find—five hundred assault rifles; obsolete, a little rusted in spite of their heavy coat of grease, but still usable—which raised George's spirits again.

George wanted to open each treasure himself, so Beverly sat on a crate and watched him. Soon Emily arrived and pulled up another crate.

They watched George fish out decades-flat Fort Neirad Beer, expired explosives, moldering fashions, rotten furs, decayed drugs, and rusted machinery. The last pallet held crates of Terran wines, some of which might still be good. Even at connoisseur prices, though, it wouldn't add up to the haul he was looking for.

George walked around the room, looking at his ruined dreams. He sighed, shrugged his shoulders, and said, "Guess it's time for breakfast," and walked out of the cavern.

He wasn't fooling anybody.

They ate breakfast in silence (the "Teryaki Chicken" rations were surprisingly good). All of the corridors were now lit by cleverly concealed lamps, and they examined the few remaining chambers, finding nothing of interest. Emily peeked out the tunnel mouth again. The storm was as bad as ever.

She came in and warmed her hands over the heater unit that George had just repaired. The three of them sat around the glowing heater in silence.

After a while, Beverly ventured, "George? Why was all the cargo on plastic pallets?"

"To keep it off the ground so it doesn't rot," he replied. "Not that it did any good. Also, if you don't have a pallet, you can't move your cargo around with a forklift."

"Oh." Beverly took off her parka and spread it out on a crate to air out. She pulled out her Anderson to make sure melting snow from yesterday hadn't made it damp, then holstered it again.

"George?" she asked.

"What?"

"There aren't any forklifts. And the door's too narrow for the pallets. Don't you think that's . . . "

George had bolted from the room before she could finish, ". . . odd?"

* * *

Beverly caught up with George in the cargo cave. He was running his hands over the far wall like a madman, cursing to himself.

Emily pushed past her, then stopped and stared at George, hands on her hips. Emily's patience lasted perhaps thirty seconds, then she demanded, "God damn it George! Stop acting like a cyborg psychopath! What the hell do you think you're doing?"

George stopped, shocked. He turned around and said, "You heard Beverly."

"And . . . ?"

"Well, would *you* use a zillion porters to carry all this loot case by case into your super-secret hideout, or would you just drive it in with a forklift?"

"But the door isn't wide enough."

"So there's another door," said George. "There's got to be. Anyway, we haven't found the hangar. Help me find it."

George went back to his search for concealed doors. Emily went to fetch a candle to test for air leaks. Beverly used rags from the cargo and swept patches of floor, hoping to find tire tracks under the dust.

After an hour of searching, sweeping, poking, and prying, Emily shouted, "I found it!" She passed her candle past a fissure in the wall, and the flame flickered abruptly.

After fifteen more minutes they had definitely identified both edges and the bottom of the doorway, but not the latch. All three of them poked and prodded at the door and the area around it, stirring up a cloud of dust but finding nothing.

Beverly began to sneeze. "This isn't working," she said between sneezes. "It's got to be something else." She retreated to the other end of the room and sat on a crate until she stopped sneezing, then got to her feet wearily to rejoin the search.

"Wait a minute," she said suddenly, remembering a story her brother Miguel had described to her. "Purloined letter: it's the purloined letter trick."

"What do you mean?" asked George.

"There are two ways of hiding things: hiding them where they won't be seen, even when looked for, and hiding them where they won't be looked for. I think the latch is nowhere near the door. And it looks like something normal."

George regarded the room. After a minute or two his eye fell on the reactor. He went to the keypad and studied it for some time, then began to try combinations.

Time passed. George grew increasingly frustrated, but continued to try combinations, teeth clenched.

Suddenly, he leapt to his feet and flung open the door to the circuit breaker box. He stared at it for a few seconds, then flipped a series of breakers.

The door opened with a low rumble, revealing a wide, dark corridor beyond.

George looked at the open doorway with satisfaction. "We really must stop using that combination," he said.

The San Vincentan crept to the crest of the wind-swept hill, raised his binoculars, and looked down at the devastation below. His two frigates—one modern, one local—were destroyed. One still burned on the pad.

Had any of his units escaped? If so, he would not be able to establish contact until after the invading troops pulled out.

They were everywhere. They scoured the burned-out barracks and warehouses. Assault boats patrolled overhead. Antiaircraft emplacements were manned and ready. And they were all the Grand Peer's troops. Jaeger troops, the only decent troops on the planet. Peer Andrew's men had probably bolted at the opening shots, leaving the handful of San Vincentans on their own, to be gunned down, or, worse, to be captured.

The San Vincentan handed his binoculars to his aide. There was nothing he could do here. Once more his luck had put him in space when the attack came, and once more he had returned too late. The Grand Peer's victory was complete. Damn Andrew Verrett!

"We should leave now, Colonel," said his aide. The Jaegers patrolled aggressively.

"I should have been there, Luis," he said, not moving.

"It wouldn't have made any difference, Colonel."

"If I had been there, I would only have been defeated. Now I am beaten."

They worked their way back down the hill and began the long hike to their ship.

The San Vincentan was beaten, but he wasn't dead yet. By the time he reached his one remaining ship, he had a new plan.

CHAPTER XVII

The wind died just before dawn. Beverly awoke to stillness. The others were still asleep. She walked to the entrance and opened the door into a grey, formless morning. Beyond the tunnel stretched a landscape of snow and fog, leaden and cold. She stood for a few minutes while the dawn brightened the landscape. The fog was thick, but perhaps not too thick. She was weary of the cavern, with its old Imperial madness poisoning the bequest of George's ancestors.

George had found his hoard. The wide corridor had opened up on a hangar, which in turn had opened up onto a concealed landing pad. The hangar had been empty except for two strato-fighters, but the spare parts it contained—two gun turrets with half a dozen spare laser tubes, a fusor, and three starship drives—represented almost enough working capital to buy the Heinz family another star ship. And the safe had held charts and encoded messages with hints of other treasures elsewhere.

The money was there, too, but it was not the ancient but still-valid Barigost currency that George had expected, but banknotes from Fort Neirad, worthless these past fifty years.

Beverly went back inside and woke the others. George's excitement had turned to insomnia, and he had only recently fallen asleep. But in spite of his weariness, he was eager to be off. Almost without speaking they packed and left the tunnel. George brought several of the bright orange packing crates with him to scatter around the hill so he could find it again later (though, by leaving the power on, he felt he might be able to pick it up on sensors). With Beverly in the lead—her compass was their only guide in the fog—they left the cavern. George locked the door behind them, and hung back for a while, tossing his crates in places where they would be visible from the air. They marched away, and the hill was soon lost in the mist.

They threaded their way through ever-taller hills. Their path took them higher and higher, and suddenly they were in sunlight. Around them they could see hilltops poking their heads above the mist, and ahead was a solid blanket of clouds. Beverly consulted her map and guessed their position. They continued, and soon descended into the mist once more.

The ground leveled off and trees began to appear; first a scattering of stunted, twisted conifers, and then a solid forest of tall, straight evergreens. Fog swirled around the trees, and the air smelled of damp and pine. Everything was very quiet.

They stumbled into a clearing with tumble-down cabin; empty, its door agape. George walked up to it and stared at it for a while.

"I think I know where we are," he said. "There should be a path through the trees behind the cabin. That'll take us home."

George found it after hunting for a few minutes. It was barely there. "This place hasn't been used in years," said George. "It was already abandoned when I was here as a little kid."

They lost the path several times in the fog, but managed to follow it for a couple of kilometers, where it met a dirt road. George was ecstatic. "We're about ten klicks from the lodge," he said. "Real food and a warm bed tonight!"

They walked quickly down the road. The fog refused to lift as the day progressed, and they could barely see ten meters in front of them. The fog swirled around them, implying movement when there was none.

Beverly was in the lead. She was tired, and kept her eyes on the ground in front of her. She almost ran into the soldier in the middle of the road.

The fog parted, and there he was; a very young man in grey-and-white arctic camouflage with an assault rifle slung over his shoulder. Two short brown braids protruded from beneath his helmet. He jumped when Beverly appeared out of the mist in front of him, and clawed his rifle off his shoulder and pointed it at her.

It looked like the starting point for a problem Beverly had studied in her self-defense class. To take out a man with a rifle, you close quickly, grab the barrel with one hand, hit him with the other hand like *so,* kick him *there*, take the weapon from his nerveless fingers like *this*, hit him in the head with the gun butt like *that*—and there you are.

There she was, with an assault rifle trained on the soldier as he lay moaning on the ground, the fog swirling around them. The soldier was barely older than she was. With a sinking feeling, she realized she was in over her head: this was a *soldier,* and soldiers never travel alone.

Someone barked, "Freeze!" and a figure loomed up ahead of her. Beverly raised her rifle, but the figure knocked the barrel aside with one arm and smashed a fist into her face with the other, knocking her to the ground. Her vision swam. There was a big, grey-bearded man above her, holding the rifle carelessly in one hand. He didn't bother pointing it at her.

She reached for her pistol, and he kicked her in the head.

* * *

"She's coming around."

Beverly opened her eyes. The forest was spinning. She felt nauseous. Her head hurt. It hurt a lot.

"Beverly?" It was Emily's voice. Emily was beside her, a hypogun in one hand. "You shouldn't have kicked her," she said to someone.

"She didn't give me a whole lot of choice," a man's voice murmured. "Are you sure she's awake?"

Beverly sat up. The forest swam, and she saw spots before her eyes. She concentrated very hard on not throwing up. After a moment she turned to Emily and said, "I'm all right."

Emily rolled her eyes. Beverly persisted, "What's going on?"

"These gentlemen are going to escort us to Heinz Lodge," said Emily, glaring at a half-dozen soldiers in grey-and-white camouflage outfits. "That is, when you and George have recovered."

Beverly was almost afraid to look around, but when she did she saw George sitting on the ground, pinching his nose shut with his hand. He obviously had a nosebleed. He shrugged at her. "Didn't put my gun down fast enough," he said.

Few of the soldiers were paying any particular attention to them. One was talking very softly into a radio, and the others were silently deploying along the road, apparently re-establishing their ambush. Only the grey-bearded man was watching them. All of them wore their hair in braids, making them look like something out of a historical drama.

"Who are these people?" asked Beverly.

"They're the Grand Peer's Jaegers," replied Emily. "His personal bodyguard and shock troops. I don't know what they're doing here, but they're apparently using the Lodge as a base."

The grey-bearded man asked softly, "Can you walk, miss? We need to get you out of here."

"I think so." Beverly allowed Emily to help her to her feet. She almost fainted, the world receded, and she sank back to her knees. She could no longer control her nausea, and began to vomit on the frozen pine needles on the forest floor.

"Never mind," said the man. He turned, and made a series of signs the Jaeger with the radio, who nodded and made a new transmission.

Emily handed her a cloth and a canteen, and Beverly, feeling deeply humiliated, wiped her face and rinsed out her mouth. Emily helped her sit against a tree.

A few minutes later they heard a small flyer approach. The radio operator changed some settings, and the flyer homed in and landed on the road. It was a small, battered twin-fan model with a chin turret and two pintle-mount door guns. After the near-silence of the Jaegers, the flier made an ear-shattering amount of noise. Grey-beard conversed briefly via signs with the pilot, gave him something in a camouflage duffel bag, then motioned his three "guests" aboard. They were allowed to keep their gear; their weapons had already been confiscated.

George's nose had stopped bleeding. He walked over to where Beverly was sitting. "I can carry you aboard," he offered gallantly.

Pride lost to practicality. Beverly didn't think she could walk yet. "Thank you," she muttered.

George picked her up without effort, although his nose started bleeding slightly again. He carried her aboard, past a door gunner, and set her down more-or-less gently on the fold-down webbing bench along the side of the compartment. Emily followed, carrying their gear, and the flyer lifted off immediately. The ground was instantly lost to view.

"I've lost my pistol again," said Beverly. All the troubles she'd been through, and she had been robbed once again. What would her uncle have said if he had known she'd twice lost his gift? Something trickled down her cheek. It had to be sweat. San Vincentans never cry.

CHAPTER XVIII

The flight to the lodge took only a few minutes. The lodge was a huge four-story square building in the middle of an immense lawn. This lawn seemed anomalous in the arctic surroundings. Steam rising from the grass seemed to indicate an extensive radiant heating system. Beverly wondered if this place showed up as a big target on infrared. Beyond the lawn was a landing field jammed with a motley assortment of aircraft, including several large military flyers and a couple of surface-to-orbit interceptors. Several gun emplacements had been hurriedly set up, while others had clearly been there all along, protected by reinforced concrete revetments and concealed with faded camouflage netting. All were manned.

The flyer dropped precipitously onto a small clear space on the landing field. The pilot shut down the flyer and climbed out of the cockpit. The door gunners stayed at their posts.

The pilot was met by a group of five people in grey uniforms. Their leader, an immaculately-groomed man of middle height, said, "Well, well, so these are the prisoners. Let me sign for them, corporal, and I'll be on my way."

The pilot looked uncertain. "They're Jaeger prisoners, sir."

"Yes, yes, I know. But who do you think you captured them for? This is clearly under our jurisdiction."

Emily whispered to Beverly, "Internal Security."

The pilot still hesitated. The Internal Security officer continued, "Look, corporal, I'm willing to sign for them. All open and above-board, what difference does it make to you? Nobody else wants them, look around." He made a sweeping gesture, which was ruined when he saw three Jaegers hustling toward the flyer.

He stared at them for a moment, then turned and hurried away in the opposite direction. His men followed him.

The three Jaegers turned out to be a sergeant and two medical corpsmen with a collapsible stretcher. The sergeant glared at the retreating Internal Security men and gave vent to a torrent of profanity. He asked the pilot something in sign language. The response, also signed, provoked another flood of swearing.

The corpsmen helped George and Emily down from the flyer, then went inside and put Beverly on the stretcher. Her head still pounded horribly and she made no resistance; she didn't think she could handle the walk to the Lodge.

The instant Emily's feet were on the ground the sergeant's cursing stopped. "We're glad to see you here safe and sound, Peer Emily, Peer George. The Colonel says you're no longer under arrest, though it looks like those Internal Security bastards— pardon, Peer Emily—those Internal Security gentlemen have other ideas." He pointed to Beverly. "Is this the off-worlder?"

"Watch you mouth, Sergeant!" snapped Emily. "That's *Lady* Beverly di Mendoza to you."

The man actually took a step backwards. "I beg your pardon, Peer Emily, ah . . . Lady . . . uh . . . di Mendoza. No offense. I just meant . . . "

"Never mind. What's going on here?" She gestured at the landing field.

"This? Well, the Grand Peer decided that this was the best staging point for the raid, so when . . . "

"The Grand Peer's *here*?" interrupted Emily.

"Yes, ma'am."

Emily looked relieved and confident. "Come on, George. Let's get this straightened out."

"Right." George, too, looked like he had the world at his feet. He hopped down from the flyer, started towards the Lodge, then stopped and said, "Oh, Sergeant! Have my bags sent up, would you?" Then he continued on his way. The corpsmen carried Beverly after them.

When they stepped off the landing pad and onto the path to the Lodge, Beverly noticed a large, weather-beaten sign:

PEOPLE'S FREE PUBLIC RECREATION AREA
#119
"Heinz Lodge"

CLOSED FOR REPAIRS

Oddly, the "Closed for Repairs" sign seemed just as old and weather-beaten as the main sign. They continued past the sign and into the hustle and bustle of the Lodge, stopping at one of the side doors. The sergeant arrived behind them, followed by one of the flyer's gunners, lugging what remained of their packs. Two Jaegers with submachine guns barred their way, but the sergeant signed in and the guards waved them through.

Beverly was surprised by the lavish furnishing of the lodge; wood paneling, hardwood floors, and servants everywhere. The lodge staff was all dressed in mock-rustic garb—neatly pressed flannel shirts and the like—and there were a lot of them. The halls were also crowded with Jaegers moving about purposefully, people in assorted other uniforms travelling with somewhat less briskness, and a number of brightly dressed, elaborately made up individuals of both sexes moving with the studied languor of sharks circling a lifeboat. These, of course, were the nobility.

Two of these popinjays detached themselves and attempted to engage Emily in conversation, but she pretended they were invisible and kept walking. One even went so far as to stuff a note into George's hand, which he dropped without a glance.

Beverly was carried into the infirmary. George and Emily followed. They had lost the sergeant somewhere; a servant now carried their gear. The infirmary had two rows of beds that were mostly full with what had to be Jaegers—judging from the braids, which seemed to be a regimental tradition. Some of these people had been seriously injured. Several whistled—at Emily, Beverly assumed—until a couple of them hissed something about "Peers." A male nurse ushered them into the examination room, where they met Dr. Hosmer, a short bald man with a Jaeger insignia on his lab coat.

He began examining Beverly's head, probing her scalp with his fingers, and looked into her eyes with one his primitive instruments. There were some modern Eight Worlds instruments scattered on the counter along with the others, but he didn't use them. He asked her brusque questions about pain, nausea, dizziness, and double vision. Then the nurse put her in a wheelchair, pushed her into the next room, and took some X-rays (another anachronism), and wheeled her back.

Dr. Hosmer was talking to Emily. "If Sandy doesn't come in to get that eye regrown, somebody's going to blind-side her one day. The treatment would only take a month. It's stupid of her to even consider going out on a raid with a handicap like that. Not that it's any of my business." He took the X-rays from the nurse and held them up to the light for a moment.

"You have received several strong blows to the head," he told Beverly, "there seems to be no permanent damage. Try to rest today and tomorrow." He didn't look at Beverly as he said this; he was busy programming a hypogun charge from a portable dispensary. He had the worst bedside manner she had ever seen.

She supposed that a military surgeon could get away with it; his patients were a captive audience.

"No strong pain-killers, and no mood-altering drugs," she said hurriedly. Her mother had told her about off-worlders' drug-abuse tendencies.

He shrugged. "It's your funeral." He changed the setting on the dispensary, pulled out a hypogun, and injected her in the arm. "You should feel better in a few minutes," he said. "You can wait here until then." He turned away to busy himself with paperwork at a desk in the corner of the room.

Soon Beverly felt the dizziness drop away, and pain receded to a dull pounding. "I'm all right now," she announced to Emily.

"I wish you'd stop saying that," said Emily. "George, we seem to have lost our escort. We need to scare up clean clothes and a shower before people find us again."

George had almost dozed off in his chair. "What? Oh, sure. Follow me." He led the way past the X-ray room to a door that opened on a servant's corridor. A pretty young servant in what might have been a maid's uniform was hurrying by, but stopped and brightened when she saw George.

"Oh, Peer George, I'm so glad you're back!" she cried. "We were all so worried about you!" Then, "You too, Peer Emily," she said cautiously.

"Constance, you're just the person I need!" said George. "Look, we all need a shower and a change of clothes. See if you can scare up a room and some clothing for these two girls. Emily, I'll be in my room. Constance will take care of you. Call me if you need me. My number's 314." He strode off down the hall, leaving them to Constance's care.

She led them away, chattering about the number of people in the building, the lack of suitable rooms, and her guesses as to what clothing might be available to suit their social station and dress size. They soon arrived at a bedroom that was reserved for

George's Aunt Brenda. Since she never visited, Constance figured that this was safe. Furthermore, Brenda was small enough that there was a chance that her clothes would fit the girls.

Emily insisted on flipping a coin for the first shower. Beverly won. After days on the tundra a hot shower was an indescribable luxury. Beverly came out of the bathroom to find clothes and a hot meal laid out for her.

Emily was shamelessly stuffing her face. "Good service here," she said around a mouthful of food. She finished the food on her plate and headed for the bathroom. "Leave some dessert for me."

Beverly tried on the clothes, which fit well enough. They were very well-made and used excellent materials, and were in the same subdued style as the clothes Emily had loaned her earlier; not at all like the peacock garb worn by the courtiers in the hallway. She wondered whether the distinction was regional, social, or economic. It might be important.

The drugs had taken away Beverly's appetite as well as her nausea, so she settled for a cup of tea, which was excellent, probably Terran.

Emily was still in the shower when there was a knock at the door. It was unbolted. Beverly leapt up (and felt relieved that she could do so without feeling dizzy), dashed to the door, and threw the bolt just as someone on the other side said, "Unlock it." The handle turned, but the bolt kept the door from opening.

Beverly edged away from the door. She really had no idea what was going on, or whether Emily and George's confidence at the situation was warranted. She picked up the phone and called George's room. He answered right away.

"George, there's someone at our door. They're trying to get in."

"Where are you?"

"In your Aunt Brenda's room."

"Ha! Good choice. Okay, don't worry. I'll send help." He hung up.

Beverly warned Emily, who cut her shower short and started dressing. "Why do people always show up when you're in the shower?" she complained.

The pounding on the door grew more insistent, then there was a sound of footsteps in the hall and the pounding stopped. Beverly crossed the room and put her ear to the wall.

"What do you peepers think you're doing?" demanded someone.

"The girl's supposed to be brought to the Grand Peer, Sergeant."

"Since when does Intelligence escort Jaeger prisoners? Get lost, before I lose my temper."

"But . . ."

"Scram!"

There was a pause, then the phone rang. Beverly picked it up, holding it away from her ear so Emily could hear it too. "Hello?"

"Begging your pardon, miss, but the Grand Peer requests the honor of your presence. We've cleared away the riff-raff from your door, and there will be a few Jaegers about to make sure you won't be bothered." It was the same voice she had heard chewing out the soldier.

"Very well. Please tell the Grand Peer that I will be down shortly."

"Thank you, miss. Good-bye."

"Good-bye." She hung up, then sat down on the bed. "False alarm, I guess."

Emily frowned. "People aren't usually this bold. Something must have shaken things up." She looked at her hair and sighed. "Nothing I can do about it now. Brenda's makeup doesn't suit me, either. I wonder if we can do something with you."

Beverly looked in the mirror. She had dried her hair and brushed it. "I'm too young to wear makeup or put up my hair."

"What an odd culture. Oh, well, you've certainly got the skin for it." She looked at her nails. "Yuck. I have to see the Grand Peer like *this*?"

There was a knock at the door: 'shave-and-a-hair-cut.' "That'll be George," said Emily. She bounced up and opened the door.

George took Emily in her arms and kissed her (causing Beverly to turn away, embarrassed; she was glad they had refrained from vulgar displays of affection until now). He looked younger after a shave, and resplendent in a fancy tunic that was almost but not quite a uniform. There was a dagger at this belt that obviously went with the outfit. Beverly realized that he must have been wearing the Peer equivalent of work clothes at Antipodes Station. Still, it was a far cry from the rainbow-hued courtier garb she had seen in the halls.

"You look great, Emily. You too, Beverly," he added diplomatically, though he hadn't even glanced in her direction. "Dad says things are almost under control here. I didn't talk to him long, but it looks like we're in the clear, and Beverly should be, too. Needless to say, Dad's excited about our find."

"We're supposed to be presented to the Grand Peer," said Emily, smiling.

"All three of us?"

"Actually," said Beverly, "I think the invitation was only for me."

"Well, it'll be easy enough to find out," said George. "Let's just wander over to the courtyard, where the Grand Peer is, as they say, holding court."

He led the way through the corridors to a balcony overlooking the huge courtyard in the center of the Lodge. Several Jaegers moved with them at a not-quite discreet distance. No one bothered them.

The courtyard was fully thirty meters on a side, and was covered entirely by grass except around the swimming pool. A number of tables had been set up. The ones around the edges were being used by bustling Jaeger staff members, radio operators, and the like. A thin scattering of courtiers formed a second ring, flagging down waiters or strolling from table to table. A third ring consisted of eight or ten important-looking people who intercepted anyone trying to get to the center.

A tall, cadaverously thin old man was alone at a table in the exact center of the courtyard. He was clean-shaven and had thin, short white hair. He was dressed in a Jaeger undress uniform without rank insignia, and was reading a large, leather-bound book, seemingly oblivious to the bustle around him.

"That's him, all right," said George. "Let's go."

As they turned to go, a sonic boom and a roar shook the whole building. Startled courtiers turned their faces skyward, and some pointed or shook their fists at something Beverly couldn't see.

"Sounds like one of the older corvettes coming in," said Emily, trying to look nonchalant (though Beverly had seen her jump).

George didn't seem particularly startled. "We really ought to make the space ships land further from the building."

He led them to a staircase and took them to the ground floor. They went through a doorway into the courtyard (which was surprisingly warm, confirming Beverly's theory about radiant heat) and started across it, only to be intercepted by one of the important-looking officials, an elderly woman in brilliant finery.

"Good afternoon, Peer George, Peer Emily," she said without warmth. "I take it that this is the Lady Beverly?" She bowed to Beverly. "I am honored to make your acquaintance. The Grand

Peer is waiting for you." She turned to lead the way towards the center. "Not you," she said to George and Emily, who had begun to follow.

"I am Peer Anitra," she continued, "I am also the Postal Minister and wield some influence over the Soviet. But today I seem to be performing introductions.

"Please try not to upset the Grand Peer. He's an old man, and the recent action has been upsetting to him. Please stick to inconsequential subjects, and humor him. Afterwards, I will make the arrangements to get you back to your home planet."

Beverly looked at the Grand Peer. His skeletal build certainly hinted at frailty. She knew that he was eighty-five years old; immensely old for someone on a planet with such backward medical technology.

They arrived at the center table. The Grand Peer looked up, placed a bookmark in his book, closed it, and said, "Yes?"

"Grand Peer, may I present Lady Beverly di Mendoza. Lady Beverly, Grand Peer Fabian."

Beverly curtsied. "How do you do, Grand Peer."

"Quite well, thank you, Beverly," replied the Grand Peer. "And you?"

Beverly took the bald use of her first name as a good sign; he would have used her title if he were planning something nasty. She hesitated a moment over her response: her brother Miguel would have said something sarcastic, while her brother Richard would have said something that did not admit the existence of dangers and discomforts. What would her father have said?

"I seem to be recovering nicely, thank you, Grand Peer," she replied.

"I'm glad to hear it." The Grand Peer gestured, and a middle-aged Jaeger officer came to the table. Oddly, his hair was cut in the same style as George's; far too short for braids. He was accompanied by a much younger officer whose arm was in a cast. Both carried large portable computers.

"Thank you, Anitra, that will be all," said the Grand Peer to Peer Anitra. She was visibly disappointed. She had been glaring at the Jaegers as if they were interlopers, but bowed to the Grand Peer and left without a word.

"These gentlemen are part of Jaeger military intelligence, and they would like to ask you some questions," said the Grand Peer.

"All right."

The younger officer detached a display panel from his computer and turned it so Beverly could see it. He placed a second panel in front of himself and tapped it. Beverly's panel displayed a photograph of a corpse.

"Do you recognize this man?" asked the older officer.

"No," replied Beverly.

Another corpse was shown on the screen. "Do you recognize this one?"

"No."

Beverly was shown pictures of twenty bodies and mug shots of six prisoners. She recognized none of them, but by the end she was convinced, somehow, that all these people were San Vincentan, and had served in the San Vincentan armed forces. They had the look.

The questioning turned to pieces of equipment: grenade launchers, anti-tank missiles, radios, laser rifles, machine pistols, and one plasma gun. The larger pieces of high-tech equipment all seemed to be of San Vincentan origin. She answered all questions truthfully. She was in the presence of professionals: she dared not do anything else. In any event, she needed the Grand Peer's goodwill.

The Grand Peer watched the proceedings silently, betraying no emotion, but without seeming to be the befuddled, sick old man that Peer Anitra had implied he was.

All this went on for some time, interrupted only once, when the Internal Security officer who had attempted to shanghai them from the flyer was escorted into the Grand Peer's presence by four Jaegers. He was wearing handcuffs and looked sick with apprehension.

The Grand Peer gazed at the face of the officer for a long moment. One of the Jaegers made a couple of signs, and the Grand Peer nodded. Then the officer was hustled away. No word had been spoken. The interruption lasted perhaps fifteen seconds.

The Jaeger officers at the table turned the questioning to more personal matters. Beverly's headache suddenly got worse. She was asked about her stay on Barigost, who she had talked to, what she had done. She began to feel sick again. They asked about the space battle.

They asked question after question about her father's mission in Valhalla, who had spoken to him on Terra, and the reason for his sudden trip to Barigost. With every question, Beverly felt sicker. She knew none of the answers.

Suddenly, a familiar voice roared across the courtyard. "God damn it, Fabian!" Peer Sandra strode into view, wearing a rumpled red-and-yellow flight suit. "You and your god damned courtiers have this place crammed tighter than a Morversarn's stockyard!"

Beverly was glad to see Peer Sandra, though she would doubtless be turned aside as George and Emily had.

Sure enough, Peer Anitra moved to intercept Peer Sandra, but stepped aside in confusion when Peer Sandra gave no sign of seeing her and every sign of walking right over her. The various Jaegers in the area made no move to stop her, either. They looked on, grinning, as Peer Sandra strode directly to the Grand Peer's table. Beverly noticed that most of the courtiers looked disapproving.

She had somehow assumed that Peer Sandra would look backward and provincial compared to the courtiers. Instead, she made the courtiers look foppish and inconsequential.

The Grand Peer smiled and said, "Hello, Sandy."

Peer Sandra sat down, uninvited, at the table. She took a look at Beverly and said, in a quieter voice than usual, "God damn it, Fabian, the girl looks like death warmed over. It's not right to sic your intelligence spooks on her after all the crap she's been through."

"It was necessary. This business may not be finished yet."

"Oh, knock it off, Fabian," she insisted. "Beverly's got more steel in her spine than an Imperial cyborg. You'll never pry a word out of her that she wouldn't have given you freely. What you *really* need to do is tell us what the hell is going on. We're interested parties. God knows we've bled enough. Give."

The Grand Peer turned to Beverly. "My apologies, Lady Beverly," he said. He paused for a long moment, then said, "I very recently became aware that a group of mercenaries had made their base here on Barigost, using Peer Andrew Verrett as their sponsor. They were by and large from San Vincento, although they claimed to be from Forret West and other worlds. They had Eight Worlds ships and were doing a certain amount of raiding.

"Last year they intercepted a Terran courier ship that was taking a large foreign aid payment to Elhild Province, beyond Valhalla. They took the money, which was mostly in gold, and tried to arrange the evidence to point to Oman Laverak, who has become active in Valhalla recently. The Terrans saw through this and recently came to me, demanding reparations, but also divulging a certain amount of intelligence. This was the first I'd heard of the theft.

"The amount of money involved was enormous, far beyond my means to repay. Furthermore, I had no clue as to the identity of the leader of Verrett's off-world allies, or where the money had been taken. The obvious assumption was that the money and men would be used to overthrow me—it wouldn't be the first time it had been tried, nor the tenth."

Peer Sandra interrupted. "Oh, so that's why the riff-raff followed you here. I was wondering. They're hoping to horn in on the loot."

The Grand Peer nodded. "Obviously, the first one to discover its location may be able to make off with it. It's likely that it's unguarded at the moment." He paused a moment, then resumed. "The Terrans and Peer Verrett were bad enough, but then we were inflicted with an odd sequence of events. Your father was appointed Ambassador to Valhalla. Fair enough; while the San Vincentans had neglected the post for a decade or so, it had been of long standing previously, and current events have piqued the interest of many of the Eight Worlds. But he would not normally have passed this way—and, indeed, from your answers had never intended to pass this way—so his presence is clearly related to my own problems."

Beverly said nothing.

"Be that as it may. I dispatched Captain Draper here"—the Grand Peer indicated the middle-aged Jaeger—"to investigate further. He went so far as to cut his braids in order to pose as a government inspector. Perhaps you can pick up the narrative, Captain."

"Yes, Grand Peer. My initial tasks were to interrogate the commissar of the Antipodes District and to examine the ambulance crash site. The commissar was party to any number of crimes, but none of interest to us now. He had been questioned at length by officials in Wrenfield, but this was after the crash. Such questioning, while pursued with unusual vigor, was not uncalled for. The crash site yielded a basic confirmation of eyewitness reports, and I proved to my satisfaction that only two people were aboard the ambulance at the time of the crash.

"I am forced to surmise that the attack on the ambulance was prompted by someone who heard the initial call for medical assistance, made by the commissar over an unencrypted radio channel. Recordings of radio traffic at the hospital indicate that the patient was identified as a survivor of an escape pod, and gave her location. If the attackers were keen on there being no survivors, as they so clearly were, this was more than enough information upon which to act.

"This left two immediately important lines of inquiry: the location of the patient, who at this point had not been identified, and the source of the attack. There seemed to be only one witness, a Mrs. Smith, but she and her husband had suddenly disappeared."

Beverly glanced at Peer Sandra, but her expression betrayed nothing.

"Nothing happens in Antipodes District," continued Captain Draper, "without the support of or instant retaliation by Peer Sandra."

"Call me Sandy," said Peer Sandra.

"Antipodes Station was my next stop, but the enemy was faster, attacking the station before I could get authorization to search it. The emergency allowed Peer Sandra to close the Station for three days, after which it re-opened suddenly, with the announcement that I was welcome to poke around. I sent a real government inspector in my place."

"He was good, too," interrupted Sandy. "He would have found something if I didn't run such a god damned lily-pure operation."

"Tracking the subject—and by this time Peer Sandra had told the Grand Peer that she was the Lady Beverly—was by now useless, due to well-known multiplicity of Peer Sandra's connections and the gratuitously large amount of air traffic that Peer Sandra mounted during the period. We decided instead to concentrate on the attackers, whose location—if not their leadership and motivation—had become known to us, courtesy of certain parties who were disaffected with Peer Andrew Verrett.

"The Colonel of Jeagers and the Grand Peer planned the assault, which was a surprise air and space attack on two small space ports near Wrenfield. The storm helped cover our attack, and we took them by surprise. Only one of their ships lifted, and it was shot down by a stratofighter. We fought a stiff action on the ground, and won it, though with surprisingly heavy casualties. We took very few prisoners; State Intelligence has them now, poor souls. We'll soon get to the bottom of things. As it stands now, it looks like we took them root and branch."

"Are you sure? Those guys were good," said Peer Sandra.

"So are the Jaegers," said the Grand Peer, "though I admit it was just as well that we achieved surprise, outnumbered them, and made good use of ship-mounted laser cannon."

Beverly didn't want to believe it. Those men were not the Grand Peer's to kill. They were hers. If her parents' killers were dead, then she was nothing but a lost girl.

"All's well that ends well," said Peer Sandra.

"Would that it has," said the Grand Peer calmly. "I still don't know where the money went or who the leader of the San Vincentans was—nor is there any way to identify the bodies of offworlders with certainty. The Terran Ambassador is at Wrenfield now. I'm hoping that he finds enough evidence to convince himself that we've done enough. We cannot afford another war with Terra."

He turned back to Beverly. His detached manner had vanished. He seemed stern and terrible. Looking her straight in the eye, he said, "Your father must have known the leader's identity. Who is he?"

Beverly couldn't hold the Grand Peer's gaze. Dropping her eyes to the table, she said, "I don't know. He never discussed business around me."

"You're sure?" There was steel in his voice.

"Yes."

Sandy interrupted, "Oh, don't badger the girl, Fabian. If she knew who it was, she'd be out stalking the son of a bitch with that pistol of hers right now."

Not a pistol, thought Beverly. *A ship. That's my true weapon.* The thought startled her.

The Grand Peer continued staring at Beverly for a moment, but his hold on her had been broken and. He abruptly got to his feet. "Very well. Lady Beverly, thank you. If you aren't too tired, you will be my guest of honor at the banquet tonight." He picked up his book and walked off, Peer Anitra and several other courtiers scurrying unnoticed after him.

Chapter XIX

Peer Rudolf Heinz led Beverly to the armory. He was a big man whose blonde hair and beard had gone mostly grey. The resemblance between him and his son was mostly around the eyes and in an indefinable similarity in attitude. He unlocked the armory door and waved Beverly in. The room had a pleasant smell of wood and gun oil.

"A lot of people carry a five-hundred Nitro-Express to show how manly they are," he said, gesturing to a rack of very large double-barreled rifles. "Most of them can't handle the recoil. For you I'd recommend a .404 Jeffery or something even lighter. That's what the Grand Peer will be carrying. Dr. Hosmer made him stop using the .500 twenty years ago."

Someone had suggested a big game hunt to the Grand Peer at the previous evening's banquet, on the basis of, "While we're here . . . " The Grand Peer had always enjoyed hunting and had allowed himself to be persuaded. Beverly had of course been invited, as had a number of the Jaeger officers, Peer Sandra, various courtiers, and a Terran diplomat who was in the vicinity. With Wrenfield crushed it seemed that a celebration was in order, loose ends or no. The attitude was that, if you shoot first and ask questions later, you shouldn't worry when you don't get many answers.

The invitation had taken place just before Dr. Hosmer had seen Beverly nodding off in her chair, ordered her off to bed, and scolded the Grand Peer for dragging her to the banquet. The doctor had come around several times during the day to make sure she stayed in bed. He had finally relented after sunset and allowed her to prepare for the next day's hunt.

Peer Rudolf was showing her the collection of archaic weapons that Barigost custom mandated for big-game hunting. He handed down the .404, which turned out to be a conventional bolt-action rifle designed for a very large cartridge. Unlike the George's assault rifle, which had been simple, workmanlike, cheap, and ugly, this rifle had been beautifully crafted. The stock had been chosen from a wood with an unusual grain pattern, and had been hand-carved with a scene depicting a hunter facing down three polar bears. For all its beauty, though, Peer Rudolf had handled the gun with no trace of reverence; just the casual competence of someone who handles weapons every day.

Beverly raised the rifle to her shoulder. While well-balanced, it was even heavier than it looked. "This is one of the light models?" she asked.

"Oh, yes. Some of them weigh ten kilograms. Here, I'll show you." He took down an immense double-barreled rifle. Beverly put the .404 Jeffry onto the table and took it from him. Its weight was staggering.

"That's what I'll be carrying; .600 Nitro-Express. Everyone but me will be shooting for pleasure. Believe me, I only fire this thing when I have to. The recoil is indescribable. Still, it will knock a therium unconscious even when it doesn't kill it, and no other hunting piece will do that."

"What's Peer Sandra shooting?"

"She'll be carrying her .505 Gibbs. I think she has the only rifle in that caliber left. Only half a dozen were ever made; it had a reputation for recoil out of proportion to its stopping power."

Beverly handed him back the .600 Nitro-Express and picked up the .404 Jeffery. "I think I'll use this one."

"Good choice. I'm sorry we won't be going to the range before we leave, but the Grand Peer is in a hurry. He has to address the Soviet three days from now. Let's get you some ammo, and I'll let George set you up with arctic gear; I have to get back to work." He handed down two cartridge boxes, which turned out to hold ten enormous cartridges each.

George met her in the "closet," a big room smelling of wool and neat's-foot oil, with a faint undertone of mold and locker-room. It was full of parkas, boots, and other arctic gear. He picked out equipment for her: electrically heated clothing, boots, parka, cartridge pouch, binoculars, and so on. She tried them on in a dressing room (and had to try three pairs of boots until she found some that fit), then a servant took the equipment up to her room. The quality was much higher than the gear George kept on his ship.

He also found a box of cartridges for her Anderson, which had been returned to her. While Beverly was aware that her pistol used a standard round, she was amazed that he could acquire ammunition for it so effortlessly. She returned George's revolver and thanked him profusely. She had the pleasure of seeing him blush.

"You'll be leaving at 5:30 in the morning, so you'd better get a good night's sleep," said George, changing the subject. "Other-wise I'd drag you to the movie we're showing tonight: *Voyage to Elhild*. You'd like it."

"I'd imagine the same advice would hold for you."

"Oh, I'm not going on the hunt. Emily and I are heading out for my ship later tonight. I had a pair of replacement control modules smuggled in on a military flyer, and a friend's going to drop us off."

"Oh," said Beverly, disappointed and a little confused. She suddenly wanted to be on board the *Northern Light* with her friends more than anything. Not here, amid all these strangers, some of whom surely wished her ill. "Well, have a good trip."

"I'll try. Got to get the ship out of there before somebody steals it, and find the Hoard and fix its position before the markers I put out disappear. Not to mention that a lot of the more expensive parts I need for the ship are right there in the Hoard—life support system, laser tubes, converter parts—you name it. I have your map, by the way. It'll help a lot. Well, anyway, good night."

"Good night, George."

Chapter XX

Two aircraft took them to the hunting site. The Grand Peer and the Jaeger hunters went in an assault boat; a heavy multipurpose craft, bristling with guns and missiles, that provided ground support, troop transport, and surface-to-orbit hauling. Beverly and the other civilian hunters flew in Peer Rudolf's rattle-trap flyer. The assault boat didn't deign to fly with the slower vehicle, but went screaming off ahead of them.

Peer Rudolf's flyer was quite a contrast to the Lodge. While the Lodge was an elegant retreat, lavishly furnished and carefully maintained, his aircraft was entirely functional. The seats were hard, the paint was dull, and the craft was shabby. Function was carefully maintained, but appearances weren't. There seemed to be a sharp dividing line between business and pleasure in the minds of Barigosters; the Lodge was a pleasure resort, while the flyer and the hunt in general seemed to count as business.

Peer Rudolf was back in the passenger compartment, talking shop with some of the customers, while a friend of his, Peer John Scidmore, did the piloting. Peer Sandra sat in the copilot's seat and talked raiding with Peer John, and Beverly wandered back and forth a few times from the unused navigator's seat to the passenger cabin before deciding that hearing Peer Sandra talk about raiding was more interesting than hearing Peer Rudolf talk about theriums, or Barigost city folk talk about parties.

A call came through from the assault boat, asking for the location of the landing zone. Peer John gave them the map coordinates, and added, "It's just west of the main fork, on the north side of the river. There's a burned-out flyer there from a crash we had about fifteen years ago. Can't miss it."

As Peer John hung up the microphone, Beverly asked, "Should you be broadcasting so freely, sir?"

"It doesn't matter," said Peer John, "we're using scramblers."

Beverly looked at the primitive radio equipment and said nothing.

An hour later they found the river valley where they would begin the hunt. The Elsee River meandered through pine-covered hills. It was a small, shallow river, full of fish that the polar bears loved and were therefore called salmon (though they resembled green catfish, as much as anything; some were mounted on the wall in the Lodge). The assault boat had already landed in a broad meadow surrounded by trees, and had disgorged its passengers, although the crew remained inside. Peer John set the flyer down near it, and everybody got out. There were patches of snow here and there. The equipment was unloaded, and Peer John locked up his flyer. The assault boat lifted, apparently intending to fly top cover; Beverly had heard Peer Rudolf asking them to stay at high altitude, to avoid disturbing the game.

Beverly noticed that the Terran Under-Ambassador, Mr. Davis, was present. She hadn't realized he was coming. She had met him at the banquet, too briefly to have formed any opinion of him.

Peer Rudolf shouted, "Everybody listen up! We've got a lot of ground to cover today, and we're short a guide or two, so everybody pay attention. We're splitting into two groups: Peer John will take Peers Jeremy, Paxton, Reid, William, Carmen, Frank, Caldwell, Weston, and Francois. I will take Miss Mendoza, Under-Ambassador Davis, the Grand Peer, Peer Sandra, Major Larsky, Captain Leech, Captain Draper, Lieutenant Ederle, Lieutenant Dunlop, and Sergeant Finster. Everybody know which group you're in? Good.

"We spotted several groups of polar bear upstream of here yesterday. There should be plenty for all of us. Remember: the guides are in charge. In particular, there's to be no firing until a guide gives the word. Don't screw around. I've had guests mauled before, and it's bad for business. We'll stop for lunch around eleven. If you have any questions, ask your guide."

The hunters found their respective guides. Beverly was relieved to note that all the courtiers had been put in the other group; hers consisted of the Grand Peer, Peer Sandra, Jaegers, and locals, plus herself and the Under-Ambassador. The Jaegers carried hunting rifles like everyone else, but wore backpacks that presumably held a small amount of military gear.

The Under-Ambassador was chattering away at Peer Rudolf, who was listening patiently. Beverly heard phrases like "exciting opportunity to participate in rituals that date back to our aboriginal past," and "Terra is of course too well-managed to allow activities like this, however educational, to take place." Someone called for Peer Rudolf, who made his excuses to the Under-Ambassador with ill-concealed relief. The Under-Ambassador, left to his own devices, opened the breech of his rifle and began to load it clumsily.

Beverly, not wanting to be caught up in the Under-Ambassador's conversation, moved to join Peer Sandra.

There was a loud explosion. Peer Sandra whipped out her hand blaster at the sound—oddly, she and Beverly were the only people present with sidearms.

The Under-Ambassador was lying on the ground, unconscious. Sergeant Finster rushed over to the Under-Ambassador, then called for the field doc unit to be brought from the assault boat. Soon the Under-Ambassador was plugged into the field doc. The assault boat's crew prepared a stretcher. Onlookers crowded around the body.

Peer Rudolf spoke to Sergeant Finster, then approached the Grand Peer, who was standing not far from Beverly. "It seems the Under-Ambassador has shot himself in the foot," he said.

Peer Sandra laughed. The Grand Peer frowned. "How bad is it?" he asked.

"The bullet hit him in the ankle, so the whole foot is pretty much gone. He's lost a lot of blood. Finster says he'd better be in the Embassy hospital in a few hours if he's going to get the foot regenerated."

The Grand Peer sighed and called to Major Larsky, a tall, tough-looking woman who wore her hair in braids. "Call Lieutenant Solter . Tell him to bring the assault boat back and fly the Under-Ambassador to the Lodge. Arrange to have a space ship take him to Ertrix on the double. Return as soon as possible."

Major Larsky objected, "According to your own instructions, you're not supposed to be without air support, Grand Peer. I suppose we could borrow Peer Rudolf's flyer."

The Grand Peer replied, "There's no need to scold me, Major. The assault boat will be back in an hour, and in the meantime no one knows where we are. All in all, the polar bears are by far the greater danger. As for *that*," he said, pointing to the unarmed flyer, "I can think of nothing that would be less useful to us."

The assault boat arrived. The patient was carried aboard. The assault boat departed.

They remaining hunters began marching a few minutes later. The two groups kept within a hundred yards of each other. Several people scanned the horizon with binoculars. An abundance of bear droppings showed that their quarry had been in the area quite recently.

They marched on. The river was to their left; a fast-moving stream in a shallow gorge. To their right were hills, lichen-covered rocks alternating with patches of conifers. In between was the rock-strewn meadow on which they were walking, covered in many places by spongy moss, and in others with knee-high grass that concealed many small animals. Ice and snow lurked in the shaded areas, but had melted wherever the sun could reach. The temperature had risen to just above freezing.

After an hour they rested before crossing a stream on a fallen log. Just after crossing the stream, Lieutenant Blaire Ederle touched Peer Rudolf on the shoulder. He held up a hand to stop his group, and Blaire pointed to where she had seen movement. Peer Rudolf motioned them all to silence, and started forward, waving for Blaire to come with him. She set down her pack and field radio and followed him.

They both moved silently toward the hills and climbed the first ridge, moving behind cover as they came up to the crest. They watched from the hilltop for a while, then Peer Rudolf shook his head. They came back down with considerably less woodcraft than their trip out.

"There was a bear, all right," said Peer Rudolf, "but we would have had to chase him up another hill or two to get a shot, so we let him go. Can't have the guests milling around while the guide's niece gets the kill. Good spotting, though, Blaire."

Blaire smiled but said nothing. Beverly couldn't see any family resemblance between her and Peer Rudolf, but she had already formed the conviction, based on the way George talked, that everyone on the planet was related to him. That a Heinz relation was an officer in the Jaegers came as no surprise.

They went on for another hour. It was clear that bears had been here recently, but none were seen. The terrain became a little rougher, and Peer Rudolf thought he saw several creatures in the distance as they crested a hill. Probably bears.

He scanned the distance for a while, then called to Peer John, who had kept his group a hundred yards behind them. "I've been hogging all the glory so far, John; why don't you take point for the next hour?" Peer John was agreeable, so he moved his group up ahead of Peer Rudolf's.

They came to a bend in the river where a cliff crowded them almost into the river. They picked their way over rocks and ridges along the bank. After a while things opened up again, and Peer John's group surged ahead eagerly. Peer Rudolf let them get two or three hundred meters ahead—perhaps out of deference to the Grand Peer, who looked a bit winded, though he said nothing.

They topped a little ridge and had a good view of a shallow, snow-covered valley, two hundred meters across, with hills on the right and water on the left, with car-sized boulders scattered artistically across it. Deep snow drifts filled the shaded areas; elsewhere patches of snow alternated with bare earth. Peer John waited for Peer Rudolf's group to catch up to within about fifty meters, then forged down into the valley, close to the water. Peer Rudolf walked down the crest until he wouldn't be silhouetted by it, then scanned the area with binoculars.

"There!" he said, pointing. "See it, Blaire? There's a breath plume on the ridge to the right. There's another one! John's going to go right on by without seeing them!" He laughed.

Beverly pulled out her binoculars to get a look; so did everyone else in the group. The boulders in question were perhaps two hundred and fifty meters away. The bears must be just behind the crest.

She quickly spotted the breath plume, then saw movement. As she watched, a shape moved in the shadow of one of the boulders, and a blinding light came from it, followed by the sound of thunder.

Laser weapons! They were being ambushed! Beverly flung herself to the frozen ground.

"Take cover!" shouted Peer Rudolf. Laser fire streaked across their position. Captain Leach was hit by the beam, his parka erupting into flame. His body fell to the snow, raising a hissing cloud of steam. More beams spattered on the tundra or into boulders, but now everyone was under cover.

Beverly crawled to where she could see the other group. Pandemonium reigned. Beverly could see three smoking bodies. Some survivors had made it to inadequate cover. They wouldn't last long.

"Pull yourselves together," barked the Grand Peer in a penetrating voice. He was sitting with his back to a large rock, watching his own people instead of the enemy. "Carmine, get their range. Blaire, call for help. Rudolf, figure out how many there are and what they've got. Chandra, Chloe, Albert; start sniping at them as soon as you get the range. Don't waste ammo. Once we've got some covering fire, everybody spread out. We're suckers for mortar fire. Lady Beverly, come over here and advise me. Sandy, hold yourself in reserve for now."

Peer Rudolf called out, "Everyone put on your snow goggles. They have flash protection."

Beverly put on her goggles. They worked – laser flashes no longer blinded her, and her dazzled vision began to clear, giving her a surge of confidence.

Captain Carmine Draper focused his rangefinder and announced "Two hundred thirty meters." Everyone adjusted the sights on their rifles.

"The snipers may fire when ready," announced the Grand Peer.

Major Chandra Larsky crawled forward to a position where only her rifle and head protruded from the rocks, and these were cloaked in shadow. She lined up her shot carefully, then waited for several seconds for someone to show himself. She shifted slightly and squeezed the trigger. She was using a double-barreled .500 Nitro-Express. The recoil pushed her a full meter backwards over the dirty snow.

"Got him," announced Carmine, who had put his rangefinder away and was spotting with binoculars. "Good shooting."

Sergeant Albert Finster and Lieutenant Chloe Dunlop started firing at the enemy position, but didn't hit anything. The others took advantage of the covering fire to spread out. The enemy was giving some return fire, but nothing found its mark.

"Chloe, your rounds are falling short," reported Carmine. "Try setting your sights for another twenty-five meters."

Beverly made a dash to the Grand Peer's position. The Grand Peer was peeking out from the side of his boulder and didn't acknowledge her arrival. He moved back for a moment, grabbed his rifle, flashed her a wolfish grin, and crawled forward.

A couple of minutes ticked by with nobody firing, then laser fire spattered the ground nearby, somebody shouted "Shit!" and the Grand Peer's rifle went off.

"Oh, well done!" said Carmine. "Knocked him ass over tea-kettle. Whose shot was that?"

"Mine," said the Grand Peer.

"Wait . . . He's getting back up. I don't believe it! What kind of armor is he wearing?

"He's still in the open, if somebody wants to take a shot at him," Carmine continued. "There's a big star fracture all over his breastplate."

"Dibs!" called Peer Rudolf. There was an immense roar as the .600 Nitro-Express went off.

"Jesus Christ, Rudolf, what are you trying to do?" called Carmine. "The guy's in three pieces! . . . Incoming!"

Everyone ducked as a furious volley of laser fire criss-crossed their position. It slowed for a second, and Chloe popped up with her .404 Jefferies to return fire. Her head was blown off instantly by a carefully-placed beam. The fireball engulfed the upper half of her body, which sank hissing into the snow, accompanied by the stench of burned plastic and seared meat.

The Grand Peer had returned from his firing position. "You getting through?" he called to Blaire.

Blair had produced a hammer and a long copper stake from her pack and was pounding the stake furiously into the ground. "No, sir. The assault boat should be back by now, but I can't raise it. I think I can reach the Lodge by shortwave if I string an antenna." She stopped hammering and connected the ground rod to her radio with a cable. She deftly tossed a loop of cord around a tall boulder and tied a reel of wire to it. This accomplished, she looked at the Grand Peer expectantly.

"Okay, listen up!" shouted the Grand Peer. "Blaire needs covering fire so she can string an antenna. It needs to be good and it needs to last a long time. Everybody but Rudolf and Carmine needs to put up covering fire. Keep it nice and steady. Rudolf, Carmine, you pick off anybody who shows himself." He turned to Beverly. "Take the position I was using. I'll try the other side."

The Grand Peer waited until everyone was in position. Occasional laser bolts were zinging past them, but none connected. The Grand Peer fired his rifle, and everyone joined in.

Beverly glanced behind her. Blaire was dashing across the tundra, unreeling her wire behind her. She was headed for a tall rock fifty meters away.

Beverly turned back and chambered a round. She lined up the sights and looked for a target. She saw no one. She saw a rock on top of a boulder that might harbor an enemy, and aimed at it. She concentrated on breath control, squeezing the trigger gently, and keeping the sights lined up.

The barrel climbed as the gun fired, obscuring her view of her target. In her concentration, she hadn't felt the recoil or heard the report of the gun, but when she worked the bolt again her shoulder hurt. She lined up again, and noticed with satisfaction that the rock was no longer there.

Just as she was about to fire a round at another rock, someone popped out from behind a boulder. Even at this range she could recognize Eight Worlds combat armor and a laser rifle. She struggled to line up the sights on the heavy rifle, and pulled the trigger just as he popped back to safety. She chambered a third round and waited for another opportunity.

Seconds later he popped up again, firing a snap shot in her direction. This time the sights lined up in time, and her shot knocked him ten feet backwards. *I've killed someone,* she realized.

Before this had time to sink in, she was startled by the Grand Peer's voice. "Damn it! Albert, see to Blaire!"

Beverly fired another shot at nothing in particular, and then her rifle was empty. She retreated behind her boulder to reload.

Sergeant Finster was half-dragging Blaire back to her position. She'd finished stringing the antenna, but she'd picked up a hideous laser burn in the hip as she was rushing back to her radio. Finster set her down and pulled a medical kit from his pack. He started with a hypogun injection that turned her from pale semi-consiousness to preternatural animation in a matter of seconds. He then started to work on the wound.

Beverly shuddered. Combat drugs! She hoped Blaire would survive the side effects.

The Grand Peer touched Beverly on the shoulder. "Assuming that these are San Vincentan naval troops, Beverly, what would they be likely to do next?"

Beverly considered. "They must have expected to burn us down in the open, sir. They didn't count on Peer Rudolf's woodcraft. In a stalemate like this the only tactical choices are to call in a strike, attack, or retreat. There don't seem to be many of them, so I'd say that they'll either unleash some air support or artillery or withdraw."

"Speaking of which," said the Grand Peer. He turned to where Blaire and Albert were. Blaire was lying on her side, talking into the radio while Sergeant Finster patched her up. She met the Grand Peer's gaze and shook her head.

Peer Sandra appeared next to the Grand Peer, smiling. "There can't be more than five or six of the sons of bitches left, Fabian," she said. "Let's get some flanking action going here."

"All right. Take three people."

Peer Sandra face lit up as if she had been given her heart's desire. "I'm taking Carmine, Chandra, and Rudolf, okay?"

"All right. If you'd had that eye regrown, you'd have an easier time of it."

Peer Sandra laughed. "I love you too, Fabian." She gave him a thump on the back and ran off, still grinning.

"Grand Peer!" shouted Blaire as Peer Sandra and her squad departed. "Word from the assault boat! They whacked on landing at the Lodge and they've just finished repairs now! ETA twenty minutes! They're scrambling interceptors and stratofighters! ETA thirty minutes!"

"Grand Peer," said Beverly, "They couldn't have known you'd send the assault boat away, so they must have been prepared to deal with it."

"Good point. But right now, let's give some covering fire to our flankers." He crawled back into his firing position.

Beverly fired four more shots near places where people might be. She saw no trace of them.

Return fire from the enemy was tapering off. Beverly used this opportunity to use her binoculars to check the other group of hunters. Little had changed; those who had found cover were keeping their heads down. Those who hadn't were dead.

A few minutes passed with no fire from the enemy, then Blaire shouted, "Grand Peer! Carmine says they ambushed a sniper. The rest had bugged out already. Should they pursue?"

"Yes! Tell them to go for it!" said the Grand Peer.

Blaire spoke into the microphone again, and then reported, "The enemy abandoned a pair of surface-to-air missiles."

"More good news," said the Grand Peer. "Sergeant Finster! Get down to the other group and tell Scidmore to go set up those missiles! Then see to their wounded."

"Sir!" Finster deftly added some final touches to Blaire's bandages, then packed his equipment with lightning speed.

Their position was looking awfully empty—only Blaire, Beverly, and the Grand Peer remained—but some of the other hunters started trooping back. The Grand Peer put Peer Frank Eaton in charge of the defense. "Keep them spread out, Frank. We want to be hard to spot from the air."

Peer Frank looked around. "That's going to be hard, with all this blood on the snow, Grand Peer."

"Damn. Well, we can't move Blaire. Does anybody have a talkie?"

"Just Peer John and Captain Draper, and they're using them," replied Peer Frank.

"Well, start scooping snow over the blood," said the Grand Peer. "And keep your eyes and ears open for aircraft."

Beverly helped the others scrape up the crusty, dirty layer of snow and dump it on the bloodstains. They dragged the corpses deep into the shadows of the boulders. They were starting to conceal tracks in the snow when Beverly heard the whine of lifters.

"Incoming aircraft!" she shouted. "Sounds like a space ship!"

Everyone dove for cover. Seconds later something roared up the river valley. Beverly at first mistook it for a jet airplane, since it had too much lifting body for a normal space ship, but it sounded . . .

"Hold your fire!" she called, "It's the *Northern Light!*"

She watched with longing as the ship approached.

Blaire started shouting into her microphone. The *Northern Light* overflew their position with an ear-splitting roar of lifters, turned around, and returned, tail-down, clearly intending to land.

"They're toast if they're caught on the ground!" shouted the Grand Peer over the roar. "Tell them we don't want a lift!"

"They aren't responding, Grand Peer!" shouted Blaire.

The *Northern Light* was landing in the bottom of the valley.

"No radio! They don't have a radio!" shouted Beverly. "I'll tell them myself!" She leaped up, leaned her heavy rifle against the boulder, and ran down the slope, her heart full of joy and fear.

The Grand Peer stood up, cupped his hands, and shouted after her, "Tell Emily that if she gets herself killed, I'll be very angry with her!"

Beverly barely heard. She waved back at him and continued running.

The airlock door opened as she approached. She could see George's space-suited figure wrestle the accommodation ladder free. The lifters were melting the permafrost, and the landing jacks were beginning to sink.

Beverly swarmed up the ladder and squeezed past George in the airlock. She heard George behind her, trying to convince the ladder's retraction mechanism to work. She threw off her parka, wrestled her feet out of their boots, and flung herself at the locker containing her space suit. George closed the airlock door, muffling the roar of the lifters enough to allow a shouted conversation."

"The Grand Peer doesn't want to be picked up," said Beverly. "We have to get out of here! Our attackers may become airborne at any time!"

"I know! I know!" shouted George, helping her into her helmet. "It's the *transmitter* that's missing, not the receiver! We're here for *you!* We got the guns working! Get up to the bridge!" He finished helping her with her gauntlets, then gave her a push towards the main ladder.

Beverly raced up the ladder to the bridge. Emily was in the pilot's seat, drumming her gauntleted fingers on the console. "Hurry, Beverly! We have to get out of here!" She began revving the lifters before Beverly made it to her chair. Blaire's voice was coming out of the speaker, asking Peer Sandra for a status report.

The ship pulled free of the ground, and Emily immediately tilted into horizontal flight mode, keeping half of her attention on the terrain and half on the instruments.

"Gear retraction okay. Engines okay. Check the guns out, Beverly."

The guns were on standby. Beverly flipped the switches that would bring them to ready, and set the display and tracking modes for short-range atmospheric work. The display showed that Emily was circling the Grand Peer's position.

The radio came into life, Carmine's voice: "Corvette! Up the canyon! It's starting to lift!"

"That's our cue," said Emily grimly. "All hands prepare for acceleration." She closed her faceplate and swung the ship in a high-gee turn into the river canyon.

The *Northern Light* roared up the canyon barely a hundred meters above the ground. Beverly switched off the pilot override system; turning the ship to aim the guns would crash the ship into the canyon wall. She set the display to full forward and waited.

They rounded a bend. Ahead of them, a corvette rose slowly into the air. Its slab-sided lines were distinctly San Vincentan.

Plumes of smoke raced into the air from the ground as the enemy's own surface-to-air missiles were used against them. Both missiles missed. The corvette rose steadily, the exhaust ports of its four turbine-jet lifters clearly visible to the people below.

Peer Sandra's voice came over the radio. "Everybody aim for the lower starboard lifter!"

Laser bolts streaked up from the ground—coming from weapons taken from the enemy's dead and Peer Sandra's hand blaster, no doubt. Someone scored a lucky shot and the lower starboard lifter erupted in flame. Part of the cowling fell off, and the lifter coughed out a wad of turbine blades that rained down like confetti. The corvette lurched and lost altitude.

"Now the other one!" bellowed Peer Sandra.

Laser fire played confusedly around the other three lifters.

Peer Sandra let out a howl of outrage. "The other *starboard* lifter, you morons!"

But it was too late. There was no repetition of the first hit. After falling to within twenty meters of the ground, the corvette's pilot regained control and the ship began limping off into the north, barely clearing the first line of hills.

Throughout this performance Peer Sandra kept up a steady stream of profanity. This was suddenly broken off with a sharp, "Incoming ship! Take cover, god damn it!"

Beverly barely heard her. She had attention only for the gunnery display. The corvette, listing to starboard but picking up speed, filled the starboard side of the display, but the guns could not be brought to bear. Emily had the ship ten degrees too far to port. "Line us up! Line us up!" Beverly shouted.

Emily turned the ship quickly—too quickly—and Beverly's shot went wild. She began lining up the sights on the corvette again. The imaging system showed the target in great clarity, and Beverly watched in helpless fascination as the corvette's turret traversed smoothly until it pointed directly at them.

Emily apparently saw the same thing, for she turned the ship hard to port and dove, pulling up only a few meters from the canyon floor, then nearly broadsiding the canyon wall as she climbed. Beverly had no chance to shoot.

Emily moved the ship back into the center of the river canyon. She kept the lifters throttled well back, but they were still moving at over three hundred kilometers per hour.

Peer Sandra was reporting to the Grand Peer over the radio. "We winged the son of a bitch, Fabian. Lifters shot to hell. They'll never get enough altitude to light the fusion drive. But if they get out of sight for more than a couple of minutes, they'll land in some narrow little god damned canyon and we'll never find them again."

Beverly kept her eyes moving from one display to the other. They had lost the corvette already, but it must still be airborne—unless it had crashed. If they could find it, the highly aerodynamic *Northern Light* was far more maneuverable than the San Vincentan ship, and with its undamaged engines it had a tremendous speed advantage. Perhaps this would compensate for the lack of a revolving turret.

The *Northern Light* raced upstream to the point where following the narrowing canyon was suicidal. There was no sign of their opponent.

"Major Belhaven, Grand Peer," came a voice from the radio. "I've got a stratofighter over your position. No radar contacts."

"They're still hedge-hopping," commented Emily. "They must have jumped to another canyon." She drummed her fingers for a few seconds, then turned the ship around, hopping over the nearest ridge as she did so.

They flew down the new river bed. The stream was a tributary of the Elsee river, and when they reached the Elsee they turned to climb the main fork, overflying the Grand Peer's position.

"Let's try the left branch this time," said Emily to no one in particular. Two kilometers later she made a hard turn to port, heading up yet another branch. No sign of the enemy.

The tension grew. Beverly bit her lip, then caught herself. She willed herself to relax, to detach herself from her roiling emotions. If anything, this familiar exercise worked better now, in real combat, than it had during simulation. She was enveloped by an alert calmness.

They came up on another fork. Emily again chose left, and put the ship into a hard turn to port.

The corvette was right in front of them! Beverly, now in her gunner's trance, was not conscious of operating the joysticks or pulling the triggers. Twin beams of destruction followed her gaze. She struck the corvette in the stern. Irregular explosions followed the beams as she struck deep into the ship's vitals.

The *Northern Light* dove toward the canyon floor. Now below and behind the corvette, Beverly turned her fiery gaze upon its belly, ripping blazing paths of destruction twenty meters long.

The *Northern Light* passed the corvette from below. Beverly's forward-firing guns could no longer be brought to bear. Emily opened the throttles wide and executed a high-gee Immelman turn that brought them back for a second pass in seconds. Unable to contain a spasm of hatred, Beverly fired convulsively. A huge explosion ripped out part of the corvette's stern. Beverly felt a terrible elation.

The surge of emotion broke her concentration. The gunnery controls suddenly seemed unfamiliar, the screen incomprehensible.

The corvette was making erratic progress at a bend in the canyon, but seemed to lack the lift to pull clear. As Beverly brought herself back under control and lined up her guns for the killing stroke, the corvette's turret fired into the *Northern Light* from point-blank range.

The gunnery display went blank. Black smoke poured from the ventilators. Emily flipped a switch to shut them off. A tooth-jarring whine ran up through the audible range and ended in an explosion—one of the lifters had run away. The ship began to buck.

The corvette disappeared around the bend in the canyon, trailing smoke and losing altitude.

"George? George? Are you all right?" shouted Emily.

"Yeah, sure," came George's weary voice over the intercom. "I'm swell. Put this thing down, will you?"

Downstream, the canyon presented no place to land. Emily turned the ship around, back toward the corvette, which had passed out of sight. She found a gravel bar that looked firm enough, and went through a landing maneuver. She set the ship down hard, but not hard enough to hurt anything. She heaved an enormous sigh and turned off the lifters.

Beverly set the guns to standby, opened her faceplate, and slumped in her seat. All was quiet.

"Medic," said George.

Both girls threw themselves from their seats. Beverly let Emily go first, and Emily slid down the ladder. Beverly climbed down after her.

George was in the engine room, which was filled with smoke and drenched with fire extinguisher foam. He had a wrench in one hand. His left arm was in a sling he had made from a length of duct tape.

"Watch your step," he said, "it's slippery." He closed a valve with the wrench. "All done," he said.

"What's with the arm?" asked Emily.

"I can't move it and it hurts," he replied. "I think it's broken."

"Let's get you up to the cargo deck, and I'll take a look at it," said Emily. "Why do your own injuries bother you so much less than other people's?"

"Dunno." George managed to climb the ladder one-handed, and the girls followed him.

Acting on a strange compulsion, Beverly opened the air-lock—the door didn't jam, for once—and looked outside. A column of smoke was rising from perhaps a kilometer upstream.

She took off her space suit, donned parka, boots, and pistol, and left the ship.

CHAPTER XXI

The corvette had landed on its belly. It had dug a trench half a kilometer long on a broad sand bar and was half-buried in the river bank. Beverly stood at the far end of the trench. Smoke pouring out of the stern obscured much of the battered hull from her view. It was well that the wind was blowing the smoke away from her, since it was probably intensely radioactive.

It was unlikely that there were any survivors, but she had to make sure. There had been so much death. This was the end of it.

She walked until she was within a few hundred meters of the ship. The fire was burning steadily. No sound reached her. The stillness was oddly peaceful.

As she watched the ship, she heard an irregular high-pitched whine. It persisted for a moment, then a smoking piece of metal fell from the hull. The whine continued, and another piece of metal fell away.

From out of the hole came a man. He stepped onto the sand, sheathed his power sword, and turned to pull another man from the ship. Both were wearing tattered space suits.

The man with the power sword lifted the other in a fireman's carry, and staggered with him for a hundred meters or so. He dropped his burden onto the sand, then pulled off both their helmets and his own gauntlets. He felt for a pulse in the other man's neck, then put the man's helmet back on, and folded the limp hands on the unmoving chest.

Beverly drew her pistol and walked toward him.

When she had closed to within perhaps twenty meters the man looked up. His hair was singed and his face was covered with soot and sweat.

"So," he said, "if it isn't little Beverly, come to avenge the family honor."

It was Miguel di Cruz.

She stopped, horrified.

"At least I'm to die like a man, shot by someone of the blood. What would they say if I were killed by a native?"

He got to his feet. Beverly disengaged the safety on her pistol. She tried to speak, but her mouth was very dry. She tried again and said, "I thought you were dead, uncle."

He snorted. "That was the plan. But I was lucky enough to be off the ship when it was betrayed to the Vradthmorn. Everyone on board was murdered, as your father intended."

"No."

"Of course he did. How pleased he must have been when word came back. No survivors, no bodies, and no one suspecting a thing. And all because I wouldn't join his damned party."

"No," she said again, remembering her father's black depression when word of di Cruz' death arrived, and his obsessive efforts to find the parties responsible. And, much, much later, his irrepressible high spirits the day he had cut short their stay on Terra, and changed their travel plans to take them to Barigost. She knew now that it had been the thought of a reunion, of forgiveness, that had brought him such joy. Her eyes filled with tears.

"When did your father tell you he'd betrayed me? My party abandoned me after I killed the Marquis di Luis for them. Did your father tell me that I went to him for help? Your father, the man whose life I saved, the man who named his second son after me? Did he tell you that he could have saved my career? But he did nothing—nothing but shove me into the arms of that murderous traitor di Grenville."

Beverly said nothing.

"He threw me to the wolves. Twelve men issued challenges to me. *Twelve men.* Their party wanted me dead. He could have stopped them, but he didn't. He told me to flee and join di Grenville. He swore to me that di Grenville was an honorable man, and left me to be butchered by a pack of Vradthmorn.

"At least, after that, I thought I was safely given up for dead. With my remaining ship and, the help of a few discreet friends in our embassy on Terra, I managed to pull off the biggest heist of the century—and your father jumped up like a jack-in-the-box to take it all away again." He was angry now, shouting. "Didn't he?"

"No," she said. She raised her pistol. The sights lined up between his eyes. She was surprised her hands weren't shaking.

He took another step forward, then looked up. Beverly heard the sound of lifters in the distance. Miguel heard them too. His shoulders sagged.

"You were always my favorite, Beverly," he said softly. "You know what you have to do." He stopped and waited.

One touch on the trigger and he would be dead. Though he had been played for a fool, he had still murdered her parents. She must avenge them. She must. It was her duty.

She didn't pull the trigger.

"It isn't easy for you, is it?" he asked. "Didn't he tell you hateful things about me?"

She shook her head.

"Well, that's something." After a pause, he said, "Quite a lot, really. Here," he said, unzipping a pocket in his space suit. "Read this when I'm gone." He tossed a small packet onto the sand.

"You have to do it, Beverly. You don't have any more choice than I did." The sound of lifters drew closer. He saw the tears running down her cheeks, behind the unwavering pistol. "Here. I'll help you."

He drew his power sword and flipped the switch. The air was filled with its high-pitched whine. He saluted her with it, then started walking toward her. After a few steps his expression changed and hardened, and he began walking faster.

She knew what he was thinking. If he could cut her down, perhaps he could talk or cut his way into her ship, and if he could get it airborne . . . it was known to the locals, they would let it go, and then perhaps he could escape. Maybe even retrieve the gold. Beverly hadn't even locked the airlock door. Di Cruz be inside before George and Emily knew he was there. They wouldn't stand a chance.

Her sights were still lined up right between his eyes.

She pulled the trigger.

EPILOGUE

The Grand Peer was in his study, surrounded by books, the windows open to let in the breeze on this warm day. His butler, Arnold, an elderly Jaeger who had not wished to leave his service, came in and announced, "Baron di Mendoza is here, Grand Peer."

Fabian set a bookmark and closed his book. "Good. Send him in, please, Arnold." He rose and crossed from the desk to the front of the room.

Young Richard di Mendoza walked in, wearing a black naval uniform. The resemblance to his father, twenty years ago, was striking.

"I'm very pleased to meet you at last, my lord," said the Grand Peer, shaking di Mendoza's hand. "Your sister spoke very highly of you."

Di Mendoza smiled. "She had good things to say of you as well, Grand Peer."

They spoke of inconsequential topics for a while, and had a glass of wine.

"You'll be wanting to get down to business. Come, I'll show you the cemetery." The Grand Peer led the way to the door, where a car was waiting. They drove a kilometer over the palace grounds until they reached a small cemetery. The chauffeur opened the wrought-iron gate for them.

The Grand Peer gestured at the cemetery around them. "This has been our cemetery for over two hundred and fifty years. All the Grand Peers are buried here. All those whose remains were recovered, at least. Your sister was quite adamant that di Cruz be buried with full honors. Her attitude mystifies me, but I did my best. Here we are."

They stopped at a grave which, in the custom of Barigost, had a simple stone headstone which read, "Miguel di Cruz." No dates, no titles, no words of comfort or of boasting.

Di Mendoza turned around. The cemetery stood near the cliffs, and had a view of the pounding surf and brilliant blue sea of Ertrix. "It's a lovely location," he said. "It's almost a shame to take him away from this."

"We'll have the casket exhumed by tomorrow. I take it that it will go to the di Cruz family plot on San Vincento?"

"No, di Mendoza."

The Grand Peer sighed. "I don't understand. He murdered your parents and tried many times to kill your sister. Yet you treat him like a beloved friend."

"He *was* a beloved friend."

Di Mendoza turned to face the Grand Peer. "In the years di Cruz spent with my father they saved each other's lives many times. Neither would have been what he was without the other. But their fate was such that they could not continue together. Father had his family's position to maintain, and di Cruz, with no family, for all his brilliant military career, could win only by playing at long odds. He played and lost."

"It's none of my business," said the Grand Peer, "but *could* your father have rescued di Cruz' career?"

"No. Yes . . . you see, Father could have gotten those twelve duels canceled or reduced from plasma guns to swords. He could have called in favors to get di Cruz put into a responsible position in the Assembly. But it wouldn't have lasted. Di Cruz had been duped by his party. He'd killed a beloved elder statesman. No amount of string-pulling would have changed anyone's opinion of him. By any real measure, he had completely and permanently destroyed his own career. Father couldn't hitch his own family's reputation to someone so thoroughly and justly disgraced. He had no choice but to refuse."

"So di Cruz killed him."

"No. Not until he was maneuvered into it by our mutual enemies."

The Grand Peer was baffled. "How much betrayal does it take to cancel a bond between people on San Vincento?"

Di Mendoza stared out at the sea. "I once told a Goan the tale of Fey Aaron. When I told of Aaron's death—how he was killed by his bride on his wedding night—the Goan said, 'Well, then she must not have loved him.'

"She killed Aaron to be with George Skelley, so that if he became Emperor, she would be Empress. It was a cold-blooded, premeditated murder. But George Skelley found her weeping over the body; Aaron's blood drenching her bridal gown.

"She loved Aaron. Of course she did. But her fate was to seek the Imperial Throne, and Aaron was in her way."

The Grand Peer shook his head, none the wiser for the explanation. He and di Mendoza rode back to the palace in silence. As they were getting out of the car, the Grand Peer said, "And what of the people who betrayed your father and di Cruz?"

Di Mendoza smiled a smile so cold and malicious that the Grand Peer actually shuddered. But all di Mendoza said was, "We shall see."

After a moment the Grand Peer shook off the feeling of second-hand doom to ask a question that meant considerably more to him. "Tell me, how is Beverly?"

"She's in the Academy now. It's something she always wanted. She's at the top of her class. And her adventure here will work to her advantage when she graduates. Few young ladies have been tested so thoroughly by events."

"Is she happy?"

"I don't know. It's not the sort of question one asks." They rode in silence, then di Mendoza continued, "I rather doubt it. She has not chosen a pleasant path."

The Grand Peer had other questions, but chose not to ask them. The money di Cruz had stolen from the Terrans had never been found. The Terrans had quietly extracted reparations from the San Vincentans and considered the case closed. But was it? The Grand Peer could not shake the suspicion that somehow Beverly had gotten hold of the money, or knew where it was. But it was no longer State business, so he kept his peace.

The Grand Peer returned to his study when di Mendoza had gone. He still found some comfort in the thousands of leather-bound volumes. They helped him while away the time as he waited for old age or a lucky assassin to take him. His life had been one long holding action, trying to keep Barigost from falling apart from within while delaying the inevitable day when the Terrans reached out their hand and took his world for their own.

He did not even have superstition to fall back upon. He envied di Mendoza his belief in fate, and the cold comfort he derived from it.

Still, he was glad he was not a San Vincentan.

THE END

www.ingramcontent.com/pod-product-compliance
Lightning Source LLC
Chambersburg PA
CBHW031941260626
47157CB00016B/1087